THE EDEN HUNTER

SKIP HORACK

A Novel

COUNTERPOINT
BERKELEY

Copyright ©2010 by Skip Horack. All rights reserved under International and
Pan-American Copyright Conventions.

Library of Congress Cataloging-in-Publication Data

Horack, Skip.
The Eden hunter : a novel / by Skip Horack.
p. cm.
ISBN-13: 978-1-58243-609-8
ISBN-10: 1-58243-609-6
1. Pygmies—Fiction. 2. Fugitive slaves—Fiction. 3. Wilderness areas—
Florida—Fiction. 4. Quests (Expeditions)—Fiction. I. Title.

PS3608.O72E34 2010
813'.6—dc22

2010017785

Cover design by Kimberly Glyder
Interior design by Megan Jones Design

Printed in the United States of America

COUNTERPOINT
1919 Fifth Street
Berkeley, CA 94710

www.counterpointpress.com

Distributed by Publishers Group West

10 9 8 7 6 5 4 3 2 1

For Sylvia

Why, ever since Adam, who has got to the meaning of his great allegory—the world? Then we pigmies must be content to have our paper allegories but ill comprehended.

—HERMAN MELVILLE

THE EDEN HUNTER

PROLOGUE

CENTRAL AFRICA. *1786. A full moon rises over the forest and the Pygmy is born. The Ota dance beneath the stars, and the clearing is beaten smooth by the poundings of their feet. A leopard coughs in the night and the child is given his name, Kau.*

Fifteen years later his sister is traded for a girl from a neighboring Ota band. A leaf hut is prepared, and she waits for him to push past the laughing crowd of older women who punch him and kick him and pinch him as he fights his way to the entrance. The girl sees that it is him—the brave one called Leopard—and she is happy because this is the young man she had hoped for. She smiles and rolls onto her stomach, giving herself to him in the way that her mother taught her. Blood drips from his torn lips onto her flawless back.

The next day he presents her family with the hindquarters of an okapi. This gift of meat is accepted and the girl becomes his wife. A near decade of happiness and children passes. His wife gives him a daughter, and then she gives him a son.

1810. HE IS HUNTING along the bank of the river when he discovers Kesa canoes hidden in the mangroves. He returns to his camp and finds it destroyed. Kesa warriors have attacked the sleeping band, and his father is among the dozen survivors who are now bound in Spanish trade irons. Twice that number are dead. Mother and wife and son and daughter lie melting in a bed of smoldering coals.

The Kesa march their chain of neck-shackled prisoners to the river and break. He follows with his bow. That evening the Kesa drink palm wine around a bonfire, and from a distance he kills them one by one by one until only a single crazed warrior remains. This last man abandons his slaves, and the Pygmy chases him away from the river and into the forest. At sunrise a poisoned arrow streaks through the trees, and the warrior is paralyzed. He can only stare as the Pygmy approaches.

The captured Ota embrace him, but when he tries to free his people he fails. They realize then that the secret to these shackles died with that final Kesa warrior. He goes to his father, but there is nothing to say.

That same night the hard rains come and the river begins to rise. He is leading them all to higher ground when they surprise a forest elephant. The bull rushes the trail and collides with the chain. Every neck is broken. Colobus monkeys scream down from the treetops. The Pygmy buries the dead in a twisted heap, then he sings an Ota song:

There is darkness upon us
darkness is all around

there is no light
but it is the darkness of the forest
so if it really must be
even the darkness is good

FROM ONE NEW *moon to the next he wanders. Kesa scouts find him*
camped near the burrow of an aardvark. They approach and he
dives into the earth. It is feared that this little man named Leopard
has become a sorcerer. Smoking firebrands are held to the entrance
of the burrow, and the Pygmy emerges, red-eyed and coughing.

He is taken to the Kesa village, but the chief is a coward who
will not order a sorcerer's death. The Pygmy is chained to a post
near the market and fed like a dog by superstitious merchants. Still,
he does not speak. Five nights later a child dies and there is a panic.
The Pygmy is traded from village to village and river to river until
finally after many days he reaches the mouth of the Congo. In the
delta barracoons he sees his first white men, and though at first he
is awed he soon finds them clumsy and disgusting. He is rowed out
to the looming square-rigger anchored in the slate and greasy bay,
but he is not afraid because inside he is already dead.

A slave ship. There is no room for him among the men, and
so the Spanish traders place him belowdecks with the women and
children moaning in their portion of the dark and crowded hold.
The enormous daughter of a murdered chief has lost her mind to
the filth of the overflowing tubs and the galling of her chains. She
beats him for his ration of cassava flour, and he latches on to her
thick neck. The big woman laughs but cannot shake him loose. His

grip constricts tighter and tighter until the giant becomes hysterical and then dies strangled, her death unnoticed until the light of morning. The body is dragged topside by a cursing Sevillano, and the woman's caught sisters begin to wail and pull at their hair.

Forty days at sea. The Africans are being made to exercise on the slave deck when rafts of marshgrass are spotted and the first birds appear. Blue water gives to green as happy sailors shoot wake-riding dolphins. The Pygmy is watching them load aim shoot, load aim shoot, when the continent is sighted. He is hungry and thirsty and miserable, but he is also fascinated. To see land and forest again somehow softens his suffering, and he decides then that he wants to survive. The slaves are ordered back into the hold save one of the prettiest girls among them. With her, the Spaniards celebrate.

The ship follows the coast of Spanish Florida, tacking against the Gulf Stream. At the wharf in Pensacola the Africans are scrubbed clean. The Pygmy has worn the same vine belt, the same foul scrap of oiled barkcloth, since the death of his people. He is stripped naked and they force open his mouth, then recoil at the sight of his cut teeth, the canines and incisors that have been filed into sharp points. The shuddering marineros *dub him El Caníbal, and a yard of coarse osnaburg is pinned around his narrow waist.*

On that Pensacola wharf an auctioneer waves a cowskin whip across the sky, dividing the surviving cargo into fieldhand lots of twenty. The Pygmy is among those purchased by an American smuggler who services Georgia plantations. These slaves are coffled and driven inland by the smuggler and his company of angry Choctaws. They follow the Escambia River north forty miles, crossing the unmarked border into the latter-day state of Alabama. They have entered the territory of Mississippi.

Northeast. On a low, swampy stretch of the federal road one of the Choctaws catches a small moccasin swimming in a flooded wagon rut. The snake is threaded into the mouth of an empty rum bottle, the neck capped with a half piece of cork. The warrior wears the bottle on his hip, and later, when two tall and scurvish slaves refuse to continue, he threatens them with the captured serpent until they rise and begin moving. The Pygmy watches this cruelty and understands that to live he must pretend obedience. And so he mimics the good slaves. He walks steadily and never balks, taking two short steps for every long stride of the coffle. The smuggler takes notice and the runt slave becomes his favorite. They have been gone from Pensacola for six days when the smuggler names him Adam.

The Yellowhammer Inn, a stopping house on the federal road to Georgia. The slaves are chained in the barn while the smuggler dines with the innkeeper and his guests. Later that night a Choctaw wakes the Pygmy with a kick, then leads him inside where he is made to dance and flash his teeth for the fascinated travelers.

The innkeeper presses a long measuring stick against him. "Four feet, eight inches," he announces. "But even that only barely."

The guests have circled him now. Only the smuggler remains at the table, quietly drinking whisky.

"He can't weigh more than a hundred pounds," says the innkeeper.

"A little monkey," whispers a young woman with strips of pale blue ribbon laced in her blonde hair. "A mischievous little monkey."

A child is present—Benjamin—the motherless son of the inn-keeper. The boy watches the tiny slave and begins to cry for him. He begs his father for the Pygmy, and because the innkeeper some-times has a soft heart when it comes to his only child, he agrees.

FOR FIVE YEARS *the Pygmy shares a cramped cabin behind the inn with an elderly slave named Samuel. The old man teaches him to work and groom horses, tend the garden and the hogs. Samuel is patient and kind with his charge, and there comes a time when the quiet world of the Pygmy is unlocked. He has a miraculous gift for mimicry and language, and eventually he learns the country English spoken along the federal road, even the Muskogean tongues of the Creeks and Alibamus and Coushattas and Choctaws who come to trade at Yellowhammer. He is the curiosity of the inn. Benjamin in-structs him on his numbers to a hundred, and the innkeeper charges his customers a few cents to see the savage dance and count. These humiliations outrage Benjamin, but the Pygmy pays for himself many times over.*

1816. THE FIRST full-moon night of the spring. The Pygmy is filling a saddlebag with oats when Samuel finds him in the tack room. It is very late and the old man realizes what he is planning. "Don," says Samuel. "Please don."

The Pygmy dumps a final measure of oats and says nothing. He is folding a horse blanket into the other saddlebag when Samuel seizes him by the wrist.

"They gonna catch you," says Samuel.

He shakes free and then ties the saddlebags closed. "Be caught now."

Samuel kneels and puts his arm around him. "Why? We got a good life here, Adam."

"A good life?"

"Ain't no one bothers us much."

The Pygmy pulls away from him again and they both rise up. "You don understand."

"I understand. You know I understand."

"Come on with me then."

"Freedom ain't livin in a hot swamp," says Samuel. *"Hidin like some panther."*

"You used to talk of runnin to Florida youself."

"And talk's all it ever be. Easy talk."

"You a coward then."

"A coward? Damn you."

"I'm goin."

"But I ain't lettin you." Samuel moves toward the open door of the tack room. The Pygmy pushes himself against the old man but he holds firm. "Be calm," he says. "You shakin like a snake rattle."

"I'll kill you."

"Kill me?"

"I would. If I had to I would."

"Lord Jesus." Samuel waves him away. *"You a devil,"* he tells him. *"All these years and I never saw it."*

Outside, Benjamin is waiting. He is ten years old now. His long brown hair is tied back in a tight pigtail, and already he is taller than the Pygmy.

THE BOY TAKES *him by horseback into the forest. Here there is a river. Since the early winter they have worked to scratch a narrow pocket into the trunk of a windblown cypress, leaving the bark untouched so that now, overturned at the water's edge, their crude dugout resembles nothing so much as a rotting log. Hoot owls are fighting like apes in the treetops, oo-aw squallings that remind the Pygmy of his lost home. It is a warm night but he sees that Benjamin is shivering. The boy is excited.* "Adam," *he says,* "we are going to do this."

The Pygmy points in the direction of Yellowhammer. "Head on home," *he says.*

"Head home?"

"Start back."

"For what?"

"I can't take you."

"What do you mean?"

"This ain't a trip you need to be makin."

"Why are you saying this, Adam?"

"Please now. Go on."

"I won't."

The Pygmy lifts a stolen hay hook and threatens him. "Go on," *he says again.* "Go."

But then the boy threatens him as well. "I'll tell Father," he says. "Make me go and I'll wake him."

The owls are in a frenzy now. Benjamin tries to move past, but the Pygmy grabs him and they stumble. They fall hard. He lands atop the boy and there is a gurgling. The hay hook is buried in the boy's throat, and he wants to speak but the Pygmy stops him. "Be still," he tells him. The hay hook slides out easily, but then much more blood comes and the boy is dead.

The Pygmy presses his lips to the boy's forehead and feels the body cooling. He rolls away and pushes his own face against the dirt. For a long time he stays like this—but finally the angry owls go quiet, and fearing daylight, he rises. Twice he swings the hay hook into Benjamin's chest, puncturing the lungs. The horse has shied off but is watching him. There are stones scattered about, and he drops handfuls of them down the front of the boy's tucked shirt. The slack corpse sinks quickly into the dark river. He watches it disappear, and he hopes that it will remain there.

Kau is in the dugout. He is drifting south. He is following the river.

PART ONE

RETURNING

South — Into the forest — Lawson

KAU SAT CROSS-LEGGED in the shaky dugout, listening to the night sounds of the forest as the river carried him farther and farther south. In the distance he could hear the yips of red wolves coursing whitetails in the hot sandhills. A whippoorwill called and he tried to answer back. Five times he whistled before finally the notes came perfect and the whippoorwill called again.

The surface of the river was shining now, and at this first hint of dawn he paddled for the shore. He beached at a sandbar, then dragged the dugout into a thicket growing along the bank. The forest had grown quieter, and he squatted low in the underbrush, forcing himself to swallow some of the horse feed. In addition to the ten pounds of raw oats, the blanket and the saddlebags, all he had managed to pilfer was a dented canteen and a small tin pot—those and the blood-flecked hay hook. He checked the crocus sack that he had taken from the boy. Inside was a leather-sheathed hunting knife and a tinderbox, Benjamin's sling and a collection of smooth stones that were each the size of chicken eggs. He added the knife and tinderbox to a saddlebag, then tossed the hay hook far out into the river. He waited for a splash but heard nothing.

Tears came as he ran his fingers along the leather sling—twin cords of finely plaited hemp joining a pocket of soft calfskin. This had been a gift from the innkeeper to his son, a weapon purchased from an Arab who did horse tricks in the Augusta circus. Kau dried his eyes against the calfskin and then folded the sling into one of the saddlebags. A distant wolf howled as he dropped ten of the round stones in with the horse feed.

He returned to the dim sandbar and found a pool of still water cut off from the muddy river. He went down on all fours and, careful not to silt the shallow pool, used his fingertips to brush the scum from its surface. A tear formed in the orange crust. He touched his dry lips to the tepid water and sucked long, steady streams down his chalked throat. He drank until his stomach felt heavy, then began spitting mouthfuls into the canteen.

The redbirds were singing as he walked back to the dugout. At Yellowhammer he had carved two short paddles from an oak plank. He took up one of them and scraped the sandy soil down to the hardpan, forming a trench alongside the beached dugout. He settled into the crumbling furrow and from across the river came cackling and the beating of wings, a turkey dropping from its roost. The hen was yelping for her poults to join her when the day arrived clean and blue and Africa hot. Exhausted, he rolled the dugout over on top of him.

Flat on his back, hidden in the dark chamber, he pressed his head against the worn saddlebags. The turned earth was cool against his skin and the scent of the cut cypress worked to clear his mind. He closed his eyes and between flashes of the bloody boy was able to think and plan. When the innkeeper discovered them both missing, he would alert the American soldiers at the fort and send for the slavecatcher. Eventually there would be a chase and for that he needed to rest. He steadied his breathing and fought to collect himself.

LAWSON. THE SLAVECATCHER. The man lived in a cabin near the fort, alone save his mules and a pack of bloodhounds. Kau had seen him only once. A smuggler had a coffle of slaves camped near Yellowhammer when there was an escape. Lawson arrived and had the runaway treed in the river swamp within a few hours. The man was brought in lashed to the back of a black mule, and all gathered to witness his punishment. A coin from the smuggler and Lawson tied the runaway's hands to the low-hanging branch of a live oak growing behind the inn, then hit him twenty times with a cat o' nine he bragged as taken from a British tent at Cowpens.

Kau remembered the runaway's skin tearing like wet paper and knew that with the boy dead he would receive much worse. Indeed, were the boy alive he could still turn back, sink the dugout and walk north to Yellowhammer. He could be asleep on his straw pallet before the sun broke the horizon. At breakfast he would tell Samuel he was sorry and they would go on about their day like nothing out of sort had ever happened between them. And when he saw the boy he would make things right there too, say I never really meant to run, and I thank you for not sayin nothin. I was gamblin that you wouldn't never. You and the Marse are good to me here. Les never speak of this again.

But the boy, of course, was dead.

BY MIDDAY THE sun was full up and he was sweating in slick sheets. His filthy slave-clothes were soaked, and the pocket of air trapped beneath his dugout had gone sour. He was reminded of the burrow of the aardvark, the hold of the slave ship, and he suffered through the last long hours of the afternoon before the day finally gave way to night and it was safe for him to emerge.

One mosquito found him and then many more came. He shed his gray osnaburgs and ran barefoot across the sandbar into the water. Blood and salt washed from his skin as he bathed in the river, scouring himself with handfuls of sand. Along the opposite shore he saw a place where the current had carved into a soft hillside. He swam to the cutbank and broke free a slick knob of red clay, then returned to his campsite and dried himself with long moss pulled from the low branches of an oak. Bats flitted past as he smeared the whole of his body with the clay. Mosquitoes still pushed against him but now they were thwarted and flew off.

He removed the leather belt from his discarded pants and cinched it around his waist. The knife of the boy hung from its sheath at his side, and he used the blade to cut a long strip of rough osnaburg from his shirt, making a breechcloth that he tucked front and back through the buckled belt. He then shouldered the saddlebags, and while dragging the dugout back into the river he saw the reflection of a clay-man painted on the shimmering water. He bent over and studied his round face, the tight curls of hair caked with clay. He shut his eyes and then opened them. For the first time in well over five years he was looking at one of his people.

HIS SECOND NIGHT on the river. The moon had just begun its descent when he heard the riders, horses galloping south along the path that followed the western bank. He hunched forward in the dugout, and after the horses had continued on he paddled himself under a willow that was growing in a hard slant out over the water. There he kept hidden, waiting for the forest to settle behind the riders' raging wake.

After that the riders came steadily. He set down his paddle and slid into the river. The water had cooled slightly with the night. He swam alongside the drifting dugout and stayed to the middle of the channel, his eyes level with the waterline as he searched for soldiers. Here and there sentinels stood solitary on the dark bank. He saw them and he thought of scarecrows.

FARTHER DOWNSTREAM THE dugout became wedged in a snag of dead and gnarled wood and he pulled it free. Soon the river narrowed, and along the bank he noticed a tiny ember glowing orange in the night—a sentinel smoking a cigar. Kau ducked even lower in the water, but still he feared that if he kept on he would be spotted. He kicked his legs and began towing the dugout to the upriver shore.

It was kill this man or leave the river, and as if to assign some meaning or purpose to the death of the boy, Kau decided that in this one moment he would not run. Instead, he pinned the dugout between cattails, then rose up carrying three pale stones and the sling of Abdullah the circus Arab.

The blue-coated sentinel stood on a gravel bank. Next to him a musket was propped against an ebony tangle of driftwood. Kau sat in the cattails and watched him. He and the boy had practiced with the sling most every day. Together they had learned to kill rats in the stables, hurl rocks a hundred yards distant. And now two separate lifetimes had funneled into this moment. That man would die or he would die. Maybe even the both of them.

He was choosing from among the sling-stones when he heard the fast clip of hooves approaching. The sentinel killed his cheroot as another soldier rode out onto the gravel. The rider was big and shadowy, and his mottled horse spun fully around as he called down to the sentinel. "Seen anything?" he asked.

"Nothing," said the sentinel. "Any word of Benjamin?"

The rider shook his head. "But they put the whip to the other nigger. He thinks they might have done run off together, might be angling for Florida."

"Why would Benjamin do a fool thing like that?"

"I bet that little ape witched him some way or another."

The sentinel sent a flat rock skipping across the river. "Better not sail past here."

"Just keep your head and mind what you're shooting at. No holes in the boy."

"Don't be worrying about me."

The rider slapped at a mosquito, and Kau heard the wet sound of flesh hitting flesh. "Ain't nobody worried," said the rider. "Just don't make any mistakes."

The rider galloped off and Kau stood. He was afraid but soon thoughts of the beaten Samuel focused him. He lifted the circus Arab's sling from his neck, then slid the loop onto the middle finger of his right hand. The other sennit tapered into a braided knot that he placed between his thumb and forefinger. He slipped a stone into the cradle and stepped free of the cattails.

The sentinel had taken up his musket but was facing the river. Kau crept closer, slowly spinning the sling to better seat the stone. At ten paces he set his feet and then, uncoiling, he swung the sling hard overhead, the weight of the stone extending his arm. He released the knot and the stone launched, grazing the top of the sentinel's high leather hat before it went careening off into the river. The struck man gave a surprised grunt and then whirled around. He was an older man, had a peppered beard. Kau flicked his wrist and the loose end of the sling snapped back into his hand. He loaded another stone, and the sentinel was struggling to full-cock his flintlock when Kau let fly again. This time the man was caught perfectly in the mouth, and there was the sound of teeth cracking. He dropped his musket and doubled over.

Kau ran forward, then picked up the musket and beat the stock into the man's skull until he could see the soft sponge of brain in the moonlight. The body was twitching as Kau dragged it across the gravel. He concealed the corpse in the cattails and then turned for the dugout, the river.

THE DAY WAS breaking hot and humid as he followed an oxbow channel behind a sliver island. He had claimed the dead sentinel's musket—that and his powderhorn, some patch and grease and ball. The boy had schooled him on firearms, and on hunting trips Kau had watched the innkeeper closely, memorizing the exact rhythms that went into loading a flintlock—the pour of the powder, the preparation of the ball, the priming of the flashpan. He examined the heavy musket as he drifted in the morning twilight. He had already learned their language, this was but another.

HE BEACHED AT a corner of the island—on a mud bank dimpled with the heart-shaped tracks of feral hogs—and was dragging the dugout ashore when he surprised a wallowing sounder of panther-scarred calicos. The wild hogs went crashing through the briers and then into the water, churning across the channel in a wrinkled line.

Later, collecting blackberries in a thicket, he was charged low and hard by a lone lingering sow. He dropped the musket and sprang for the rough trunk of a dogwood, pulling himself from the ground just as a torn ear grazed the bottom of his bare foot. The sow hit the still-bubbling water, and he eased down from his perch. Deeper in the thicket he found her abandoned farrow, eight slink piglets that were dead but not yet cold. He took one of the stillborn shoats back to the dugout, then ate great handfuls of acrid blackberries, translucent slices of raw white pork as succulent and tender as the flesh of some clear-water fish.

HE DREAMT OF the boy. A quick dream that came like a snakebite, a flash of heat lightning on the horizon. A brief vision of Benjamin tumbling along the river bottom, wispy threads of blood trailing him like smoke, his wet hair unraveled and in tendrils, gas bubbling from the holes in his small chest.

And then he awoke to a memory. Benjamin and the innkeeper are on horseback, quail hunting in the uplands, and he and Samuel follow in the wagon as lemon setters quarter off-cycle acres of lespedeza and ragweed. In a hayfield a young dog rouses a bedded spike buck, and the deer goes bouncing toward the hunters. The innkeeper dismounts and drops the buck with a close blast of fineshot from his fowling piece. The boy cheers but then his father reloads and passes him the shotgun. "Once more," says the innkeeper to his son. "In the head." Benjamin takes the flintlock into his small and freckled hands, but then he hesitates as the buck drags its lifeless hindquarters across the field. Black hooves are stabbing black dirt when the bird dogs arrive. The snarling setters pile on to the wounded deer, and the angry innkeeper orders the boy not to fire. The spike buck is bleating like a fawn as Kau cuts its throat with the innkeeper's knife. There is the metallic smell of blood, and Benjamin is told to remain with the wagon. "Ride with the niggers," his father tells him, "ride with the niggers until you are ready to be a man." The innkeeper canters off after his dogs and Benjamin weeps. Kau helps Samuel butcher the deer. "Don be cryin now," says Samuel to the boy. "Killin ain't no easy thing." The boy says nothing, just climbs on to his horse and heads in the direction of Yellowhammer.

Kau watches him leave, then wraps the slippery liver in a cut piece of hide. Crows caw as the distant pop of a shotgun announces that the innkeeper has scattered the morning's first covey.

AT DARK CAME the chitter of coons night-fishing the shallows. He crawled out from under the dugout and the startled coons fled. A shooting star streaked across the southern sky and burned into nothing. It was time to move on.

HE WAS ALL night on the water before he rounded an elbow bend and saw the blockade. Two wide flatboats sat anchored across the river, the pine barges illuminated by the false-dawn glow of torches. Soldiers leapt from boat to boat, and in the center of the flotilla he saw the slavecatcher, Lawson, a leashed hound in either hand. Kau watched him and thought of a thing that Samuel would sometimes say when a bad man slunk past Yellowhammer.

That fella there be the Devil's own pirate.

Kau backpaddled against the current, straining to avoid the place where the dark ended and light began. A dog barked but then went quiet. Kau made for the western shore, and he was guiding the dugout through a field of bone-smooth cypress knees when something hard and fast and hot tore across the slope of his shoulder. A musket boomed, and beneath a shoreline shower of flint-sparks and smoke stood a moonfaced soldier. Kau rolled into the water and unsheathed his knife. A great black cloud of mosquitoes lifted, and he was splashing toward the shore when the soldier threw down his spent musket. The man turned and ran in the direction of the downriver blockade. He was yelling in a high and winded voice, screaming, "Don't shoot, it's Jacob! He's back there! He's back there!"

There were constant hollers down the line as the soldier retreated. Kau grabbed the musket and saddlebags from the dugout, and a hunting horn sounded as he began moving away from the river.

HE WAS A quarter mile from the blockade when dawn burst and the hounds picked up his trail. He had already jettisoned the horse feed—the cooking pot as well—yet still they gained. He doubled back on a low ridge and inspected his shoulder. The musket ball had sliced a furrow through the caked clay, leaving a shallow red scrape but no real damage. He pressed clean green leaves against the cut and sat down with the musket. If they were trying to kill him then they must have found the body of the sentinel, maybe even the sunken boy. He lifted the frizzen to check the prime on the flashpan. The powder looked dry but he added a little more from the powderhorn. The hounds would be ariving soon. He laid the musket across the front of his breechcloth and he waited.

IN THE GRAY light he saw the blurred mass of the main pack pour into the draw beneath him. They continued on, then were followed in a short while by a bell-mouthed bitch—pregnant, her teats heavy with milk—carefully working the scent with an occasional bawl. The old slavehound was nosing through the dry leaves when she came to a stop. She sat on her haunches with her head tilted, and then Kau whistled low and she let loose a howling bay, long and deep. He knelt on the ridge, cocking back the hammer of the musket as she came in a lumber. The bellowing hound was almost to him when he thrust the musket forward and pulled the trigger. The flashpan hissed before finally the muzzle load caught. There was an explosion and then a sharp, quick yelp. He opened his eyes and saw the hound sliding slowly down the hill, her frothing jaws clicking so that for a moment she looked like some enormous dying insect.

The main pack went silent at the shot, and he pulled the powderhorn from a saddlebag and began reloading the musket—a four-count measure of powder, a ball wrapped in a greased patch of cloth and fitted into the muzzle. He pushed the ramrod down the barrel and was priming the flashpan when the hounds started up again. They were moving west still, staying true to the trail he had laid, and this helped to settle him. He tucked the powderhorn through his belt and stood, shouldering his saddlebags as he started out in a straight southern jog.

The hunting horn sounded, but the hounds were overeager and refused to quit the hot trail. Twice more Lawson tried to call in his dogs to check their pursuit. Each time they ignored the slave-catcher's horn. Kau pushed forward, running, and soon the river-bottom graywoods rose into green pinewoods as the whole of the morning sun emerged in the golden east.

IN A SKELETON forest of fire-scarred pine he stopped again. A lightning-struck longleaf had snapped near its base, and he crawled carefully atop that jagged and oozing pedestal. Behind him he could see quick streaks of hide as the hounds came like monkeys moving through a canopy. He pinned his saddlebags between his feet and waited.

Before long five hounds had collected at the burnt and broken stump, clawing at pine bark as they tried to reach him. He shot a young male point-blank in the chest, then pulled patch and ball from a saddlebag and reloaded as quickly as he could manage. Another point-blank shot and Lawson began to scream. Kau could hear him clearly now. "Where the hell are you?" the slavecatcher hollered. "I'm a-coming, nigger."

Kau fired again, and the surviving pair of hounds skulked off whimpering and ruined just as the slavecatcher appeared in his torn buckskins. He was tall and thin and bearded, had black hair veined with gray. Lawson saw the three dogs lying dead at the foot of the broken pine and hurried forward in a hunched trot. At thirty yards the exhausted man raised his longrifle, the black barrel cutting small circles as he tried to take aim. Kau finished seating another ball, then waved the ramrod in the air as he spoke out across the distance between them. "Lemme alone," he said. "You miss and I'm gonna kill you."

"So it talks," said the slavecatcher.

Lawson rushed his shot and there came the hollow echo-knock of a lead ball burying itself into a faraway tree. Kau leapt from his pine stump and the slavecatcher turned to run. The two remaining hounds shied as Kau pursued their master. He primed the musket's flashpan on the sprint, then let the powderhorn fall to the ground. At an arm's length he shot Lawson low in the back, the barrel so close that for a moment the man's greasy buckskins caught fire. The slavecatcher collapsed, gutshot and smoking, and Kau came sliding down beside him.

Lawson's pink stomach was split across the middle and showing cords of intestine. His mouth cracked open. Two of his front teeth were missing. "Well, you've gone and done it," he whispered. "Done what the lobsterbacks never could."

Kau ran his fingers over the stock of Lawson's longrifle. There were stripes and curls in the amber wood. "I gave you a good choice in this," he said.

"Turning tail from some rag-wearing nigger wasn't no choice."

"You done ran though."

Lawson called for the two hounds but they stayed huddled together and frightened among the already dead. Kau watched them and thought of the calmed lions in one of Samuel's Bible stories. Lawson cursed the dogs and then he cursed him. "You son of a bitch," he said. The slavecatcher coughed and a trickle of blood escaped the corner of his scabbed mouth. He started to shiver. Sweat had pooled in the hairless hollow of his chin.

Kau touched him on the shoulder. "I can go and cut your throat if you want that."

"Well," said Lawson. "I don't."

"Be a long while fore they findin you."

"I ain't afraid."

"You gonna be. At the end."

Lawson spit blood at him but missed. "What I might fear ain't no concern of yours."

Kau nodded and the two of them sat there in silence, thinking. A fox squirrel chattered as he unsheathed his knife. He had realized something. "I should scalp you," he said.

"Now why?"

"Them soldiers maybe go thinkin redsticks about." Kau moved closer. "Lose they heart for chasin me."

The slavecatcher sighed a scratched breath. "Play Indian with your possum teeth. I ain't gonna die begging."

"I'll kill you fore I do it."

"Well, thank the good Jesus for that." Lawson sneered and then spit more bright blood. "You kill that boy?"

Kau looked up, searching the blackened forest for danger. "Not wantin to."

The slavecatcher repeated the words, mocking the thickness of his accent. "Ain't what I asked," he said.

"You go and whip my friend?"

Lawson nodded and Kau smelled shit, piss. "I was a scout for Marion, spied with my own eyes that British bastard Tarleton making a Patriot widow dig up her dead husband." The slavecatcher shook his head. "Least that was a war."

"That means you ready?"

"Don't mean that at all."

"You won't feel nothin."

The slavecatcher laughed a high chopping laugh, and a red mist sprayed from his mouth. "Get on," he said. "This has become an ugly world."

Kau pressed the blade against the loose and wrinkled skin folded across Lawson's throat. "I know that," he said.

"Well, then you go on and live free in it awhile," said the slave-catcher. "See if it treats you any better now."

A land forfeit — Redsticks — Florida

DAYS OF WANDERING. He buried the slavecatcher's scalp in a bobcat den and walked south, moving at night, following the stars to Florida. The clay that had once coated him dried into brick dust and fell away, and his skin was left stained red and itching. His breechcloth was now dyed the color of rust.

It was easy country to traverse and at times he grew angry with himself for not bolting long before. He crossed pine flatlands that in low spots dropped off into thin finger forests of virgin oak and elm—beech, sycamore and chestnut—shady hollows where clear springs flowed and he could escape the stunning heat of the day. The cut on his shoulder from the musket ball scabbed and then healed.

As a distraction from thoughts of Samuel and the boy, he collected arrowheads as he walked—chert bird-points and deer-points.

This was land forfeited by the Creeks to the Americans at the end of the Creek civil war, but still the Indians lingered. He could see their scattered sign and surely they his, and yet one did not cause harm upon the other. A peace persisted. Some understanding that he was only a traveler passing through. A visitor laying no claim. A small man who would leave no lasting mark of any consequence, no evidence that he had ever even existed. This was a wilderness.

HE HAD TRADED the dead sentinel's musket and accessories for Lawson's longrifle and hunting pouch and powderhorn. Kau brought the longrifle to his shoulder and his finger only barely reached the trigger. Though lighter than the musket, the flintlock was as long as he was from brass buttplate to muzzle. Still, he stared down the barrel and nodded, supposed that he could continue to kill at very close range and that maybe—one day and with practice—he would be able to shoot with the skill of the innkeeper, a man who could snipe a fish crow from the top branch of a cross-river cypress, tumble a running fox.

ON HIS WALK he saw many deer, sorrel in their spring coats, and though he needed to test himself with the longrifle he thought it even more important that he move in a whisper through this strange land. He foraged for his food at dawn and at dusk, collecting ripe berries and fat white grubs, stabbing pine snakes and woodrats with a three-pronged gig sharpened from a hickory stick. He was tracking a diamondback through sugar sand one morning when he encountered an old Indian woman sitting alone near the entrance of a tortoise burrow. She was a Creek, he decided. Her lined face was the color of dark cedar, and she was wearing only moccasins and a faded British redcoat decorated with broken pieces of mirror. Though he made no effort to hide, she did not seem aware of his presence.

He spoke out to her in the faltering Creek he had learned during his years at Yellowhammer. "Grandmother," he asked, "is this Florida?"

The woman gave a vague and toothless smile but said nothing in reply. Nearby a gopher tortoise—its scaly hind legs hobbled together by the end of a long rope—struggled across the sand, fighting to return to the burrow that it had been stolen from.

He stood watching the woman, and after a while another tortoise emerged. The woman rushed forward like a statue gone living and flipped the tortoise onto its back. She tied this second tortoise to the other end of the rope and then lifted them both up so that they hung like fish on a stringer. The rope was placed atop her balding head like a tumpline, and the kicking tortoises bounced against her small hips as she disappeared down a thin scratch path that meandered through the clumps of pale green wiregrass.

MOST NIGHTS IT was humid and hot like some darkened day and the snap of a broken stick would cut the stillness with a sound like a whipcrack. Other nights it would rain and this was in fact best because he could move through the forest trackless and without sound.

To sleep was to dream. And to dream was to see the dead boy.

Late afternoon. Upon rising for his tenth night of walking south he spotted a thickening thread of smoke in the near distance. He folded his horse blanket as he considered whether to keep on or investigate. Soon he would have the cover of darkness, and in the end he decided that perhaps in seeking out that fire he would come upon some clue as to whether finally, after so many nights of travel, he had at last crossed over into Florida.

THE NIGHT BREEZE was in his face and he could smell the wood smoke as he walked. Before long he came to a clearing in the pines where pioneers had cut a shallow potato field in the poor soil. Across the way stood a small barn, and beside it a cabin was burning down to its gray-rock chimney. In the glow of the orange fire an enormous Indian was pushing himself against a bent white woman. A smaller figure leaned against a toppled middlebreaker, watching, and a man lay dead and mutilated in the nearby dust with killed daughter and killed son and killed plow mule. The shock-struck wife made no real sound as the giant forced his way inside of her.

Kau hid himself and decided that these two Indians were Red Stick Creeks—the villains of all those Yellowhammer stories, the terrors of the federal road. The smaller Indian moved away from the middlebreaker, and Kau saw that she was a young woman. She called out to the giant and he quit with his raping long enough to slide the pioneer's long dress free from her milky body. He threw the dress high into the air, and as it came ballooning down the red-stick girl caught it. She laughed and then danced as she pulled the dress on over her head.

He remained hidden until they took out their knives, then was turning to leave them when he saw an Indian crouched and watching him from a few feet away. Kau lifted his longrifle but this third redstick charged forward and knocked it from his hands.

Kau was wrestled out of the forest and into the potato field. He lay sprawled in the dirt and in the firelight he saw that the full tip of the redstick's nose was missing. The Indian was bare-chested and wore a breechcloth, beaded leggings and moccasins. A crimson war-club hung from his side and ashes swirled around him. The deformed redstick put a foot on Kau's stomach, then called to his companions with a single whooping holler. Kau turned his head and saw the other two redsticks come running. Behind them the pioneer woman kept at her writhing. Her heels seemed to have been cut. Twice she tried to run but both times she fell.

The redstick girl had wild brown hair that fell down past her waist, and was maybe half the age of the two men. She laughed and tugged at Kau's breechcloth, then he heard her wonder in Creek if this tiny clay-tinged man could be the son of the master of breath himself. The cut-nosed Indian smiled and the redsticks all moved closer. Both the cutnose and the girl now held what looked to be big-bored Jaeger rifles. The giant wore only a breechcloth and moccasins, carried a red club of his own but no rifle or musket. His long face and broad chest were painted in a division of black and bright red. Like the cutnose his head was shaved. He stared at Kau and seemed never to blink.

THAT HE WAS a negro and knew much of their language perhaps saved his life. And of course his size intrigued them. When he saw that they would not harm him he asked carefully for his longrifle, and the cutnose fired the flintlock into the air before returning it to him empty. Kau was told to wait, and so he sat alone in the potato field while the pioneer woman was at last scalped and then killed by a blow from a war-club that split her skinned head.

LATER, ALL THREE redsticks stood facing him in the potato field but he would not look at them. He stared at the burning cabin instead until finally the girl spoke to him in Creek. "Do not be afraid," she said. "Our war is not with you."

The cutnose nodded. "You are running to Florida?"

Kau answered in Creek. "I am," he said.

"Then we will bring you," said the girl. "We go there as well."

"I do not need that."

The cutnose shook his head. "No," he said. "This is our land. And we will guide you through it."

THE BODIES OF the pioneers were thrown into the fire, and after the redsticks stole some oats the barn was torched as well. Kau was then led back into the forest to where three stallions—a white, a gray and a red—stood hitched to scrub pines. The cutnose told him that his name was Little Horn. "And you?" he asked. Kau said his own name, and Little Horn copied him slowly. "*Kaa-ew?*"

"Yes."

Little Horn nodded and then climbed on to the white horse. "Kau," he said again. The redstick offered his hand, and when Kau took it he was lifted in a rush so that in an instant he was sitting straddled and felt like a child.

THE REDSTICKS RODE south, talking. The young woman was called Blood Girl. The giant, Morning Star—a prophet who spoke only to Blood Girl. When Morning Star had a thing to say to the others he would point to Blood Girl. She would ride to him and he would whisper into her ear, stare off at the stars as she shared his message.

"You are one of the caught ones?" asked Little Horn. "An African?"

"Yes." He could hear whistles of air passing through Little Horn's clipped nose. What Kau knew of redsticks he had learned from the soldiers who came to Yellowhammer to play cards and drink whisky. He turned and touched his own nose. "Horseshoe Bend?" he asked.

Little Horn poked him in the side. "What do you know of that place?"

"I heard that the Americans took noses to count the dead." In fact he had seen a glimpse of them once, a sack of some six hundred shriveled scraps of flesh. The soldiers had gambled with them as faro checks.

"So they did." Little Horn wiped away the snot that had collected above his lip. "I have seen the whole of the war between my people."

They rode on and Little Horn began to speak of his life and his battles. The redstick had been in Tukabatchee five years earlier when Tecumseh came down from the icy lands in the north, splitting the Creek nation with his calls for war and a return to the ways of the ancestors. The Shawnee chief showed them a comet and then promised an earthquake—and when the village shook that same autumn Little Horn took up the war-club of the redsticks, fought for the prophets at Burnt Corn and Fort Mims, Tallushatchee and Talladega. The war ended at Horseshoe Bend. Little Horn was left shot and unconscious in a tangled carnage field when they came for their cut count. He awoke with a young soldier sitting on his chest, and after the boy had finished with his sawing Little Horn took hold of the knife and killed him. Blood of Indian mixed with the blood of the boy, and as the stabbed American screamed all eyes witnessed the quickening of the dead redstick in the slippery gore. General Jackson himself ordered the dirty goddamn heathen devil killed at once, but Little Horn survived the hacking gauntlet of soldier and militiaman and Lower Creek and mercenary Cherokee. He threw himself into the river like a diving mink, and when he surfaced on the other side of the Tallapoosa this time all shots missed.

BLOOD GIRL MANEUVERED her chestnut stallion alongside Little Horn and held out a canteen. "Water for the child of the master of breath?" she asked. Kau's own canteen was empty and so he accepted. He drank and stared back at her, listening as she started up a chant that told of the creation. How at one time the entirety of the world lay underwater, the only land a hill. On this hill lived the master of breath, and from the clay of the hill the master of breath molded the first people. A man and a woman.

Kau grunted and Blood Girl sat sideways on the bare back of her red horse. "Is that what your people believe as well?" she asked. The pioneer woman's blue dress was gathered around her young hips and he saw that it was trimmed with lace. She pulled it over her head and let it fall from her fingers. Beneath that dress she wore another. This one made from the finely woven fibers of some plant or tree. She was pretty and seemed strong and able—perhaps the closest thing he had seen in this second world to the wife he had lost in the first.

"No," he said finally. "But what we believed was not so different."

She dropped the reins and began gathering her chocolate hair into a topknot. She was sideways and facing him still, but her horse stayed the trail, following that of Morning Star. "They are gone?" she asked. "Your people?"

He nodded and then the path made a sharp turn. The redsticks banked their stallions quickly—so quickly that, for a moment, they all seemed to be spinning in place.

THEY TRAVELED THROUGH the night and then until late the next day. Along a wide spot in the trail he saw where the trunk of a big live oak had been notched twice with an axe. Here they at last halted. Little Horn dismounted and patted him on his leg. "Florida," he said, stomping down hard on the earth.

AT DARK THEY left the trail and made their camp at the far end of an oak grove. He spread his horse blanket out beside the fire and sat down. Morning Star and Blood Girl were across from him; Little Horn was already on his back and sleeping.

Kau watched through the smoke as Blood Girl began scrubbing the war paint from Morning Star's skin with the torn corner of a charred quilt. The redstick prophet whispered to her, and she looked over at Kau and spoke: "He tells me that we have many more to kill."

"White men, you mean?"

"Yes."

Kau folded his blanket over so that he was cocooned within it. He was through with killing. "I have heard that there are places here in Florida where there are still no white men," he said. "Is that true?"

She balled the quilt in her hands and handed it to Morning Star. "I think so," she said. "But at one time you could have said that about the whole of this land."

"I only need a piece of it."

He saw Morning Star shake his head. The prophet rose up holding the quilt, then walked with Blood Girl away from the fire and into the darkness. Soon there came sounds like those made by small animals tussling, and Kau stared at a far southern star as he lay listening to the snarls and squeals of their lovemaking.

IN THE MORNING he watched as Little Horn took a knife to Lawson's longrifle. The redstick unscrewed the buttplate and shaved down the stock. When he was finished Kau lifted it to his shoulder, and though the balance was off it did fit him perfectly. He lowered the flintlock and motioned toward Morning Star. The prophet was wandering among the hobbled stallions.

"Yes?" asked Little Horn. "What is it you want to know?"

"Why does he not carry a flintlock?"

Little Horn brushed the curled chips of wood from his lap and shook his head. "He follows the old ways in everything."

"So only the club?"

"Yes."

"And you?"

Little Horn laughed, then he bent the brass buttplate over onto itself and threw it into the fire. The full sun had appeared in the sky, but the air was still cool within the shade of the oaks that surrounded them. "I am no prophet," he said.

Little Horn and Blood Girl both gave him lessons with the longrifle—teaching him the proper powder load and how to shoot with some accuracy. On occasion he made to leave but always the redsticks delayed him, convincing him that he needed more rest and more food, more training with the longrifle before he should continue on his journey. At night they built great roaring fires without concern, but when he asked if here at last was a place where men need not fear discovery the redsticks only shrugged and said no but let them come. We fear no one.

HE SPENT ALL of the day with the longrifle, concealed within briers near the fork of a deer trail. Late in the afternoon a doe appeared, and when she paused to glance back the way she had come he pressed his cheek against the longrifle and peered down the barrel, closing his left eye same as the redsticks had taught him. The front sight was a thin blade of silver, and he lined it up with the groove of the rear sight, fixing on a spot just behind the doe's shoulder. At present the doe continued on, and when she was about twenty paces from him he released a level breath and squeezed the trigger. The doe collapsed onto her side, then began to paw at the air with slow and rhythmic kicks. He pushed his way through the briers and ran toward her. His ball had flown wide but she was shot through the neck.

AT DUSK HE sat by the fire with the others. Little Horn had cut himself a long green stick, and the redstick was roasting the deer heart when he made a clucking sound with his tongue and pointed. "Look there," he said.

Kau followed his gaze and in the fading light he saw a spotted fawn walking alone in the oak grove, cold-trailing its dead mother through the leaves. The fawn trotted into the camp like a pet goat, then began to nuzzle the wet doe hide that lay crumpled nearby.

"Sad," said Little Horn.

Morning Star threw a coiled length of rope to Blood Girl, and she tied the confused fawn's leg to a sapling. She walked back to Morning Star, and the fawn folded itself atop the comforting deerskin.

Kau looked across the fire at Little Horn. "If there had been a child with me, would you have killed him?"

Little Horn bounced the deer heart over the flames. "What kind of child?"

"A white child. A boy."

"A baby white child?"

"No."

"How big?"

Kau placed the flat of his hand two widths higher than his own head.

Little Horn laughed and the fawn's head lifted at the sound. "That is no child," he said.

HE SAT UP that night watching the caught fawn sleep, wondering whether the creature knew that its mother was dead, whether the little deer realized that it was only waiting for the moment of its own slaughter. Morning Star was tossing through a nightmare, and Kau saw him shiver and then kick at the ground. The fawn awoke with big blinking eyes and though Kau considered slipping its noose he knew that there was no point, that tether or no tether it would never leave this place that smelled of its mother.

MORNING. THE REDSTICKS woke late and lazed in the camp eating venison and passing pipefuls of tobacco cut with sumac. The deer meat had begun to ripen in the sun, so a rack was fashioned from green limbs. The hungry fawn went to bleating as they smoked the remains of the doe, and its cries brought a horned owl swooping like some gigantic bat. The owl settled into an oak, watching the fawn until the owl itself was spotted by a crow, and then these ancient enemies fought in the treetops like courting dragonflies until more crows came calling and at last the day-roving owl was chased off.

The redsticks watched all of this and after a while even they could no longer bear the cries of the starving fawn. Morning Star whispered to Blood Girl and then handed her his ball-headed club. The fawn cowered as she walked toward it.

THAT NIGHT THE three redsticks planned their next raid while the skewered fawn cooked on a crooked length of dogwood that had been stripped of its bark. He listened to them plot. A company of thieves was living in a cave back across the border, not far from the federal road. The redsticks would kill these highwaymen and ride to Pensacola, buy weapons and supplies from the Spanish and then fall in with the other redsticks—those who had already fled deeper into Florida. Little Horn bit at his fingernail. "We will find them and together we will fight a running war. I have learned from our mistake at Horseshoe Bend."

Kau watched the eyeball of the skinned fawn begin to bulge and then split from the heat of the embers. He sat up on his horse blanket and the redsticks looked at him. He was thinking that maybe there was another lesson to be learned that day at Horseshoe Bend. "What if the Americans cannot be defeated?" he asked.

Little Horn leaned closer to the red coals, and his flat skull-face gleamed in the firelight. After a long while he spoke. "Your tribe must have been a very peaceful one," he said.

Kau nodded. "We had no enemies," he said quietly. "Not until the end."

The Ota and the Kesa

NO ENEMIES UNTIL the end.

The redsticks pressed him on this comment but he gave no answers. The entire truth was that he had brought those enemies and that end, same as he had brought about the death of Benjamin, the torture of Samuel. The fawn was pulled from the fire and consumed, and as the night wore on the redsticks finally left him alone save Morning Star. The prophet rose up from beside Blood Girl and went to sit with him. At first Kau was nervous but then he relaxed. He stared at the fire and thought of his lost home, of an emerald forest cut by swift rivers.

THOUGH HE AND his band of Ota roamed the forest like bees, they seldom strayed very far from the Kesa settlement of Opoku, trading wild meat and wild honey for the vegetables and fruits of the village fields. The Ota and the Kesa were separate, but they were also the same in that each depended upon the other for their survival—still, while the Kesa viewed the Ota as something like allies, they did not consider the tiny forest people to be their equals. And for their part, Kau and his tribesmen, they too were not without arrogance.

But the arrogance of the Ota was akin to the quiet satisfaction of a spy who continues to escape detection. Moving among the Kesa, the Ota were shy and deferential because an Ota is a mimic. What he knows of survival is learned in the forest and—just as a stalking Ota huntsman copies the bark of duiker, the chatter of monkeys—the Ota long ago traded their own language for that of the Kesa, doing what they must to gain access to that village world of plenty they had grown to covet. Only when the Ota were alone in the forest was their true nature revealed. Here, with the last remnants of their dying language, they described those things for which the Kesa had no words or understanding. And they mocked the villagers, a superstitious people who presumed evil spirits and witchcraft to be the cause of every ill.

The villagers' fear of the forest was above all a confusion to the Ota, as the Ota trusted in the forest. The Ota saw the forest as benevolent and kind and believed that when there was a hardship it was only because their guardian had fallen into a slumber. During these bad times the Ota would send for the sacred molimo that they kept hidden high in a treetop, and with this wooden trumpet they would call out to the forest so that it would then awake and continue to protect them. There would be singing and dancing, a celebration of the happiness soon to return.

OCCASIONALLY IN THE long history of their association, the condescension of the Kesa and the deception of the Ota caused minor clashings between the two peoples. Insignificant disagreements and confrontations that were always soon resolved.

But then one day Kau's wife was caught foraging in the village cassava fields. Her name was Janeti, and she was the mother of their young daughter Tufu, their infant son Abeki.

The farmer who seized Janeti had long desired her from afar—as it was a fact that most Kesa men found the small and cheerful Ota women to be more attractive than the sullen females from the village. And with her shiny skin and wide hips Janeti was even prettier than most. The farmer wrestled her to the ground and then clamped his hand over her dark lips. Janeti's barkcloth fell away, and when she returned to the Ota camp that evening she was dirt-caked and crying and bruised. There was outrage among the Ota, and though they were not warriors some of the younger men took up their hunting bows and threatened to attack the village of Opoku. Kau himself was leaving the camp when his mother and his wife locked their arms around his leg. At last his father intervened, asking that the elders be allowed to speak. The women and children withdrew to their leaf huts, and the men held council until a consensus was reached. Because it was the Ota way, they would make a bid for peace—the Kesa would be given the opportunity to punish this farmer themselves.

And so the next day Kau went to Opoku and requested an audience with the Kesa chief, a massive man named Chabo. The chief had a leopard skin draped across his broad shoulders and wore a necklace of sun-bleached cowrie shells. He listened in his hut to the grievance, and then the farmer was sent for.

The farmer was an honest man, and when Chabo repeated Kau's accusations he admitted to the rape. "But it was justified," said the farmer. "Who knows how long that woman has been taking from me? How much I have lost because of her? How much food has been stolen from the mouths of my family?"

"But what of my wife?" said Kau. "What of my wife?"

The farmer looked to Chabo, then punched at the air with wild arms. "Do we not kill the monkeys caught in our fields? She is fortunate."

Chabo's head gave a slight nod, and though again Kau protested this time he was silenced. The chief pointed at him. "It was wrong for your wife to steal from this man. Do you agree?"

Kau could not deny the truth of that. Though the Ota shared everything among themselves, he knew that this was not the way of the village. "Yes," he said. "That was wrong."

Chabo then addressed the farmer: "But you, by taking his wife you have taken all that you are owed." The farmer began to argue but Chabo stopped him as well. "It is settled," he said.

The farmer was leaving the hut when Kau spoke. "One is not equal to the other," he said.

Chabo tilted his head, annoyed. "Explain to me what you mean."

"One is not equal to the other," Kau repeated. "My wife is worth more than any amount of cassavas taken from this man." He turned to the farmer. "I will replace with meat twice over all that you have lost. Would you accept this?"

The farmer shrugged. "I would."

"But in exchange," said Kau, "I must be allowed to bring one of your wives into my own hut. Only then will all be truly even."

Chabo laughed. "You are very bold."

Kau slapped his hands together. "Is what I suggest not an equal trade? Is a Kesa woman somehow worth more than an Ota woman?"

"Yes," said the farmer. "Much more."

Chabo started a speech but then faltered and checked his words. "I have made my decision," he said at last. "It is time now for you to return to the forest."

THAT AFTERNOON KAU brought the news of Chabo's verdict to his camp, and although there was again much anger and posturing for battle, the small band knew that to make war with the Kesa would only bring about their own destruction. "No," Kau told the elders. "He said return to the forest, and that is what we should do." And so it was decided.

EARLY THE NEXT morning the Ota began their exodus. The band traveled north for several days, journeying into a part of the forest that only the oldest among them had ever visited. In this new land they built new leaf huts, and it was not long before Kau, hunting alone, heard the angry trumpetings of elephants fighting in the distance. He started for that far-off battleground in a steady trot, and the sun was setting when he finally reached them. From a downwind treetop he watched an enormous male humiliate a broken-tusked bull, then raise its trunk to celebrate the banished king's retreat into the darkening forest.

Kau began to stalk the solitary old bull, and at spots along the trail he would cover himself with handfuls of the elephant's steaming dung, replacing his own smell with that of his prey as the doomed creature cut a great meaningless circle in the forest.

On the third night he decided that the time to kill had arrived. He tracked the bull to a clearing in the forest, then watched as the weepy-eyed beast licked at an oozing gore hole. The elephant drifted off into a motionless and standing sleep, and a stray breeze rustled high branches as Kau crept across the clearing. The pale legs of the bull rose like columns in the moonlight, and through these columns Kau passed. He drove a short mahogany spear up into the elephant's gray belly, piercing its bladder with a succession of quick jabs, then ran back into the forest as from behind him came a bellowing song of sadness and pain and rage.

It was another night before the crippled bull finally bled out, yet another before Kau found his way back to the camp. He was clutching the severed tail of the bull, and news of this great fortune was taken by the elders as a sign from the forest. It was agreed that they would never again trade with the village of Opoku.

THOUGH OF COURSE the meat of the elephant was one day exhausted, the forest continued to provide, and among the band this time in isolation was a period of great comfort and plenty. Fifteen full moons passed before Chabo's taste for honey won over and he relented. The Ota were joined in their camp by a delegation from

Opoku, and a terrified woman was presented to Kau. "This is the wife of the farmer," said a Kesa warrior. "She is yours to have until morning."

Kau looked to his own wife Janeti. Her eyes were wet but she nodded to him.

Although many within the band argued for the acceptance of the Kesa woman, in the end Kau would not take her. A man often thirsts for that which he is never meant to have, yet Kau felt the pull of something even greater. Pride. The woman was sent away, and ten nights later the Kesa attacked the Ota camp.

A teeth cutting—A return to the Mississippi Territory—The remains of a buffalo— On black panthers

THE NEXT DAY the redsticks revealed to him what they knew of the highwaymen. They had learned of these white thieves two months earlier—from a muleskinner captured north of the port city of Mobile. Facing death, hoping to save his life, the man had told them a tale of land pirates and treasure.

The highwaymen had laid claim to a cave near the Conecuh River. Assisted by men seeking commissions—collaborators like the muleskinner himself—they targeted wealthy travelers along the federal road. In his own broken Creek the desperate muleskinner had convinced the redsticks that he knew the exact location of that hidden cave, describing a cleft in a particular broken hillside so well that he made his own survival irrelevant.

Kau sat sweating on his horse blanket beside a dying fire, watching as the redsticks prepared to depart that safe camp for another distant blood field. A company of cursed souls doomed to spend their days cutting warpaths across borderlands, a back-and-forth revenge life of ambush then pursuit. The night before, Little Horn and Blood Girl had both asked him to join them. His answer had been no, but now, studying on the redsticks, he was less certain. In a way he envied their lives of purpose, their forever war. He himself had felt nothing at all since the killing of the boy, nothing save the blank hope that if he continued pushing across Florida he would someday find a silent corner of forest that reminded him of his home, a place he could come to treasure as much as all that had been taken away from him.

The stallions were freed from their hobbles and Little Horn asked him again. Once more Kau explained that he intended to strike out on his own, and Blood Girl stepped forward. "You are not listening," she said. "Morning Star believes you must come with us."

Kau looked over at Morning Star. The prophet was standing beside his horse, and the old gray was refusing to eat oats from the flat of his hand. Morning Star nodded, and Kau turned to Little Horn. "I have no choice?"

"No," said Little Horn. "In this you do not."

Kau knelt and began to slowly place his things into his saddle-bags. He could smell a coming rain. So, he realized, it seemed that he had somehow become a slave again.

IT WAS DRIZZLING when the redsticks finally broke camp and rode off west to kill the highwaymen. The light rain washed the very last of the clay dust from his thick hair, and steam rose from the ground. Little Horn offered him a place on his horse but he declined. His thighs were still sore and blistered from the bareback night ride of the previous week and so he swore off horses, preferred instead to follow on foot, tracking the unshod stallions alone through the damp and dripping forest.

Several times while trailing the redsticks he considered turning around and trying to escape them. Twice he backtracked for a near mile before again changing his mind. Were he his younger self, were this a forest he knew as well as the one he had been stolen from, he thought he might have had the courage to break away from them. As it was he did not. These redsticks were not white men. If he ran he was certain that they would find him and so he kept on.

HE WAS ANXIOUS for more real practice with the longrifle, and so when he came upon a wild cow wallowing in the muddy path he crept to within a few downwind paces of the big speckled beast and then shot it in the head. The cow sighed as it rolled over in the mud. He drew his knife and cut loose one of the backstraps, a thick length of meat that reminded him of a python.

It was dark by the time he reached the camp. The redsticks had built a fire and were waiting for him. He washed the backstrap in a creek that ran nearby, and Little Horn walked over from the fire. "It was you who shot?" he asked.

"It was," said Kau.

"A cow?"

"Yes."

"I thought you lost our trail." Little Horn tapped at the creek with the toe of his moccasin. "Or that maybe you decided to leave us."

Kau dried his hands on his breechcloth and then began cutting the wet backstrap into steaks. "You do not need to worry," he said. "I will not run."

A smile played across Little Horn's scar-slick face. In the firelight Kau saw Blood Girl and Morning Star spread out on horse blankets. They were watching him as well. Kau brought the meat to the fire and saw that the girl had a bare and glistening leg draped over that of the prophet. Morning Star put a finger to his open mouth and she laughed. "He wants you to cut his teeth," said Blood Girl. "Can you do that?"

"Why?"

"He says that we have things to learn from you."

Morning Star pushed her leg away and sat up on his blanket. Blood Girl clapped her small hands.

"Now?" asked Kau.

"Yes," said Blood Girl. "Now."

He hesitated but then removed a scavenged arrowhead from a saddlebag, that and one of Benjamin's oval sling-stones. "Hold him," he said to the redsticks. "He will want to kill me." He looked into Morning Star's black eyes as he said this. Nothing. The prophet lay back and allowed Little Horn to pin his massive arms to the ground, and then Blood Girl slid a hand under his breechcloth, distracting him. Kau held a stick out sideways, and Morning Star bit down onto it with straight teeth that were stained the color of honey. The big man's brown skin was smooth and unscarred, and Kau straddled his wide chest, holding the deer-point in one hand, the river stone in the other. Morning Star shut his eyes as the tip of the arrowhead came to rest on the edge of an incisor, and Kau began tapping at the base of the arrowhead with the stone. Blood Girl grunted behind him, and flakes of enamel fell away as the front six teeth of the prophet were sculpted.

It was slow work, work that he had not done in many years. Morning Star's gums were cut here and there from mishits, but still he did not cry out or even open his eyes. Occasionally the prophet would turn his head to spit blood and bits of tooth and flint and stick, and before long a paste had formed in the dirt beside them. Kau finished with the final canine and rose up, then Morning Star pulled the stick from his mouth and ran his tongue across his cut teeth. Blood Girl passed him a cracked hand mirror that had been stolen from the dead pioneer woman, and the prophet knelt with it beside the fire and examined himself for a long while.

At last Morning Star dropped the mirror and rolled his head in a wide, slow circle. Kau heard a popping sound, and was not sure whether it came from the fire or from somewhere deep inside the body of the prophet. Little Horn had a beefsteak cooking on a hot rock in the coals, and Morning Star grabbed the rare meat in his big hands. He turned to Kau, then bit off a chunk of the sizzling steak and smiled. Pink blood-juice spilled from the corners of his mouth as Little Horn let out a series of war whoops. "He likes it," said Blood Girl in a low voice. "He likes it very much."

EVENTUALLY THEY CHANGED their direction from west to north, and though he saw no real difference in the land, the redsticks told him that they had crossed back over the border and were once again traveling through the territory of Mississippi. After several days the pinewoods fell off into an immense canebrake, a great green sleeve that choked both banks of the dark and peaceful Conecuh. They made their way through the slender cane, following a confusion of game trails. The serried stalks rose fifteen, twenty feet from the moist black soil, filtering out the sun so that Kau came to feel as if he had joined with some party of burrowing tunnel-dwellers.

The canebrake teemed with deer and bear that crashed off unseen before them, and in an ancient salt lick Little Horn found the large and gnawed bones of what Kau thought must be more wild cattle. But then Morning Star crouched beside them and traced a long finger in the dirt. The prophet drew the crude outline of some big, short-horned animal, and in Kau's mind those bleached bones took proper shape. Morning Star whispered to Blood Girl and she began to describe a creature that seemed so much like the forest buffalo of Africa that Kau felt his heart quicken. "*Tupi*," he whispered.

"*Yuh-nuh-suh*," said Blood Girl.

Kau stared at her. "Are there many here?"

Blood Girl shook her head and told him that even Morning Star had seen only two in his entire life, a cow and calf in the rocky foothills far to the north. "But that was very long ago," she said.

Kau knelt among the familiar bones. He figured this could only be a message from the forest, a sign that he was on the proper path, that perhaps he was indeed meant to try this angry killing life. He searched the scattered remains until he found a long bone half buried in the loam. He pulled the bone free of the earth and brushed it clean.

"What do you want with it?" asked Little Horn.

Kau slapped the bone against his palm and then pointed to the war-club that hung from Little Horn's waist. The redstick smiled, and that night they helped him dye the bone in a crimson broth made from boiled pieces of oak bark and root that Blood Girl had went off to collect in the uplands. The bone was painted with thin coats of pine resin, then placed by the fire to dry and strengthen until morning. They slept and at dawn Little Horn tested the reddened bone against the thick skull of the buffalo. The skull cracked and he handed the bone to Kau. "Now take it to Morning Star," said the redstick. This was done and after the prophet had mouthed some silent blessing or curse over the virgin weapon it was returned. Kau fixed a hard loop of rawhide to the back of his belt and then slid the bone club into place.

HE WAS LESS than a mile from the salt lick yet again he was alone, separated from the riders. Along a wet section of trail he saw where Morning Star had paused to draw another buffalo in the mud, that and a little stick man Kau realized was meant to be him.

He was studying his image when there was an eruption in the canebreak. He full-cocked his longrifle, then watched as a velvet-horned buck stumbled out into the path with a tawny and growling panther attached to its back. The cat raised its head from the buck's neck and stared at him, then left the deer for the shelter of the cane. Buck hair filled the hot air like sparks from a kicked fire. The bloodied deer lurched forward and Kau pardoned the wobbly creature. "Go," he said in Kesa. "You were lucky today." The buck gathered itself and then bolted. Kau watched it bound back down the trail. There were other deer close by—keeping still in the cane—and as the wounded buck fled these others spooked as well so that soon Kau could hear deer moving all around him.

He sat down in the trail. Because his name was Leopard these New World panthers were of great interest to him. He cupped his ears and listened, thinking that maybe, if he waited long enough, he might just hear the big cat scream from somewhere in the canebrake. No scream came, but waiting for some sound from this panther soon made him think of another panther—the black African leopard that had once visited him while he slept.

THE LEOPARD HAD been a female. Small but cunning, she was introduced to the flesh of humans by the carelessness of the Kesa. Before the destruction of his people, before the rape of Janeti, before the births of Abeki and Tufu even, there had been this man-eater.

But the leopard did not become a man-eater until the arrival of a Kesa child—a blind child, the son of one of the poorest farmers in Opoku. It was the custom of the Kesa to cast out such misfits, and for that reason the condition of the infant was a secret kept close by the mother and father. The child was raised in the hut, and somehow three years passed before an aunt finally spoke out and word reached the chief. Chabo sent for the boy.

The delay of the parents only made their loss more profound, as the boy was walking and even speaking by the time Chabo's men came for him. He had a name and a personality, a preference for bananas over plantains, for goat meat over chicken. Even Chabo was stalled, but then he consulted the witch doctors and was compelled to act in accordance with tradition. The boy was pulled from the arms of his mother, then brought deep into the forest and released to wander.

And wander he did. The child's whole world had been a small round hut and to be taken from it terrified him. The next day he was walking through the village calling for his mother. Chabo heard his cries and again the boy was seized.

After two days in the forest the child was found by Kau, hunting. He carried the milk-eyed boy back to Opoku and was scolded by the Kesa villagers. "Do not involve yourself with our affairs," Chabo told him.

For a third time the boy was carried off into the forest—though even farther now toward the rising sun, to a distant place separated from the village by an impossible maze of trails. But by now Kau had developed an interest in the unfortunate child. He lingered in Opoku until the Kesa warriors had returned, then backtracked to where the boy had been left to die. When he arrived the child was already gone, stolen by a leopard. He studied the abundant sign:

The leopard had arrived that same day, perhaps attracted by the cries of the boy. Kau saw that at first she was only curious and had sat in the shadows, watching. She was not hungry—he found where earlier she had killed a nesting chimpanzee—but as time passed she grew bolder. She crept closer and walked a tight circle around the blind boy—brushing against him, perhaps even teasing him with her tail—and the shock of her presence sent him dancing little nightmare steps that left random dimples in the soft earth. The boy then rolled himself into a ball and the leopard slapped at him, her hooked claws kept hidden, retracted. The cat played until finally the terror-stricken boy collapsed. He lay flat on his stomach, digging his fingers into the dirt as the leopard sniffed him. When death came it came quickly. She touched her fangs to his neck and squeezed her jaws closed.

Kau thought of the blind and banished child and wondered whether there was a moment before that killing bite when he believed he might be spared, that maybe he had met a friend in the forest, that maybe he would be adopted by that leopard and raised by her, go on to live as a wild boy.

At that time in his life Kau was still cursed with the curiosity and courage and foolishness of a young man, and so he began to track the leopard. In a sun-dappled clearing he spotted the stiff arm of the buried boy pushing up from kicked leaves. He tensed and looked around, and then he saw the cat asleep within the plank buttresses of a giant fig tree. She was an all-black, a coloration that was almost unknown among the leopards of the forest. He sat and watched the dark sleeping cat for all the afternoon, then slipped off in silence as night began to fall.

SHE WAS THE only black panther he would ever see—though in the Mississippi Territory the white pioneers and settlers would speak of them often. Black panthers killed hogs. Black panthers stalked travelers on the federal road. Black panthers screamed like dying women in the night. But not so long ago an Alibamu mystic had assured him that the white men were all wrong, that no such creature really existed in these forests. There were indeed panthers but not black panthers.

He had come upon the old Indian sitting alone on a stump in a field behind Yellowhammer and had stopped and visited with him for a while. Though Kau knew much of his language, the Alibamu spoke good English and so eventually they settled upon that tongue. Somehow their talk turned to black panthers, the Alibamu insisting that white men saw them for the same reason people sought to name the shapes of clouds and the clusterings of stars—a beast akin to that shadowy form lived in their imaginations and their fears. "But that does not make black panthers real," said the Alibamu. "No Indian will ever claim to have seen one, at least not before the invaders came."

Kau told the Alibamu that black panthers were in fact in Africa—that he had killed one himself, a man-eater.

The Alibamu stared at him. "Is that the truth?"

"It is."

"Maybe you say that because you have lived a long time with the whites, are owned by them even."

"No, that black cat done come first."

The Alibamu rose up and began to shake a loop of clicking snake rattles. When he finished he climbed atop the stump and looked down at Kau. "You should be very careful," he warned.

"Why you sayin that?"

"Because you must come from a place where the dreams in their heads live," explained the Alibamu. "Be careful that in the end you do not become just another one of their wicked creations."

THE OTA MEN were gathered around a fire, listening as Kau told of what he had seen. When they at last retired, the leopard entered the camp and looked into the leaf hut of the sleeping storyteller. She brought her face almost to rest against his own and watched him— watched him like he had watched her and then stole off, returning to the forest.

In the morning Kau saw her pugmarks in the dust and thanked that same sheltering forest for protecting him. The elders pointed at where the cat had stood over him and laughed at his luck. Only a visit, they told him, from his namesake.

AGAIN HE TRACKED the leopard, and before long he saw where she had ignored the fresh spoor of a crippled bongo to instead return and begin feeding on the remains of the child. Something had changed within her, and that night in the Ota camp Kau shared this news with the others. The leopard was headed in the direction of Opoku. A man-eater was now hunting.

EVERY FEW DAYS thereafter the leopard visited upon the Kesa, waiting all night at the edge of the burnt-back forest, in the thick borderland where their cassava fields pushed up against the beginnings of the tree line. At sunrise the farmers would leave their huts with the fatalism common among those reigned over by others, and once they had worked themselves far enough into the fields the leopard would attack, hauling off a half-dead catch as the more fortunate of the Kesa raced for the village.

At night goats were left staked throughout the forest, broken legged and bleating, their hides soaked with poisons. All these the leopard ignored.

Chabo began to station the best of his warriors in the fields with the farmers, and these men kept guard but without effect—as they could never know the exact place or moment or victim of the next attack. When the black cat appeared they were always unprepared, and the closest they came to killing the man-eater was an errant spear thrown into the chest of a mauled farmer.

Five more men were taken before Chabo asked for help from the Ota. He called upon the Ota even though he knew of their relationship with leopards. Like all people the band lived by certain codes, and among their beliefs were prohibitions against the killing of particular animals. Generations of Ota had shared the forest with leopards, and though on occasion there would be incidents between the two forest-dwellers, for the most part they existed together in peace. That leopards allowed the Ota to live in their midst was a gift from the forest, and so to kill a leopard would be an insult to that blessing. Chabo asked and the Ota refused. In their minds this problem belonged to the Kesa alone.

More villagers died. The Kesa witch doctors conferred and blame was placed on the young Ota man who called himself Leopard—the one who had first returned the blind child to Opoku. The black cat was his sister. He had somehow brought this killer, and therefore it fell upon him to destroy her. Chabo declared that the Kesa would not suffer this alone. The Ota were not welcome in the village so long as the man-eater lived.

AMONG THE OTA were some who had begun to adopt the customs and superstitions of the Kesa. These younger men spoke out in support of Chabo, arguing that the black cat was a mistake of the forest same as the blind child had been a mistake of the village—an unintended creature. The Ota were hunters; the forest was their home. It was their duty to kill this man-eater and restore the balance of things.

In the end there was a compromise between the young men and their elders. Kau alone would help the Kesa. If the leopard must be hunted then it should be done by the one she herself had chosen to visit. Perhaps in this way there might come forgiveness from both the leopard and the forest.

THOUGH HE HAD feigned reluctance for the sake of the elders, in truth Kau was eager to test his skills against the animal whose ancestor had appeared at his birth and thus given him his name. In her decision to spare him while he slept he had come to see not a kindness but a challenge, and so he took up his bow and went to Opoku.

SPRAWLED IN THE shade of a hut, he passed the time with the extraordinary patience of the Ota. After two days the leopard made another kill. Kau was dozing when she came, and he awoke to the shouts of farmers running for the village. He hurried into the fields and was brought to the place where the man had been attacked. The turned earth was splashed with blood, and a shallow rut in the dirt led into the forest. A warrior pushed him forward. "Go," he said. "Hunt."

Kau ignored the warrior and instead returned to Opoku. There he spent the morning coating the tips of his arrows with poisons while the impatient villagers glared at him. The leopard would feed and then she would rest. Once the forest grew hot he would seek her.

SHE CARRIED HER kill far, far away, beyond the boundaries of his own known world. Though the farmer was very heavy Kau saw that the leopard dropped him only once, placing the body beside a creek so that she could drink. When she was finished the man-eater rearranged her grip and continued on, straddling the corpse as she walked so that to Kau, tracking, her pugmarks seemed situated like little villages on either side of a wide, drag-path river.

He began to gain on the leopard, and so he strapped his bow across his back and scanned the forest for any glimpse of the black cat—a flicked ear, a twitching tail. A Kesa warrior had lent him a long spear affixed with a rusty iron point, and Kau held it low out in front of him as he tracked, swiveling his hips from side to side, moving in tiny measured steps.

A leopard has a weak nose—though it still works much better than that of a man. And what a leopard lacks in smell it gains in eyesight, hearing. Such is the way with all animals. An elephant might see only in shadows but it can also listen to the beatings of its own massive heart, wind a hunter from a mile off. Soaring eagles spot prey from soundless heights. A snake tastes the world with a tongue flick. So what then is a man? An animal with poor eyes and poor ears, a near-useless nose. Hairless. Fangless. Clawless. How is it that this pitiful creature—a creature that should not ever have been able to survive among beasts—has come to lord over so much?

It was almost dark when he spied the dead farmer lying high up the slanted trunk of a fallen tree. A blanket of flies covered the half-eaten corpse; moths drank from still-damp eyes. Kau looked around, processing the forest in sections. Nothing. She was still resting, he decided. She was resting, and at some point when she was once again hungry she would return to resume her feeding. By the light of the moon he would kill her.

And so he readied himself. He walked up the sloped trunk of the dead tree and stepped carefully over the mangled farmer. At a place well past the ripening corpse he stopped and bent branches for a blind, and then he set his spear and quiver down close where he could reach them. The bow was in his hand, and he selected the best from among his arrows, then went as still against the tree as a day-lazing moth.

Darkness fell over the forest as day pulled away. He remained motionless in the tree, waiting for the man-eater to appear. A hyrax shrieked and was soon answered by another. The ebony sky was speckled with bright stars. The moon rose and he closed his eyes, listening for the sound of claws scratching bark.

THE LONG NIGHT passed without any sign of the leopard, and as dawn came he spotted the first of them—a colony of driver ants was moving through the forest, a dark brown band of butchers coming million after million. They swept closer and the base of his bent tree divided the river into halves. He saw a sprinkling of foragers ascend the tree trunk, following the stink trail of the cat-killed man. A single ant perched itself on a rib bone of the corpse. It reared back on hind legs, seemed to celebrate before retreating. Some collective intelligence clicked and both columns shifted and then doubled back. They met at the tree and soon ants covered the dead man. The leopard had lost her kill.

And Kau was trapped. He knew the colony would stay for several days now, would not leave until the farmer's bones were all that remained of him. An ant latched onto Kau's ankle and he flinched in pain. He broke off the body but the stubborn head remained, the jaws still clamped to his skin. He pulled the head loose, and then he threw his spear and quiver and bow down to the forest floor. More ants were on him. He jumped, touched down on the balls of his feet and crumbled into the leaves. He was on his knees when he spotted her. The black cat was crouched and staring, close enough for him to see the tip of her pink tongue. The snaking mass of ants flowed between them.

The leopard's black coat shined almost blue in the glow of morning, and watching her Kau was certain that he would die. He waited but she stayed crouched even as her tail danced above her. The Kesa spear was impaled in the ground beside him, and when he slowly reached for it so came the man-eater over the wide scramble of ants. She leapt once and then twice as he lifted the spear. The iron point went in at her chest, and then the spear twisted free from his hands. He rolled away and watched as the screaming cat raked at the shaft with her claws. Finally blade nicked spine and the leopard went limp. She stared at him with fluttering yellow eyes, until at last her bleeding slowed to a trickle and she died.

He stood and looked down at the dead leopard. Only now could he see the splash of rosettes hidden deep within her black coat—rosettes the same as a typical and ordinary leopard. The first few driver ants had discovered this new kill, and he watched as the insect river divided itself yet again. This would not be so horrible, he thought—to be devoured by the forest. He knelt and with the wet spearhead he sawed off the man-eater's tail, his proof for Chabo.

A beam of sun pierced through the canopy, and Kau felt his body being cut by light. He tied the soft black tail in a twist around his neck and let himself be warmed. He could sense the forest watching him, and he trembled as he began walking toward the village.

Hungry Crow—The Conecuh River—
An unknown killer—The highwaymen

THAT AFTERNOON HE overtook the three redsticks, and they
halted their horses as he told them of the panther. When he was
finished speaking Morning Star rocked back on his mount. His gray
horse was coughing now, and a lump had formed on the left side of
its neck. The prophet rode on ahead, and Blood Girl galloped after
him. When she returned it was to report that Morning Star had
shared a vision. She circled Kau on her horse and then looked down
at him. "Stay close to us," she said. "Another redstick is coming."

HIS NAME WAS Hungry Crow and he rode a black horse. They were
making a fire for the night when he galloped into their camp, his
longrifle held high above his head. This fourth stallion was quickly

challenged by the other three that stood hobbled nearby, but then Morning Star rushed over and the horses all calmed.

Hungry Crow was both taller and thinner than any man Kau had seen in the whole of his life, taller even than Morning Star. Kau was introduced but Hungry Crow ignored him.

"He can speak our language," said Blood Girl.

Hungry Crow dismounted and walked over to him. His dark hair had been shaved save a narrow roach running from his forehead to the nape of his neck. He lifted a finger to Kau's mouth but Kau stepped away. Finally the redstick spoke: "Those were your small tracks?"

Kau nodded.

Hungry Crow contorted his bony face into a sneer. "I wondered," he said. "I thought a child was wandering lost."

HE CAME TO understand that Hungry Crow lived alone in the canebrake as an angry hermit of sorts, and was a stranger to all of the redsticks save Little Horn. Blood Girl explained that both men were from the Tallushatchee village, had fought together when the Creek War started at Burnt Corn, and now Kau sat listening by the fire with the others as Little Horn told Hungry Crow their purpose in his hideaway, asking what if anything he knew of the men they had come to hunt.

"Thieves," said Hungry Crow. "Nothing more."

"So you do know of them?" asked Little Horn.

"Of course."

"And their cave?"

"Not far. Two day's ride." Hungry Crow pointed at Kau. "Maybe two moons of walking for the little one." The redstick started to say more but then went silent. Morning Star was scraping at his cut teeth with the frayed end of a twig, and Kau saw Hungry Crow look from the prophet to him and then back again. He is jealous, Kau realized. Hungry Crow kept on staring and Kau heard a hissing sound. Morning Star was laughing now. The closest he had yet come to speaking beyond his whisperings to Blood Girl.

THOUGH HE SEEMED to hate all men Hungry Crow was also a redstick, and so in the end he agreed to guide them and kill with them. The next morning the redsticks mounted their horses and rode off in a single-file string. Kau lingered in camp until they were gone. A breeze came and the river cane swayed all around. He heard water frogs in the distance and could smell the river. It felt good to be alone and so he lingered still. The sun was over the trees when at last he shouldered his saddlebags and took up the longrifle. He followed after the four stallions in the running walk of an Ota huntsman, hurrying to overtake the redsticks before they turned and came to find him.

HUNGRY CROW TOOK the redsticks even farther north through the canebrake, and then late in the day Kau saw where the riders had angled to the west. He discovered them waiting for him near the bank of the broad Conecuh. The sun was beginning to set.

"Do not make us stop for you again," said Hungry Crow.

Kau kept quiet and prepared for the crossing. He wrapped his blanket around his longrifle, then passed the bundle up to Little

Horn with his saddlebags. The horses began to swim the warm river, and Kau splashed after them. He worked his hands around the coarse tail of Little Horn's stallion and was towed past Blood Girl. She laughed in the failing light, and they were halfway across the river when Kau saw orange muzzle-flash appear on the hillside that rose up beyond the canebrake in front of them. There was a great sucking sound as Blood Girl fell backward from her horse into the river, and Kau reached for her but she sank and was gone.

Little Horn gave a warning and the remaining redsticks lay flat against the strained necks of their hard-swimming stallions. Kau tightened his grip on the horsetail, letting himself be pulled, and once they had reached the shore Hungry Crow led them all into the cover of the cane. Kau saw Morning Star begin slapping at the crown of his shaved head, and the prophet's horse had ropes of drool hanging from its open mouth.

As the winded horses settled Kau looked out over the river. He saw Blood Girl's stallion on the opposite bank. Twice the red horse started to swim the Conecuh and join them—but each time the stallion turned back until finally it quit altogether. The riderless horse melted into the forest, and Kau supposed that perhaps one day it would shake its Indian bridle, wander game trails and learn to forage, live a free and mustang life.

THEY WALKED THE three horses downstream through the canebrake, away from the shooter on the hill. It was night now, and the redsticks agreed that any further attack would come in the morning or not at all. They dried their rifles, then each took a turn keeping watch while the others slept.

KAU HAD THE last guard, and at dawn he heard the screams of wood ducks leaving cypress roosts for hidden backwaters and sloughs. These were local birds, ducks somehow born without the instinct to migrate north in the spring. They darted across the chalk sky in twisting, drake-hen pairs.

He woke the others and they readied themselves. It began to rain, light at first but then much heavier. No sunrise raid came and the redsticks relaxed some. Hungry Crow tried asking Morning Star who was hunting them, but without Blood Girl the prophet was now silent and useless. Hungry Crow asked again but Morning Star turned away, walking off in the rain with his sick horse.

KAU VOLUNTEERED TO scout for the shooter. None of the redsticks objected and so he went off alone down a trail that ran along the edge of the canebrake. Here a hill of iron hardwoods rose up from the lowlands. He sat in the rain and watched. Soon three jake turkeys came working across the wet hillside, scratching for rising worms, and Kau waited until the last of them had vanished over the crest of the hill. The turkeys never spooked, and this satisfied him that the shooter was gone.

He left the muddy trail and began to cut for sign. Midway up the hill he found a plug of spent spit tobacco. He took it into his hands and watched the brown leaves break apart in the rain. The wind picked up and rainwater creeks formed in the furrows of the hill. Suddenly there was thunder on top of lightning and he was chased back into the canebrake. He ended his search and returned to the redsticks, announcing his approach with a cardinal whistle that was smothered up by the slapping rain.

Hungry Crow and Little Horn sat huddled beneath the wide stomachs of their stallions; both Morning Star and his horse were missing still. Hungry Crow called out, but Kau ignored him and instead went to Little Horn. He knelt beside the hobbled horse and spoke. "I believe that we are safe now," he said.

"Was it a white man?"

"I think. But his tracks are gone."

Hungry Crow had left the shelter of his own horse and joined them. The redstick's wet strip of hair was pasted flat against his skull. "Gone?" he asked.

"Yes. Washed away by the rain."

"So you say, baby slave."

Kau nodded and then walked off. There was a cypress on the riverbank that had been killed by pecky rot. Lightning flashed all about, yet he took refuge inside the hollow tree without regard. He draped the damp horse blanket over his shoulders, then began to squeeze water from his breechcloth. He was exhausted and miserable, and a piece of him wondered if to end his life here—beside a rain-dimpled river, inside a warm tree—was about the best he could dare hope for in this second world. There was a shimmer of blue light, and for a single second he saw Benjamin alive and standing in the hard rain. The hay hook dangled from the boy's throat, and his thin white shirt was red with blood. Then thunder boomed and it was dark again. Kau pressed the tip of his knife against his bare chest and was not afraid. There was comfort for him there, knowing he had that one power still—the only absolute power that any man ever truly possesses.

IN THE QUIET that followed the thunderstorm he returned to the camp and found Little Horn stabbing at the wet ashes of a fire with a crooked stick. The redstick looked up at him.

"Where is Morning Star?" asked Kau.

"He has left us for now." Little Horn shrugged. "I think he will go searching along the river for Blood Girl. That would be important to him."

Kau sat down on his heels. "But not important to you?"

"I have seen many deaths."

"And him?"

"Him, too," said Little Horn. "But he has let them stir at his mind."

"You do not believe he is a prophet?"

"I suppose he could be many things." Little Horn drew a cross in the dead ash. "But does it even matter?"

WITHOUT MORNING STAR, Kau came to doubt that they would ever learn exactly who had killed Blood Girl during the crossing. Little Horn suspected the highwaymen but Hungry Crow disagreed, promising that they were still at least a day's ride from the cave where the white thieves lived. In the end Kau decided that it did not matter really. She was dead and had died poorly, shot like a deer in a bean field.

Hungry Crow and Little Horn rode north, following the river, and he trailed after them for all of the next day. That night they made a fireless camp and then, at sunrise, left the two remaining horses secured in the canebrake. A short stretch of creek led them to the foot of a steep ridge, and Hungry Crow pointed to where bits of stone showed through a thick green layer of wild grapevine and creeper, explaining that the whole of that broken ridge was hollow, that inside was the cave they were seeking.

"And the entrance?" asked Little Horn.

They crept forward and took cover in the branches of a fallen magnolia. Hungry Crow aimed his longrifle at a rent in the side of the ridge. "There," he said. "Hidden."

Midday a thin white man dressed in fine clothes emerged from the cracked earth. Kau saw now that a series of ropes had been woven into the tangled vines, forming a sort of ladder that fell down across the side of the ridge. The man slung a sagging feed sack over his shoulder, then began to climb the twenty yards of rope ladder one-handed. Two pistols were tucked through the red sash that ran around his waist. Little Horn full-cocked his Jaeger rifle but Hungry Crow stayed him.

The man made the climb to the top of the ridge, then stretched and removed a silver length of metal from some hidden pocket inside his loose shirt. He sat down on a stone and lowered his head, blew a long and steady whistle that confused the birds, and for a moment, quieted the forest.

Soon Kau saw movement at the far end of the ridgeline. Four stocky ponies came trotting from right to left along the rise, and the man poured oats for them. He emptied the sack and then patted the mud-splashed neck of the closest pony.

Kau watched as the man stood atop the ridge and surveyed the forest below. The sun was at his back and he seemed afire. Finally the man took hold of the rope ladder and began his descent. Once he had returned to the hollow of the earth, Hungry Crow spoke. "We will come for them tomorrow," he said.

A HUMID NIGHT in a dark camp and then came dawn the next morning. Hungry Crow knew of a path that led from the canebrake around to the top of the ridge, and after hiking for about three hundred yards they reached the feeding place above the cave. The redsticks scraped two deep troughs in the black dirt, then Little Horn settled into one and Hungry Crow into the other. Kau concealed them with handfuls of oak leaves, then retreated alone down the ridgeline.

HOURS LATER THE same lank man emerged and began to climb the rope ladder. Kau issued a series of squirrel barks to alert the redsticks, and when the white man blew his whistleflute Little Horn and Hungry Crow erupted from the dry leaves like graved corpses come alive. Kau ran to join the two redsticks. The man had begun to scream, but then Little Horn swung his war-club and all was silent.

THE HIGHWAYMAN WAS a gaunt man with wide-set mole eyes, a short blond beard and enormous ears. Little Horn knelt to cut the scalp as the summoned ponies appeared on the ridge, and if they smelled death yet they did not show it. The boldest of the four ponies pushed Little Horn aside with its muzzle, then began to nudge at the feed sack that lay resting in the turned leaves.

THEY DESCENDED THE rope ladder like scrambling spiders, and Hungry Crow motioned for him to go first into the dim cave. Kau had strapped his saddlebags to his body, and his longrifle was now pinned against him. He slid the flintlock free, then turned sideways and began to shuffle through the thin crack in the earth. There were words scratched in the rock walls, and he stared at them for a moment, wondering what they might mean.

The narrow entrance soon opened into a wide chamber. He crept to the center of this square cavity, and as his eyes adjusted he peered into the corner shadows and spotted two blunderbuss muskets wedged into a cairn of piled rock, their belled barrels aimed at the opening of the cave. He turned and looked back toward the glow of the yellow entrance. The floor of the cave seemed to sparkle, and he realized then that he had somehow walked safely through a shimmering web of silk trip lines. He dropped down to his stomach, and had started to call out a warning when Little Horn entered the cave. The redstick took a step into the chamber before he seemed to sense the trap. He stopped but then Hungry Crow pushed past him in a rush. Kau saw a moccasin connect with the first of the triplines, then both spring guns threw sparks and roared. Smoke and dust filled the cave, and he began to cough and then choke as he felt around for his dropped longrifle. Finally his hand found the barrel and he pulled the flintlock to him.

From the dark heart of that hollow ridge an angry highwayman yelled out, and when the air cleared Kau crawled forward and saw that Little Horn was dead. His bare chest was riddled like the breast of a shot duck, and blood seeped from the socket of his missing nose. Hungry Crow was laid out beside him. The redstick had taken beads of lead to the fronts of his spindly legs and could not walk. The highwayman yelled again, and Kau watched as Hungry Crow dragged himself to the entrance of the cave. The redstick had his longrifle in his lap. "Do not run," he said, but then he slumped over and was dead.

Kau shoved Hungry Crow aside and then slid his own longrifle back between the cinched saddlebags. He squeezed out of the cave and sunlight blinded him as he stumbled gasping into the day. The ground dropped off beneath his feet, and as he fell he reached out and caught hold of the rope ladder. Something clattered off the rocks beneath him—the longrifle, lost—and more shouts came as he began to climb.

At the top of the ridge he looked down and saw that three dusty white men had emerged from the cave and were now climbing one by one toward him. He began to saw at the rope ladder with his knife, but then a black-haired man aimed a pistol up at him and so he fled. He circled back down the ridge, following Hungry Crow's path to the canebrake and then the river. Morning Star was on the opposite bank, watching, and his diseased horse lay dead in the shallows. The prophet motioned for him to cross the river, but Kau hesitated until he heard the highwaymen entering the cane behind him. Finally he splashed into the water and began to swim. The saddlebags threatened to sink him but he was able to push on.

He reached the other side of the Conecuh and found Morning Star kneeling on the bank. The prophet smiled at him, revealing his own cut teeth, and then he began to sing, his long silence finally broken. Kau listened and was reminded of the songs of the Ota. He tried to make sense of the words being chanted over and again:

> I will fly with the winds
> I will swim with the rivers
> I will return
> to some far corner
> of the world

Morning Star seemed almost to be screaming now. Shots were fired at them from across the river, and finally Kau took off running into the forest. He would be traveling alone again, he realized. The prophet was singing a death song.

Across Florida—Honeybees— Lorenzo Dow—Another cave

SOUTH, THEN EAST. With the longrifle lost he kept slow, vigilant and—as if engaged in some barefoot child's amusement of balance—walked heel to toe in the way of his people, the bone club held loose in his hand, his breechcloth snug against him. Water was plentiful, and his saddlebags still held some of the smoked venison; it would be days before he needed to hunt again.

This was a Spanish territory in name, but he saw that more than anything it was an everyman's land. Country where a lone Ota trespasser walking with the pole star off his left shoulder belonged as much as the assortment of runaways and filibusters and renegades who shared the forest with him. On occasion there were shots in the distance, sometimes even the hollerings of men, and he saw that all but the ignorant or fearless moved after sunset, eyes averted from the bright moon to maintain their night vision.

Most travelers rode horses and came so rank and noisy that he could avoid them with ease. Only the runaways moved on foot, and at certain moments in the dark flatwoods strangers would each become aware of the other approaching. Like the warm-water sharks that had once circled his slave ship, as they neared they would both veer slightly so that to a next-day tracker it would appear almost as if the first had careened off the second, that directions and destinies had been forever altered by that chance encounter.

FOUR NIGHTS AFTER the clash with the highwaymen, the deaths of Little Horn and Hungry Crow and Morning Star, he arrived upon a place where the pine forest was split by a wide creek. He was filling his canteen when there came the pungency and then the whinnies of upwind horses. He made to run and hide himself but then he grew very angry. He was tired of playing the coward, and so instead he pushed open his saddlebags and removed Lawson's hunting pouch and powderhorn, the boy's tinderbox. These pinewoods had not seen rain in many days. A great flash of light and then a fire began to spread slowly through the dry forest. He stowed the tinderbox and walked away, crossed one creek and then a second.

MUCH LATER THAT night he looked back and saw that the entire western horizon was glowing orange like some false sunrise. He shimmied up the trunk of a high pine, and for a long time he sat among the branches and watched the forest burn. This was yet another horrible thing to have done. Somewhere on the other side of that fire, Samuel now slept alone in a slave cabin, and the boy lay dead at the bottom of a river. He thought of them both and he wept.

IN A DOGHAIR thicket of loblolly he came upon a family of runaways asleep among the dense young pines. A large woman rose up and he went still. She was scolding him like he was her son—saying, "Don you go wanderin, Toby"—when she registered her mistake and screamed. All souls scattered and for the entire night forth, like a cock quail gathering a busted covey, the desperate father whistled from a nearby hill, pleading with his family to come and join him.

HE WAS LYING on his stomach in a purple field of blooming meadowrue, his face buried in the folds of the saddlebags so as to block out the midday sun, when he heard the low buzzing of a honeybee. For a moment he wondered if all his pining for his home had finally confused his mind. He turned his head and opened his swollen eyes. The bee was hovering close, and he reached for it as if somehow hoping to prove the reality of the thing. His finger brushed against a fragile wing, and the frightened bee zigzagged and then bolted. Kau sprang to his feet and began moving through the towering stalks of meadowrue. As he searched the blossoms he encountered yellow jackets and even hummingbirds—but it was a long while before he again saw a honeybee, a lone worker leaving the field for the woodlands. Kau bent a flimsy tree limb to mark this spot, then collected his saddlebags and returned there to wait.

REPORTS OF THE blooming field soon reached the honeybee colony, and as the bees arrived and then departed, he followed. Losing sight of one he would sit and wait for the pollen-heavy next, on and on like a lost and frantic captain chasing seabirds across open water, all the while praying for land.

HE SKIRTED A small forest lake and was led to a flat sweep of high ground. Here the trees thickened. He noted the change, recognizing that long ago this had once been a clearing, a settlement. He saw where stones had been laid out in the shape of a large cross, but now nothing else remained, nothing save the descendants of those dead Christians' honeybees.

The colony had laid claim to the hollow trunk of a fallen beech, near enough to the ground that he could approach and peer inside. It was almost dark and the hive was full, a wet and golden mass that pulsed like a heart with the tusslings of the bees. Were he in Africa, back in that time before his world was destroyed, he would now blow on a honey whistle, calling for his band to come and share in this. He unsheathed his knife and dug a fire-hole in the soft dirt. Again he made use of the tinderbox, igniting bits of pine shavings that Benjamin had soaked in kerosene the day before he died. The small blaze grew as he added twigs and then branches. Soon a solid fire was burning.

He covered his fire with a cut bough of damp cedar. The evergreen burned slowly, releasing a steady stream of smoke that he blew in mouthfuls over the resting bees. He coaxed the colony into a torpor and then began to cut away at the entrance of the hive until the honey was revealed. He brushed the stunned bees aside and broke loose a small piece of dark and dripping comb that he crammed into his mouth. This was his first taste of honey since Africa, and it was different somehow but still good. He sat on the smooth trunk of the fallen beech, and the more that he ate the more that he trembled.

He kept on until his stomach was full and then waded into the tannic water of the moonlit lake. There he tore loose wide sheets of lotus and lily that later he slathered with honey and then folded into tight envelopes. He placed the bundles into his saddlebags and looked back at the hive, wincing at all that he would be leaving behind.

Still, he thought, this was a gift from the forest indeed.

He smothered the fire and gathered his things. A solitary bee stung his neck as he walked off into the darkness, departing forever that forgotten place where once there had been a Christian community.

CHRISTIANITY. WHAT HE knew of the white man's religion had been taught to him at Yellowhammer by Samuel and a lone crazed preacher named Dow.

1814. He had been sweeping the inn's chimney when a pair of Irish travelers came seeking the innkeeper. Their first language—the one they only spoke between themselves—was a strange language, but the men knew English as well, and if Kau concentrated he could mostly understand them. He would learn later that they were from Ireland, and he crouched in the cold hearth and listened as they told of having been surprised by a wildman while cutting wood that morning along the federal road. According to these Irishmen, the stranger had been skinny and filthy and a little bit hunchbacked. The man had approached them, and they had demanded that he state his business or else leave as he came. Finally one of the Irishmen had recognized him. "I swear to you I saw that fellow preach once in Dublin," he said to the innkeeper. "It was Lorenzo Dow himself."

And so he was. The itinerant preacher had leapt onto a fresh-cut stump, and then he promised that at high noon exactly one year from that day he would return to that same spot and preach a sermon.

"Those were all the words he spoke," said the taller of the two Irishmen. "We looked away for but a second, and he disappeared like we had both gone and dreamed him."

A drunk soldier glanced up from his dented tin mug. "Hell," he slurred. "You Irish are superstitious as niggers."

The innkeeper was not religious, but still he had the Irishmen bring him to the oak stump. That same afternoon Kau and Samuel helped him mark that place with a signboard, and one year to the day later the inn was full and a congregation had formed. Soldiers and settlers, Indians and slaves, pioneers and traders. Pilgrims, even.

THE FALL OF 1815. Kau and the boy had climbed a tree to see this Lorenzo Dow. Benjamin caught a small lizard, and they watched as it bit at his hand. Samuel was standing beneath them, and Benjamin dropped the lizard so that it fell twisting onto the old man's head. Samuel shook his fist up at them, but it was clear that he was happy, excited that he would soon be hearing a sermon.

At solar noon, Dow showed. He was as the Irishmen had described him—a longhaired man with a tangled beard and patched clothes. Some in the crowd heckled him for his appearance, but they were soon shouted down by the righteous. There was a brief silence before he opened with a false story:

On the last day of the last century a young Dow was traveling in Vermont when he was caught in a blizzard and lost the road. He wandered the forest until finally he saw the light of a cabin tucked in the woods. A woman answered the door and Dow begged that she take mercy on his miserable soul.

"I'm sorry," the woman told him, "but my husband is away for the night. I can't ask in a stranger."

Dow explained to her that he was a preacher, that he was asking her to save his life. At last she relented and a place was made for him in the cabin, in a corner separated from the main room by a partition of rough wood.

That night Dow awoke to whispers and giggles. He peered through a crack in the partition and saw the woman and a man sitting alone at a table lit by a single candle.

So the husband has come home, thought Dow. He smiled at the scene, at the love between two people in a warm cabin in a cold forest. He lay back down to sleep and soon there came a great banging at the bolted door. Again Dow's eyes went to the partition crack. A large barrel sat beside the woman's spinning wheel, and

Dow watched as she helped her lover inside of it, burying him under a cloud of flax tow. The man at the door sounded drunk. He was cursing and shouting.

So the husband has come home, thought Dow (and here there was much laughter from the Mississippi crowd).

Her lover hidden, the woman opened the door and was pushed aside down by her red-faced husband. "Where is the scoundrel?" he demanded.

Dow was pulling on his shoes when he heard himself identified. "There is a preacher staying here tonight," said the woman. "He was caught in the storm."

At this Dow appeared from behind the partition with his Bible in hand. "And good evening to you, sir," he said.

The husband pulled a knife from his belt and took a step toward him. "That true, son?" he asked. "You a preacher?"

Dow nodded and lifted the Bible higher. "That is indeed the truth, sir."

"All right," said the husband, "then quote me some scripture, preacher."

"Now?"

"It would be real bad if you couldn't."

Dow thought for a moment. "I can do better than scripture," he said.

"That right?"

"I can raise the Devil himself," said Dow.

The husband waved his knife at him. "Mind your tongue," he said. "Mind your tongue if you care to keep it."

Here Dow paused and apologized to the crowd. "That drunk man said other things," he confessed. "Things I could never repeat in front of you good people."

"Bet he threatened to cut off his pizzle," shouted a young man. Many in the crowd laughed, and even Dow smiled.

"Why, sir," said Dow, "don't you sound just like that drunken husband." The laughter grew louder as the shamed man slunk off, and when the crowd had once again quieted Dow continued with his story.

"Now you watch," Dow told the husband, "and I will raise the Devil."

"You had better do it soon."

"That's a preacher you're speaking to," said the wife.

"Woman, you shut your mouth."

"I must warn you," said Dow. "When the Devil comes it will be in a flaming fire."

The husband sneered at him. "Of course," he said.

"Open that door, sir. You don't ever want to be caught in the same room as the Devil."

The husband did as he was told. "But you make a move to leave this cabin," he said, "and I'll go and cut you open."

Dow went to the fireplace and lifted a burning coal with the iron tongs. "Are you ready?" he asked.

"I'm ready." The husband stabbed the air with his knife. "Are *you* ready?"

The wife screamed (and the crowd cheered) when Dow dropped the ember into the cask of oily tow. There was a flash like a pitch torch lighting, and the howling lover leapt from the flaming barrel, his clothes afire as he ran out the open door and into the snowy night.

The husband had thrown down his knife, and now he pulled his crying wife close to protect her. "Dear Jesus," he said.

Dow capped the barrel to smother the fire, and then he turned back to him. "Do I finally have your trust?" he asked.

"You do," said the shaken husband. "Yes, preacher, you do."

"Very well then."

Dow began to gather his few things but the husband stopped him. "But what of the storm?" he asked. "You'll freeze. I know that you'll freeze."

"No," said Dow. "I will manage."

"But you can't leave us," pleaded the husband. "Not with the Devil about."

"There is nothing more I can do for you," said Dow. "Only one thing alone will guarantee your safety."

"Anything. Just say it to me."

"Never drink again," said Dow. "It was your weakness for drink that allowed the Devil into your home."

The husband dropped his head and his pretty wife hugged him. "I know that to be true," he said. "I'll beat it yet."

"Promise me."

"I promise," said the husband. "I'm through."

Dow then looked to the woman and spoke: "He'll need all your help as a wife with this. Do you believe you can do that, ma'am?"

"I can," she said. "Yes."

Kau watched with the boy from atop the tree as Dow raised his worn Bible. The crowd clapped and whistled for the parable, and Dow stood beaming from his oak stump. He then started into his sermon, and for two hours he held forth. He spoke on every vice and every virtue, until finally a Georgia man who traded mules along the federal road begged for him to stop. Benjamin asked what was happening but Kau had no answer. Dow continued and the muleskinner began to kick at the earth. Convulsions took hold all around. Women fainted. Men fell to their knees as if struck. A cavalry officer went about on all fours, barking like a dog. Kau saw the innkeeper plug his ears with tobacco as the muleskinner began to sprint round in a tight circle and claim that he was doomed. An orgy of faith. Such was the state of the crowd when Dow locked eyes with Kau sitting high up in that distant tree and smiled. A woman shrieked as the preacher began to speak on the subject of men owning men.

Said Dow, "As all men are created equal and independent by God of Nature, slavery must have moral evil for its foundation, seeing it violates the Law of Nature, as established by its author. Ambition and avarice on the one hand, and social dependence upon the other, affords the former an opportunity of being served at the expense of the latter, and this unnatural state of things hath been exemplified in all countries and all ages of the world from time immemorial."

The cavalry officer cocked his head and went still, listening. Kau looked down to check on Samuel, but the old man was no longer standing there beneath the tree.

Said Dow, "The exercise of an absolute sway over others begets an unnatural hardness, which as it becomes imperious, contaminates the mind of the governor—while the governed becomes factious and stupefied like brute beasts which are kept under by a continual dread."

The innkeeper removed the tobacco from the hollows of his ears and took a single step closer. After so many years as his slave Kau knew the man's temper well, and it was clear to him that his master was very angry now.

Said Dow, "Pride and vainglory on the one side, and degradation and oppression on the other, creates on the one hand a spirit of contempt, and on the other a spirit of hatred and revenge, preparing them to be dissolute and qualifying them for every base and malicious work."

The collapsed crowd began to stir, rising from the ground as if Dow had both killed and then quickened them.

"That is the Lord's word," Dow concluded. "This evil must be antidoted before the storm gathers and bursts."

"That's just *your* word," shouted the innkeeper.

In the end Dow barely escaped with his life. He was pelted with sticks and rocks but refused to run. A party of soldiers saved him. Dow was led under their protection toward Georgia and this time his promise was that he would never return. The last Kau ever saw of Lorenzo Dow, the wildman preacher was standing in the middle of the federal road, quoting Luke at the enraged innkeeper as he slapped the dust from his bare feet. "I leave this wicked place as a witness against you," said Dow. "And I pronounce you all cursed."

KAU STAYED WITH Benjamin in the tree until the crowd was gone, and once they were alone he spoke with him for the first time about leaving Yellowhammer. To be free again he would need the help of the boy. There was no other way that he saw. Three weeks later they found the dead cypress that had blown down near the river. They returned with an axe, then began making the cuts for the dugout.

WITH THE HONEY came strength. Miles of sunset to sunrise walking. Hot days of restless sleep followed by long warm nights afoot, letting the stars guide him further east into Florida.

Yet sometimes he still wandered. Early one morning the pinelands dropped down into a dry floodplain, and instead of concealing himself until nightfall he followed a clear river south to a place where it vanished into the earth. This was something he had never seen before. He looped around the pool and then crossed over a jagged heap of limestone. The rocks were splattered with batshit, and in a gap between boulders he discovered the entrance to a cave. He had been walking for many hours and he was tired. Here was shelter yet still he hesitated before entering this next hole in the earth. He wondered whether somehow this had become his lot—to venture from cave to cave forever. A hunted lifetime of hiding and emerging.

He gathered wood for a fire. At the cave opening an ancient circle of stones surrounded a bed of fine gray ash. He removed the tinderbox from a saddlebag, and soon he had a small flame dancing within the blackened rocks. Wood hissed and cracked as he ate a wide strip of venison drizzled with the last of his honey.

AFTER HE HAD finished eating he lit the end of a length of resin-rich fatwood that he had cut from a pine stump, and then he smothered the fire and crept deeper into the cave.

The walls of the cave glowed yellow in the flickering torchlight. He came upon a rimstone pool alive with salamanders and realized that he was tunneling between the forest above and an aquifer below. Overhead he could see where the gnarled roots of a magnolia had broken through a thin ceiling of rock. The ceiling dipped lower, and he grabbed hold of one of the roots. It felt alive in his hands, seemed almost to throb and to struggle.

He waded across the shallow pool and crawfish nipped at his feet. Here the cave descended with the sinking river, and soon the ceiling disappeared from view altogether. The cave opened wider still and led him into a cavern. Round layers of stone rose up from the floor like great piles of wax. The fatwood torch was threatening to burn out and he worried that he would be thrown into darkness, lose his way. He turned back and was again approaching the rimstone pool when he stumbled over the petrified bones of cave-dwellers blanketed by the dust. His flame trembled as he searched for some clue as to the identity of these broken skeletons. They seemed a small people. Small like him, small like the boy. He riffled through the bones but finally the torch went black. He had not found anything more. No tools. No weapons. No art. These are like the remains of some long-dead animal, he thought. A creature that leaves this world owning nothing at all.

HE SPENT TWO days and two nights resting within the hollow core of that natural bridge. He had masked the entrance to the cave with moss-draped branches, and he sat watching as occasional travelers moved across the land. East to west and west to east.

Only once was he himself spotted. An Indian woman looked through his wall of branches and surprised him lying on his horse blanket beside the cold fire. She hurried away, and he took up his knife and his bone club, stood waiting for her men to attack.

But the fight never came. He thought of his mother and of his wife Janeti. He remembered them both begging that he not go to Opoku. Had he listened then all might be different now. He looked out over the empty forest and pondered that special wisdom of women, their understanding that some things were more valuable than the pride of their men.

BY THE THIRD day he was without venison and honey both. There were small alligators in the river, creatures he remembered from his long-ago trek from Pensacola to Yellowhammer. He lured one into the shallows with a stone-struck cave bat, then dove forward and seized it in his hands. With his knife he skinned out the still-twitching tail, and he saw that the flesh was as rosy and firm as that of the crocodiles that swam in African waters. He captured another and then another, and that night when he could risk the smoke he cured meat until his saddlebags were once again full and he was ready to leave the cave, ready to keep searching for some safe place that was even more like his lost home.

The Apalachicola River — Elvy Callaway

AFTER TWO DAYS of careful night travel through a forest of pine and mixed hardwoods he came to a swollen and muddy river. A river wider than any he had seen since Africa. Glistening black logs floated past him like the lost toys of children, and he realized that in this land of sandy creeks and sluggish bayous here, finally, was a master river—a river that gathered many others and would at some distant point pour itself into a green sea. On a brown-sand beach he stopped and looked east out over the water. To cross a river such as this was perhaps to put the whole of one tragic life behind him.

HE FOLLOWED THE river south to where the current eased into a slight bend, pushing against a series of high bluffs on the far bank. That afternoon he ate the final scraps of his alligator meat, and then he fashioned a crude raft of vine-lashed driftwood. He set off just before sunset, at a time when it was still bright enough for him to make his way safely.

The river took quick hold of the small raft and he let himself be dragged along with it, binding his hands in the cut vine so as not to lose his grip. The water was cool and thick and he kicked his legs, taking aim for a spot downstream where a narrow ravine divided the bluffs. After several hundred yards of drift he hit his mark perfectly. The raft slid onto the sand shore and he rose up, dripping.

There was a wide groove in the beach where a clear creek spilled down through the ravine and into the brown river. He knelt to drink. The creek water was very good, and he filled his canteen before gathering the rest of his things from the raft. Out in the river an enormous garfish rolled in a pocket between currents. Kau pushed the empty raft free and then stood watching as it was swept away spinning.

He was climbing the steep riverbank when he heard a voice ordering him to stay right where he was, don't you move none. A woman in a torn yellow dress was looking down on him from atop the riverbank, and she had a musket leveled at his chest. He reached for his bone club but the woman hissed at him. "Told you not to move none," she said.

"Please."

The woman frowned and stepped closer. "You fall out the sky?" she asked.

He said nothing. In the softening light he could see that she had white-blonde hair and cornflower eyes. Her dirt-streaked skin was sunburnt, her lips split.

"I could kill you if I wanted. You'd admit that?"

"Yessum."

"Lord Jesus, what have you done to your teeth?" She jabbed at the air with the musket. "You trying to be a demon of some sort?"

"Ma'am?"

"Get on out the mud."

He climbed up from the riverbank.

"I don't want to shoot you," said the woman. "But before I put this musket down you have to promise me you'll remember this kindness, spare me like I spared you."

"I got no call to be hurtin you."

"Not what I asked."

"I promise not to hurt you none."

"You got a thick tongue." The woman lowered her musket, and he saw now that it was rusted useless. "Fetch your things," she told him. "I know you're hungry." She began walking away, but he stayed where he was. She turned and looked back at him. "Come on," she said. "I have supper enough."

Finally he slung the canteen around his neck and lifted the saddlebags. She led him away from the river, down a worn path that ran alongside the babbling creek and into the ravine. He closed the distance between them and considered whether he should take his knife to her back, smash her skull with the bone club. The red-sticks, he admitted, already would have killed her twice over.

Still, he kept his word. He was not a redstick. He had tried that life and was through with it.

They entered a dense green pocket forest of magnolia and oak. The walls of the ravine rose at least a hundred feet on either side, and the air cooled as they moved deeper into the forest. She took him through a laurel thicket alive with the rustlings of ribbon snakes and the cracklings of cicadas. Softshell turtles bolted for dark creek-holes; mink tracks lined the bank. The humid air was sweet with the tea-smell of rotting leaves, and then from somewhere ahead came the faint scent of wood smoke.

The woman lived at the blind end of the ravine, in a small stone hut built against the side of a rocky cliff. The roof of the hut was thatched with palmetto fronds woven through twisted lengths of willow, and at the base of the cliff the pure water of the creek bubbled up from the earth. They stopped here and she looked down at his breechcloth. "Ain't you got no real clothes?" she asked. "You gone Indian?"

"Nome."

"Need any?"

"Nome."

She shrugged. "Fine then," she said. "Sit." She pointed to a collection of stumps arranged around a crackling fire. Five stumps in all, as if he were simply the first of many guests to arrive. They sat beside each other, staring at the fire as night fell upon them. She asked him about his bone club, and he told her that he had found it in the forest. He could tell that she did not believe him.

"You livin here by youself, ma'am?" he asked.

"Yes."

"No men?"

"No men, not no more." She patted him on his knee. "We're alone. Don't you be afraid."

A dented kettle dangled over the fire, suspended from a tripod of rusty iron rods. She filled two metal bowls with a pearl broth containing white chunks of fish meat. At last she introduced herself. "My name is Elvy," she said. "Elvy Callaway."

"I am Kau."

"Cow like a milk cow?" She laughed and he saw that her teeth were somehow quite white. "You got a Christian name?"

He shook his head.

"Ever want one? I'm a wizard at naming things."

"Nome."

She smiled and handed him his bowl. "You lack the talent for conversation," she said. "Have no gift for it at all."

He took a cautious sip of the soup, then coughed as it burned at his throat. His horse blanket was wet from the river crossing, and she took it from him and laid it out to dry across the thatched roof of the hut. He thanked her and then, in the manner of some people too long in solitude, she grew anxious to talk. As they ate she began to tell him her story. The story of how she had come to exist alone in that dark valley.

"I am a witness for the Lord," she told him.

ELVY CALLAWAY HAD also once lived along the federal road, though farther to the east than he himself had. Her home was near the Chattahoochee River crossing, the border between Georgia and the Mississippi Territory. She was the madam of a brothel house, and her establishment had been quite famous. In a shy way Kau admitted that he had overheard more than a few tales of Elvy's Den.

She nodded. "God have mercy on our sinning souls," she said.

Though five women called the Den their home, Elvy herself was far and away the prettiest and healthiest of the lot. She dressed in Charleston finery befitting her station as a madam, and refused her own favors to all but the occasional wealthy traveler, a few officers from the nearby fort. For trysts with these select men she kept a small cabin hidden in the forest. Visits to Elvy were carefully arranged, and so great was her discretion that no customer could ever be certain of the identity of another.

Such was her life until a cold night in December 1814 when she was surprised in her cabin by a knock at the door. She was not alone. A young British lieutenant, gentleman prisoner of the Americans at Fort Mitchell, was spread out beneath her. The lieutenant had lost a hand to grapeshot in the defeat at Pensacola, and for this one evening with Elvy he had cut all of the silver buttons from his uniform.

Elvy went naked to the door, and when she flipped open the wrought-iron Judas viewer, she saw a shabby and hollow-cheeked man staring back at her with sad eyes. "Whoa now," she said to him. "Who are you?"

The man sneezed into his sleeve and then spoke. "I'm a preacher, ma'am. A preacher in need of lodging for the night."

"This ain't no inn."

"Have you really nothing, ma'am?"

"I have plenty," she said. "Backtrack to that big cabin on the road. You can share a room all night with one of my girls if you show her enough coins."

The preacher's face went high pink. His frail body seemed to tremble. "You are the owner of that place?"

"I am indeed."

At that the preacher slammed his fist against the thick door so hard that the one-handed lieutenant hurried to her side. "Is this man badgering you?" he whispered.

She touched his hand. "I'll tend to him," she said. "But thank you." She was moved by the young officer's concern, his willingness to reveal his presence. In truth she had thought him to be hiding under the bed.

The preacher had calmed himself. "Who is with you?" he asked.

"Mind your business," she told him.

"I will pray for you both."

He turned to leave but she would not allow him the final word. "We don't need your prayers," she said.

The preacher stopped and looked back at her. "Tell me," he said, "tell me truthfully. Do you ever pray?"

There was something about the way the question was asked, something heartbreaking that drew her in. As a child she had been religious, but of course that was long ago. "No," she allowed. "I don't pray."

"And your companion?"

The lieutenant still had his pale body pressed against the door, listening. Elvy glanced over and he shook his head. "No," she said again. "Him neither."

The preacher nodded and reached into the pocket of his patched coat. He pulled out his hand and she saw that he was holding a fistful of half dollars. She watched as he counted the coins with crooked fingers, clicking them down across the flat of his other hand. Once he had them all stacked in three equal piles he looked up. "Nine dollars," he said.

"That it is. Lot of money for a beggar."

"And it's yours to have," he told her. "So long as you both can make me one promise."

"Well?"

"Promise me that you will never ever pray." The preacher held the coins out to her. "Simple."

"Have you lost your senses?"

"Perhaps."

"What kind of preacher are you?"

"Does it matter?"

Elvy looked over at the lieutenant and he shrugged. "All right, mister." She reached her hand out through the Judas viewer. "I promise you."

The preacher smiled. "And your friend?"

"He promises."

"I need to hear him say it."

She grabbed a handful of the lieutenant's bare flesh and he spoke. "I promise that I will never pray," he said, rushing the words.

The preacher raised a wispy eyebrow. "An Englishman?"

"Still none of your concern. Now pay me."

"Very well." He let her take the coins from his outstretched hand, then made for the path that led back to the federal road.

Elvy watched him go and felt a small measure of sorrow for taking advantage of what only could be a lunatic. She called out after him. "Head on up to my place," she said. "Tell the girls I promised you a room till morning. They'll leave you be."

The preacher had retreated down the path and into the night. She could no longer see him, but suddenly she heard his voice speak out to her in the dark. "I'll manage," he said, and then it was quiet again.

Nine dollars. Elvy split the coins with the lieutenant—even sewed the buttons back onto his uniform—and in light of their bizarre windfall she came to see herself as fated to a lifetime of happiness with this war-wounded man. Their relationship became something more than it had been, and one week after the visit from the crazed preacher the lieutenant dropped to a knee on the dirt floor of her cabin. "Marry me," he begged. "Marry me, Elvy Callaway."

"Of course," she replied.

The lieutenant then told her of a British fort downriver—across the border in Spanish Florida—and promised that if she helped him reach that place they would one day sail together to England. "Your next home will be a castle," he promised her. "A castle with silver and servants and silk." The lieutenant held her and she fell asleep trying to conjure up what an English countryside might look like. In the morning she awoke in a brilliant mood and went down to the wharf, taking into her confidence a milky-breathed riverman she had twice turned away from her cabin. For an hour in the boathouse plus nine dollars exact he furnished her with a canoe and supplies.

The journey south with the lieutenant was the great adventure of Elvy's life. They traveled at night, the only moment of real danger coming as they eased past the bonfires of the Choctaw mercenaries stationed at the final American outpost on the river. At last they reached the point where the Chattahoochee gathered the Flint and became the Apalachicola. "Florida," said the lieutenant, and the two lovers gave a great sigh of relief and accomplishment.

ELVY BROKE FROM her story and he saw that she was crying. "That was nineteen months ago," she said.

"So he gone?"

"I killed him."

"Killed him?"

"Cut his veins while he slept."

He sat watching and as she began to explain herself it registered, the animal wildness in those blue eyes. She wiped her nose and told him how the lovers had stopped at this same valley. She had been collecting water while her fiancé gathered roots and herbs and berries in the pocket forest. The lieutenant had happened upon the abandoned stone hut and called out to her. It was late in the afternoon and so they decided to make their camp. That night while the lieutenant slept beside her she had a dream—a dream in which all she had begun to suspect during their long cold hours on the river was revealed to her as truth. In this dream she was alone and in hell, burning. There was the sound of a man laughing, and as her skin melted away she saw him—the preacher at the door. She awoke holding a knife and covered in warm blood. The one-handed lieutenant was dead, his stumped wrist sliced open at its base.

Kau watched as she began to shake. Fish soup splashed from her bowl down onto her bare feet. "Now do you see?" she asked him.

"See what?"

She dabbed her wet eye with the hem of her filthy dress. "Never mind."

"You really don recall killin him?"

"I don't."

"Then maybe it weren't you."

She was staring at a heap of rocks piled beside the hut, and he realized that suspended in the dirt beneath those stones were the bones of her lieutenant. She tilted her head back and spoke to the stars. "May the Lord and God forgive me," she said.

Kau set his own soup down on the ground by his feet. "Why you sayin all this?"

"My God," she said. "You still don't see what we did that night?"

He shook his head.

"The preacher," she said.

"What of him?"

"I believe we met the Devil that day."

"The Devil?"

"Think now, heathen. Who else would have tempted us so?"
She punched at her neck with a fist. "I woke up that morning and
just knew I was damned."

"But why stay here?"

"To repent. To beg for the Lord's forgiveness."

"Forever?"

"I suspect."

"How come you ain't been killed youself?"

She laughed. "By?"

"Indians?"

Elvy waved a limp hand. "I see them now and again," she said.
"They look down at me from atop the cliffs, throw pebbles for
sport. Nothing too fearful."

"Someone be comin for you one day. You must know that."

"So let them come." Elvy sighed and then spread out her arms.
"I imagine this is only the first of many hells I will suffer."

FOR A LONG time they sat in silence beside the fire. Elvy fixed him
a mug of wild tea and asked that he drink, promising that it would
give him strength. He thanked her and she stared at him. Her own
tin mug was up against her lips, and so when she spoke her words
made a light echo. "There's something I've been wanting to ask
you," she said quietly.

"Yessum?"

"How goes the war?"

"The war with the British?"

"Yes."

"Done ended."

"Ended? When?"

"A year ago. At leas a year ago."

"Who won?"

"Americans say they won. But I also heard some sayin ain't neither side."

Elvy rubbed at the side of her head as he sipped his drink. The tea was bitter and hot with the lingering taste of some root or herb he could not quite place. Finally she told him that she was going into her hut for the night, but then soon after she called for him.

Kau pushed aside the blanket covering the entrance to her hut and saw that she had changed into a cotton nightgown.

"All right," she said. "Now get on in here."

"Nome. I'll jus make a place for myself outside."

Of course he was thinking of the killed Englishman, and he watched as she lifted a walking stick that was leaning against the wall, then hurled it at his chest. She missed and the stick went sailing past him like a spear. "Then leave," she said.

He moved away and pulled his horse blanket from the roof of the hut. The night was warm but with a breeze. He followed the path along the creek to the river, and in a fern grove he stumbled upon a long canoe half covered in leaves. He flipped the canoe over and a bedded boar possum scurried off through the emerald ferns. Daddy longlegs came spilling out of the hull so that for a moment the canoe itself somehow seemed alive. He watched them leave in a great twitching wave, then go marching silently across the forest floor on their hair-thin legs.

When the canoe had emptied he collected the two paddles he had discovered hidden beneath it and stepped inside. He could hear the water music of the nearby creek, and he lay on his back, listening. High above him, this second full moon of the spring was the color of bone. It had been a month since he had left Yellowhammer, killed the boy. He could make out the moon's mountains and craters and oceans, the open-mouthed laughing man Benjamin had once taught him to see, a man who would keep on watching him no matter where he was taken, ran to or hid.

HE AWOKE TO movement in the forest and sat up holding his knife. Elvy was walking the trail in her nightgown. She came alongside the canoe, then looked down at him and smiled. The moon was framed atop her head like a balanced ball, and he waved at her with the knife. "You go away," he said.

Elvy pulled the nightgown off and threw it aside. She was still smiling when she turned and stepped into the shallow creek. He looked on as she knelt to dip a rag into the water. She washed her legs and then her stomach, bathing herself. He watched her and she called out to him. "Please," she said. "Come and let me clean you once." He gave no reply and she kept on. She ran the cut cloth over her chest, and water dripped down across her white breasts. He felt himself hardening. He unbuckled his belt. The breechcloth fell away and he stepped free of the beached canoe. He went to her and she grabbed him by his wrist. "Good," she said. "Now hold still." He stood there with the knife in his hand; cool water ran over and past his ankles as she scrubbed at his body with the rag. She was taller by a half foot at least so that as she washed the dirt and sweat from his skin he felt more like her child than a man. He tossed his knife onto the creek bank, and she put her hands between his legs. Her fingernails were long and sharp, and he shivered as she pulled at him. He tried to slow her, but she refused and then dropped to her knees in the water. He closed his eyes and came quickly before opening them again. He looked down and she stayed there, her cheeks working steadily as she sucked him dry. He felt weak and so he pushed at her head. Finally she released him. She swallowed and then spoke. "Stay," she said.

He splashed onto the bank, then watched as she lay back in the creek. Her body divided the current, and her long blonde hair flowed with the water. He found his knife and picked it up. A jagged part had now formed along the center of her scalp, and she seemed asleep, dead even.

Again she asked him to stay but instead he turned away from her. He was dragging the heavy canoe toward the river when she let loose a raw and devastated scream, a lonely shriek that silenced the cicadas.

PART TWO

THE NEGRO FORT

Down the Apalachicola River—
A negro farm—A general presents

HE SPENT TWO nights and two days on the river after departing the valley of Elvy Callaway, and though he was without food he stayed to the river and pressed on, did not sleep and did not eat.

ON THE THIRD morning the east-bank forest finally thinned, and he saw green and gold fields of wheat and corn. He was very tired and very hungry and so he put to shore. A distant rooster crowed as he muscled the big canoe up onto the bank. He gathered his canteen and saddlebags, then made his way through a cornfield.

The rich lowlands soon gave way to poor sandy soil, and here the cornfield ended. A small cabin stood to the left of a sturdy post oak, and there was a man hunched over beneath the tree. Kau lay flat in the boundary stalks of corn, watching as the negro took a file to a rusty plowshare. A pretty woman came out onto the porch and called to the man in Spanish, a language Kau recognized but did not speak. The man waved back at her, and then the woman walked barefoot across the dirt yard to a scrap-wood chickenhouse. She opened the door and two dozen clucking Dominickers came parading out.

The black-and-white hens were followed by a colossal rose-combed rooster. The hens scratched the dirt for insects and seed while the rooster stood with its head cocked to the morning sky, searching for hawks. The woman slipped into the chickenhouse, then came back out with an armful of brown eggs cradled against her stomach. The rooster charged after her, and the man stopped his steady filing to laugh.

"*Gallo bobo*," said the woman to the rooster. It came at her again and she kicked the bird hard in the side with her foot. Barred feathers flew and the rooster shied off. "*¿No comprendes?*" she said.

The rooster gave a series of violent squawks but quit the fight, joining a group of hens clustered in a far corner of the yard. The farmer had stood and seemed to be jeering it. "*¡Nunca capitulas!*" he shouted.

The woman smiled and rocked her hips from side to side, and Kau thought he heard her say the tall man's name—Pelayo, she called him. She pretended to throw an egg at her husband, and he pretended to duck.

"*¡No más, Elisenda!*" said the farmer Pelayo. He dropped the file and raised his hands up over his head. "*¡Capitulamos, Elisenda! ¡Capitulamos!*"

This woman Elisenda went back into the cabin, and Pelayo returned to the plowshare. Kau kept on with his spying. The sun rose higher and the day grew hot. Pelayo pulled his osnaburg shirt off, and Kau saw the whip scars of a runaway latticing the length of his back. Free negroes. The first he had seen since Africa. They live as farmers, he realized, farmers like the Kesa.

MIDDAY, TWIN GIRLS in simple cotton dresses—children eleven or twelve years old with boy-short hair—emerged from farther down the cornfield carrying a dead rabbit. They laid the rabbit on the porch of the cabin and went to Pelayo. He said something that Kau could not hear, then handed one of them the long, curved knife that he wore on his side.

"*Gracias, Papá,*" sang the girls.

A nail had been driven at a slant into the side of the post oak, and the big rabbit was hung upside down by a slit foot. The twins then began to argue over the knife, and Pelayo scolded them until it was passed. The second girl brought the blade to the rabbit's neck and cut off its head. Dark blood spilled down the rough trunk of the oak to collect between twisting roots.

Back and forth the knife was traded. The girls took turns sawing through the rabbit's feet, then one peeled the pelt while the other removed the bowels. They finished and the carcass dangled from the nail. The girls carried the hide and guts and head behind the cabin, and Kau heard happy pigs squeal. After the hogs went silent the girls returned to the front yard with a bucket of water collected from some hidden cistern or well. They took the rabbit down from the tree, washing the carcass and then their hands in the water. One girl quartered the rabbit and took the pink sections of meat inside. "*Bueno*," said Pelayo, and the remaining daughter nodded as she cleaned her father's knife.

Soon the dry and dusty cornfield became too hot for Kau to bear, and so he returned to his canoe to think. Across the river the land was unsettled and lush, and he wondered if there, at last, was the quiet forest that he was seeking. He figured that he could hunt in those across-the-river pinewoods, maybe even trade with this farmer Pelayo for corn and milk and eggs. But how to approach him? He took a sip from his canteen, then dragged the canoe halfway into the river. The corn grew close to the bank, and he could see bent stalks left by crop-raiding coons. He stole four or five of the raw ears for himself as a line of clouds passed over the sun and the whole world darkened.

He made his camp on the western bank, a quarter mile or so inland into the pine forest. As night fell he took up the tinderbox and risked a small fire. He had left the unshucked corn soaking in a shallow pond rimmed with pitcher plants and flytraps, and after the fire had burned down he laid them carefully over the bed of white coals, turning them from time to time just as Samuel had once taught him. He shook his head. Those five years at Yellowhammer now felt as distant to him as his old life in Africa.

The corn cooked as he sat on his horse blanket and thought of the valley-dweller Elvy Callaway. He had been trying to keep her out of his mind, but now finally she forced her way in. On that full-moon night the American had both washed him and tasted him, and he considered the strangeness of that for a long while—how after the death of his wife Janeti he could go so many years without the touch of any woman only to then have such a thing happen here in this land. He remembered the white woman screaming, how she had begged him not to leave her. He remembered the feel of her mouth around him. Just as Elvy was doomed to remain in her valley, he seemed doomed to wander. In the end all he could conclude was that he was a man destined to travel between worlds, to spend a first life moving through one and then a second life struggling through another.

He used the bone club to push the roasting corn free of the coals, and the fire coughed sparks as he waited for the steaming cobs to cool. Satisfied, he picked up the closest of the ears and removed its blackened husk. The meat of the hot corn was swollen and yellow, and he finished with the first ear and then went for another. Soon none were left and it was time for him to sleep. He stretched himself out and saw the chopped face of Benjamin's man in the moon. A god-giant peering down at him from between a gap in the skeletal pines. In Africa Kau had seen many things revealed in that same moon—animals and trees and rivers—but never once a man.

HE HID FOR two days in the forest across the river. It was pine savanna, and the tall trees were mostly longleafs, the flatlands below a green patchwork of wiregrass and saw palmetto interlaced with game trails. When the wind blew the pines swayed, and from the high canopy there came a sound like the roar of the ocean he thought he had forgotten.

At dawn he would hunt with the sling, and on the second morning he watched a blue heron come circling down through the pines to settle onto the bank of the pond. The slate bird was stabbing at the shimmering water when Kau sent a river stone flying. There was a hollow thumping as the round rock hit the heron hard in the breast. It collapsed stunned but kicking and he ran for it.

THROUGH THE HOT hours he would rest in the shade of the pinewoods and then, at night, cross the river to steal corn from Pelayo's field. Sometimes he would linger, listening to the sounds that escaped from the cabin.

SUNSET. HE HEARD laughter in the cornfield and crept toward it. On a small patch of stubbled ground he came upon Pelayo and Elisenda, alone and kissing. A warm breeze blew in from the river, riffling the surrounding cornstalks, and he watched them as they undressed. Elisenda laid herself down on a spread quilt, then giggled as her husband went to her.

Finally Kau turned and crept off, the whole time thinking of his nights with Janeti, the way she would smile at him when the children fell asleep. He pushed his canoe out into the current and yet still he could hear moanings from the cornfield. A new torture. He hooted like an owl calling but of course they did not quit.

THE FOLLOWING NIGHT he was carrying more stolen corn to his canoe when he spotted Pelayo's twin daughters walking along the dim riverbank. The barefoot girls were thin, yet not so much shorter than he himself was. They were talking and laughing, but then they came upon his canoe and went quiet. Kau set the corn down in the dirt and eased back into the field. Here he waited, crouched low and listening, willing his quick breaths to settle.

Soon the twins began to call for their father, and then Kau heard them bolt toward the cabin. He was pulling his knife from its belt sheath when they both came tearing through the corn and slammed into him. He dropped the knife, and the surprised girls screamed as they all fell to the ground together. They were locked in a tumble, and for a flash instant he thought of Benjamin and his bleeding neck. Kau rolled away from them, his eyes now filled with dirt, and began to stumble blind through the cornfield. His breechcloth had come untucked from his belt and was gone.

And then Pelayo's deep voice cried out from the direction of the cabin. "¡Ramona!" he called. "¡Marcela!"

A terrified girl answered back: "¡Papá!" she shrieked. "¡Ven por favor!"

"¿Qué paso?"

"¡Un ladrón! ¡Ven ahora!"

Kau wiped dirt from his eyes and could see the corn ahead thinning. He had almost reached the river when he was swallowed up by the arms of the farmer Pelayo.

THE COLLISION IN the cornfield had somehow swollen the eye of the twin he heard them call Ramona, and so Pelayo took vengeance with the bone club. The farmer and his girls struck blow after blow until finally Kau lay still, refusing to fight them. He felt the tickle of blood leaking from his left ear, a bone in his nose breaking. So this, he decided, will be the death of me. Soon he felt nothing as they beat him, nothing save the numb sensation that he was being hammered like a fencepost into the warm earth. He let himself believe that the farmer was indeed planting him within that turned field, that he would cycle with the crops and fall back in with the natural rhythm of the world. So yes beat me then, he thought, beat me until nothing remains.

He might have been strangled or even drowned had it not been for the arrival of Elisenda. Pelayo had dragged him all the way to the riverbank, but she pried her husband's fingers from his throat and calmed him. *"Por favor,"* she said. *"No lo mates."*

MORNING. HE AWOKE naked and hogtied on the shit floor of the hot chickenhouse, his hands bound to his feet, and the hens slept in their nest boxes while the angry rooster paced. Now and again the cock would rush forward to peck and spur at his legs, and soon they were badly scratched and bleeding. He rocked onto his side and the rooster retreated. A girl laughed from somewhere close, and Kau craned his neck, searching for her.

The door of the chickenhouse had been propped open and there sat black-eyed Ramona on an overturned bucket. Spread out behind her was his knife and bone club and belt, his canteen and saddlebags. She said something harsh in Spanish, and he tried to speak to her. He moved his lips but no words came, his damaged throat unable to mold his breaths into anything more than a reptile hiss. There was a constant ringing in his left ear, and he could feel shards of bone jostling in his nose. Again he tried to speak and this time the girl mocked him with hisses of her own.

He began to cough and his mouth filled with salty blood. He spit, then watched his blood and saliva mix with dust and chicken-shit. He spit and the girl spit. A speck of her fluid settled onto his eyelash and shined like a prism; for a moment the rays of sunlight that pushed through the cracks in the chickenhouse seemed to spar-kle and glisten. He blinked and the world returned to clear.

The girl called for her sister Marcela and there came a muffled response from somewhere beyond. He had his good ear pressed to the stinking ground, and could hear a slight pounding in the earth as she came running. Marcela joined her sister at the entrance to the chickenhouse, and he watched as, together, they regarded him. Ramona then cleared her throat and spit on him once more, impress-ing her twin. They made a game of it. One would spit and then the other, and when he finally he rolled away from the both of them he was attacked again by the cornered rooster. The twins laughed and crept closer. The rooster flew to the high rung of its roost, and the girls raised their short dresses. Elisenda was shouting for her daugh-ters as the first hot splash of piss hit the side of his face. A shallow cut that ran across the bridge of his fractured nose began to throb and sting, and he shut his eyes and then turned onto his stomach, waiting for these girls to finish, waiting for these girls to be satisfied.

LATER THAT DAY a shackle was fastened to his ankle, and at last he was untied so that he could move about the chickenhouse. A chain ran from his shackle up into the rafters, and he felt like a dog on a leash. The shackle was small—could only have been meant for a woman or even a child—and he wondered why, if this was truly a place without slaves, Pelayo would ever possess such a thing.

BY EAVESDROPPING ON the chickenhouse whisperings of the twins, he would soon learn that their mother had been awoken from a dream on the night that he was discovered in the cornfield. His visit to their farm—his very appearance, even—had tracked all of the important details of that dream. The superstitious woman had seen his small size and sharp teeth and thought him a death angel come to take one of her daughters. It was good that he had been caught—of that she was certain—but whether it was proper to execute an angel, that was not for simple farmers to decide.

HIS SECOND NIGHT on the chain he killed and ate the rooster, and again Pelayo beat him. For all of the next day he was given neither food nor water. He drank raw eggs to quench his thirst, burying the broken shells to avoid another punishing.

HE PILED FEATHERS to mark the days, and over the three weeks following his capture word spread and every manner of negro man, woman and child came to behold him. A few Indians, even. Some of the negroes spoke Spanish and some spoke English. They would give Pelayo a basket of vegetables, some ribbon for his wife, and in exchange he would throw open the door of the chickenhouse, allowing them a look at his *ángel de la muerte*.

THE PRIMARY AMUSEMENT of these visitors seemed to be the challenge of somehow making him speak. They would pelt him with rocks and jab him with sticks, threaten him with fire. He tried to communicate with them, pointing at his bruised throat while at the same time shaking his head. He did this time and again but they never once caught his meaning. A young negro flinched and then cursed him. "No suh," he said. "Don you go puttin no spells on us."

A FOURTH WEEK passed. The ceiling of the chickenhouse was lined with the panpipe nests of dirt daubers, and he watched the black wasps come and go.

His visitors dwindled to the occasional curious Indian, then soon stopped coming altogether. Food was brought rarely now, and he was dependent upon the eggs of the chickens, even the lice in their feathers. It became clear that no one truly believed him an angel anymore. He imagined that he would be killed soon, that Pelayo and his daughters would finally come for him.

To keep his mind he mouthed the names of every member of his Ota band. They came easily and so he moved on to recalling the names of every Kesa and every Indian and every slave and every white man he could recall. He whispered Benjamin last and fell into a sort of half-sleep trance. He saw the boy in the river, dead but moving. Benjamin has walked the Chattahoochee south to the Apalachicola and he is here, underwater and waiting, level with Pelayo's farm.

One night as the moon rises Benjamin emerges onto the east-bank shore. The blood has drained from his body and most of his flesh is missing. Still, Kau sees him and he has hope. The boy has forgiven him; the boy is coming to save him. He calls Benjamin's name over and again to guide him to the chickenhouse, and Benjamin leaves the shore for the cornfield. Looking down on the world from somewhere above, Kau can see the collapsing of cornstalks as Benjamin weaves his way closer. Yes, he is coming. Kau says, Benjamin, Benjamin, Benjamin, loud as he can manage and finally the boy steps out onto the dirt of Pelayo's yard. Benjamin looks at the chickenhouse, then brings two fingers to his lipless mouth and whistles. The door to the cabin opens and Kau sees Marcela and Ramona. The twins leap from the porch to the yard, and the three children meet by the post oak. Together they all turn for the chickenhouse.

AFTER FIVE MORE days in the chickenhouse he awoke somehow knowing that his voice had begun its slow return. He whispered, "I am a man," but there was no one there to hear him. He thought maybe he should try to cry out but then checked himself, deciding instead to think on just what it was that he might say should he ever have the opportunity to speak.

AT LAST PELAYO did come for him. The farmer tied Kau's hands behind his back, then slid a long metal key into the butterfly shaft of the slave shackle. The coupling fell open, and Kau was led filthy and naked out into the sun-baked yard. He looked to the cabin and saw that Elisenda and the twins were watching him from the porch.

A copper horse had been hitched to the post oak, and a pair of brindled hounds lay panting in the shade. Beside the horse stood a powerfully built man with almond eyes, high cheekbones and coal skin. He wore white breeches and black boots, a British officer's redcoat and sword. The man was staring at Kau and seemed fascinated. He spoke to Pelayo: "*¿Con los pollos?*"

"*Sí, General*," said Pelayo. "*Robó de mí.*" The farmer pointed to the porch, then moved his finger from silent daughter to silent daughter. "*Y atacó a mis chicas.*"

The man came closer and Kau saw that they were about the same age. His hair had been twisted into braids that spilled down from under a battered black tricorn. "*¿Español?*" the man asked him. "English?"

"Yes," said Kau. "English." His voice was scratchy and weak, but when he spoke Pelayo stepped back and then crossed himself.

The stranger muttered something to Pelayo in Spanish, and in turn Pelayo yelled to his wife and his daughters still watching from the porch. Marcela and Ramona disappeared into the cabin, but Elisenda remained and seemed to be praying.

The man put his hand on Kau's shoulder. "I am General Garçon," he said. "I decided I should come and see you for myself."

Kau nodded.

"Is it true?" he asked. "Did you attack his children?"

"No, not like he meanin."

"Well, then did you steal from him?"

Kau glanced at Pelayo and then nodded again. "I was hungry and took me some corn."

"I see." And then this general named Garçon gave a thin smile. "So he made you his chicken."

Pelayo appeared confused and also smiled. Kau looked toward the cabin. The twins had walked back onto the porch carrying his effects—his canteen and saddlebags, his bone club and belt and knife—when suddenly Garçon punched Pelayo hard in the stomach. The farmer sank to both knees, and Garçon slapped him across the face. "*¡Papá!*" said the twins. They made to rush to their father, but Elisenda grabbed them both.

Garçon drew his sword, then told Kau to hold still as he sliced through the rope binding his hands. The rope fell away and Kau rubbed his raw wrists. Garçon offered him the sword and Elisenda screamed. Pelayo covered his face with his hands.

Kau hesitated and Garçon spoke to him. "Only if you wish," he said.

The frightened twins were now crying, and their sobs sounded almost like the squeals of the gut-eating hogs. Ramona's eye had healed, and Kau could no longer tell the two girls apart. "No," he said finally. He started to say more, but again his voice had left him.

Garçon shrugged. "Then collect what is yours," he said. "I will take you away from this place."

It was Pelayo who brought him his things, and then one of the twins walked slowly down from the porch carrying a small stack of clothes. Garçon smoothed her dark hair back with the flat of his hand, then whispered something in her ear. Kau saw that she was trembling as she held the clothes out for him to take. "*Toma,*" she said to him. "*Lo siento.*" He lifted the shirt and pants from her arms and unfolded them. These were the osnaburgs of a child, but they were also clean. With his breechcloth lost he had nothing else, and so he nodded and put them on.

A fort—Beah—
The biography of Garçon

H E WAS WEDGED between Garçon and a fresh bear hide and taken south through the farms that lined the river. Negro families gathered along the narrow and dusty road as they passed by atop the gelding. These farmers cheered their general and threw scraps to his hunting dogs. Kau recognized some among them as visitors to the chickenhouse, but when he locked eyes with them they were careful to look away.

It was growing late and he was fading with the day. Garçon had asked him about the bone club and even his teeth, but Kau still could not speak loud enough to even give his own name. Twice he had fainted and slid off the back of the horse, and now his ankle was badly sprained. A bugle sounded, and when he opened his eyes he thought that maybe he was dreaming. Cornfields had given way to an immense dirt field planted with potatoes and turnips and onions. The thin road bisected the plowed land, and farmers leaned on their hoes and watched them. To the east was a smoking cutover and then pine forest; to the west he could see the brown river. From somewhere beyond came the lowing of range cattle, the bray of a mule. A speckled flock of guineafowl was moving through the weed banks of a drainage, scratching for a few last ticks before sunset.

In the dim southern distance the land rose up and a long row of barked pickets ran east from the river like a high fence. A fort, he realized. A breeze came and from atop a tall flagstaff he saw flapping fragments of white, blue and red. Garçon slapped the reins and the gelding sighed under them.

A stagnant moat surrounded the fort with a horseshoe of river water. At a small wooden bridge Garçon gave a broad wave, and a gate swung open to reveal a rectangle of six or seven dusty acres sprinkled with white tents, a few low-slung cabins and structures. A skinny negro soldier touched the curled brim of his felt hat. It was black and round and lacquered. The soldier wore a redcoat and loose white trousers, held a long musket fitted with a bayonet. He stared up at Kau as they passed.

The gate closed behind them and Kau looked around. He saw no one else; the fort appeared mostly empty, abandoned even. Garçon laughed as they made for a far corner. This general seemed able to hear the thoughts in his head. "They come when I call them," he said. "They are my warrior farmers."

THE INFIRMARY WAS a small cabin with four beds, and it was vacant except for a fat negro woman with a thick head of bushy black hair. Garçon helped him onto a camp bed, and Kau studied the woman. She looked just a few years older than he and wore a great sack of an osnaburg dress. He heard a name—Beah—then she caught him watching her and whistled through a gap in her front teeth. "What the Lord you bringin me here, General?"

"A hurt man," said Garçon.

"Looks like an African, jus smaller."

"I believe that he is."

"My, my, my. This baby got a name?"

"He does not. Not yet."

"How's that?"

"You see the bruises on his throat?"

Kau shifted on the canvas bottom of the camp bed, looking on as Garçon pointed down at him.

"I see them fine," said Beah. "Got a crooked nose, too."

"True. And a bad foot."

"He knowin English or Spanish?"

"English. But do not talk him to death."

"Me?"

"Indeed." Beah smiled, and Kau thought she seemed about to say something more when Garçon stopped her. "I mean that," he said.

She laughed but did not speak.

"Let him rest," said Garçon. "And then you bring him to me when he is better."

Kau watched him leave and thought of Samuel. What would he have made of all this? A fort under the control of a negro? A negro fort. Chances were fair that the old slave was still alive, would outlive him even—but he wondered whether Samuel would have accepted it. Whether even if Samuel were with him to see these negro soldiers he would just shake his head and say, No suh, I don't believe that at all. Them look like white man's uniforms, I say.

HE WOKE AND the nurse Beah rushed over. "Keep still," she told him. "You been sleepin for two days."

The cabin was very hot. He tried to sit up but she pushed him back down. The sleeves of her dress had been cut off to accommodate her huge arms, and her flesh jiggled as she held him pinned.

"I mean it," she said. "Gotta be easy on that foot, hear me now?"

He stopped fighting her and looked around. His skin had been washed clean of dust and chickenshit, and he was wearing a child's cotton nightshirt. He tried to tell her his name but his voice only crackled. She put a finger to his lips.

"Rest that, too," she ordered. "Else it won't never get no better."

He soon learned that it was true—Beah did not know how to be quiet. The ringing in his ear was gone, and he listened as she told him how lucky he was that the General had found him when he did. She teased at the gap between her teeth with the tip of her tongue. "Lucky, lucky, lucky," she said.

This had begun to annoy him, how she liked to say simple things in threes. "Who is he?" he asked. The words cut at his throat and he winced.

She pinched his arm. "Hush, African," she said. Then, later: "You really don know?"

He shook his head and she leaned into him. Her heavy breasts pressed against his shoulder, and she smelled faintly of molasses. "I know all about that man," she said. "Morn anybody, I spose." She looked around the empty room, then lowered her voice to a whisper. "What I could tell you about the General would curl your little toes."

"Go on with it."

Again Beah pinched him.

"Don be doin that no more."

She rolled her brown eyes. "You wantin me to tell you or no?"

He nodded.

"Then quit all your fussin and listen." She pulled a chair closer and poured them both a mug of water. He took a sip. The water was cool but tasted of sulfur. Beah spoke. "While back he spent two weeks in here crazy with fever," she said. "Whole time runnin his mouth like a madman, talkin every language—English and French, Spanish and Indian." She tapped a thick finger against her temple. "And I don forget nothin, at leas not the English."

THE THINGS BEAH told him about the General seemed more akin to myth and legend than truth—things as difficult for him to believe as they were impossible for him to confirm. The tale she told him held that even the man's name was in fact uncertain.

According to Beah, the negro who now called himself a British general was born to the name Gustave thirty miles up the river from New Orleans. His master had been a Creole sugar planter named Trépagnier, and the boy Gustave was Trépagnier's favored slave—something close to a son for a man whose young wife died before she could give him any children of his own. Picture a negro boy in a crushed velvet suit sitting cross-legged under the table. Picture him being handfed dainty scraps of grillade and pigeon, warm bread and sweet praline, cool slices of raw mirliton.

It was obvious that the child possessed genius, and on a wager with a neighbor Trépagnier himself taught Gustave how to read and to write. By age twelve the boy could speak three languages, and soon he was studying and composing poetry. Beah had memorized the final lines of a long poem that the General would sometimes mumble pieces of to her in English. She cleared her throat, then sang the words out carefully:

> The world was all before them
> where to choose they place of rest
> and Providence they guide
> hand in hand, with wanderin steps and slow
> through Eden they took they solitary way

The narrative Beah recited secondhand held that for Gustave's eighteenth birthday Trépagnier had promised his emancipation in three years. The young man kissed the hem of his master's coat and began to live free in his own head. In Gustave's mind he was already a gentleman living in New Orleans. His mother was a field slave, and sometimes he visited her in the crowded quarters at night, promising that he would not forget her, that he would one day purchase her own freedom from the blessed Trépagnier.

Of course the others heard Gustave's talk and became jealous. A quadroon slave had captured the master's heart, and this beautiful young woman now thought to ask after her own liberation. Her name was Simone, and she and the widower Trépagnier would play all-day games in his room.

The planter had a four-post bed as perfect and square as a cube. His greatest pleasure was to lie spread-eagled on that wide, moss-stuffed mattress, and then Simone would come calling with lengths of torn silk, binding his wrists and ankles to each nearest corner. Trépagnier was in such a state one autumn afternoon when she took to him with a peacock feather. She ran the quill down the length of his naked body, across each arm and across each leg, from the dimple of his chin to the hollow of his crotch.

"I am more to you than that boy," she told Trépagnier. "Am I not, Maître?"

Simone changed into one of his dead wife's purple dresses and then kept on. The planter began to shiver and twitch and moan. He begged her to stop but whenever she did he ordered her not to. Gustave watched all of this from behind the cracked door of his master's enormous armoire. He did this often.

Simone started up again with her shiny feather, teasing Trépagnier in her soft-spoken French. "There are many, many things I could do to you," she told him. "But only as a free woman, Maître."

"Tell me," said Trépagnier.

She slipped the purple dress from her body and leaned closer. Her dark tresses fell across Trépagnier's damp face, and Gustave saw her begin to lick at their master's ear. She whispered something that Gustave could not hear, but whatever words were carried by her hot breath made Trépagnier gasp. The planter pulled against his silk restraints. "Please," he said. "You must."

"Oh, but no," said Simone. "I will not."

She changed back into her slave-clothes and then turned to leave. The long feather dangled from her fingers, and she let it trail along the floor as she walked toward the door. She was smiling, seemed to wink at nothing as she left the room. It was only later, much later, that Gustave realized she had been well aware of his presence, that she had known he was there but simply did not care.

Within the week Simone was given her freedom. A room was prepared for her in the house, a bedroom that connected to that of Trépagnier. On cool and breezy evenings she would stroll with a parasol through the oaks. Gustave would see her preparing to leave the house and rush to throw open the door. They had been child-hood playmates, were in fact cousins of some degree. He was very much in love with her and she knew this. She would sneer as she sent him on some small task or errand. "Fetch me a glass of water," she would tell him. "Find me my comb at once." After he brought her one comb she would send him for another. "No," she would say. "The pretty one made of tortoise."

To these humiliations Gustave would only dip his head and say, *Oui, Mademoiselle*—thinking all the while that soon, very soon, they would be equals again. He would be free and he would go to New Orleans and he would send for her. One, two, three went this plan of his.

KAU LISTENED TO Beah and realized that she was having her fun with this story of Garçon's, embellishing the details, manipulating the facts. So it is with all storytellers everywhere, he figured. And then he closed his eyes as she continued.

THE BIRTHDAY. IN the morning Gustave takes breakfast to Trépagnier on the back of the veranda that belts the big house. It is March and the weather is pleasant still. Sugarcane runs for a green half mile before giving way to marsh, and slaves are toiling in the fields. Gustave places a silver tray gently on a wrought-iron table and then grins at his master. He thinks he can smell the linger of Simone's perfume on Trépagnier's pale skin. The planter thanks him, and then he opens his linen napkin with a violent snap.

Gustave grins wider. "Is there anything else I might bring you, Maître?"

The planter appears to think for a moment. He shakes his head. "No," he says finally.

Trépagnier finishes his breakfast and then dawdles in his library until the early afternoon, writing letters to family in France. At two o'clock he takes a nap in his room until three o'clock. At three fifteen the stable boy has his horse saddled and waiting exactly twenty paces from the front steps of the house. Gustave watches from the window as his master rides out to survey the fields. He hears footsteps behind him and turns. It is Simone and she is smiling.

"Happy birthday, my sweet cousin," she tells him.

Gustave nods and then thanks her.

Simone stands there, expressionless and silent, volunteering nothing. She is waiting for him to ask his question. He yields to her. "Does he remember, Simone?"

"Mademoiselle."

"Mademoiselle."

She smiles again, licks her lips, pouts and then laughs. It is all too much for him. He takes her and he shakes her. She keeps on with her laughing and plays a child's game, letting her giggles rise and fall with the rhythm of his thrusts. She goes *uh* and *uh* and *uh* like a little girl amused, until at last he turns her loose and hurries outside.

Gustave stands alone on the veranda. He can see Trépagnier silhouetted atop the distant levee. The planter has checked his horse and looks to be staring right back. The sky is darkening. Gustave grows bold and waves, but his master gives no reply. Trépagnier spurs his mount and pushes on along the river. The birthday slave remains on the veranda, watching horse and rider move farther and farther away.

A month passes. The field slaves have been at him, and Gustave thinks even his mother finds some entertainment in their taunts. Finally he cannot bear the waiting any longer. Trépagnier is reading in the parlor when Gustave makes his shy approach. "Maître," he asks, "may we speak?"

Trépagnier sighs and puts down one of the leather-bound books from his library—*Discours sur l'origine et les fondements de l'inégalité parmi les hommes*. A book of ideas. Perhaps the first such book Gustave himself was ever allowed to read. "Certainly," says Trépagnier. "What is it?"

Gustave stares at his feet. He has started to sob. "It was my twenty-first birthday," he says. "Thirty-three days ago."

"I see," says Trépagnier.

"Yes."

"This is not at all proper, Gustave. Not at all proper."

"And I beg your pardon for that, Maître."

"Listen," says Trépagnier. "Circumstances have changed. I need you here. You are just too important to this house."

"Maître?"

"I think you understand."

Gustave begins to speak but his master stops him.

"No," says Trépagnier. "We are finished."

Gustave leaves the parlor and Simone is there in the great hall. She has been listening through the door, that much is clear. She brushes the back of her small hand across his wet face. "I am so sorry, my cousin," she coos. He takes hold of her wrist, and she ticks a finger in the space between them. "Do not make me scream for your *maître*," she tells him.

That night Gustave packs his few things into a pillowslip, and he is almost to the door when Simone catches him. He looks at her and sees her soften. They go together onto the veranda and she kisses his cheek. She promises that she will say nothing to Trépagnier, that she will distract him for as long as she is able. Even as Gustave runs he imagines her in the planter's room. It is morning, yet still their master's head moves between her sleek legs. By the time Trépagnier notices that his favorite slave has gone missing, the trail will be long past cold.

The outlier years. Gustave steals a pirogue from a trapper cabin, then takes to the brackish marsh that separates the river from Lake Pontchartrain. As a house slave he knows nothing of nature, and he spends several days lost in the tangle of marsh channels. Finally two negro men out gigging flounder happen upon him. Too weak to stand, he is sprawled in the pirogue catching raindrops in his mouth. These maroons tie his pirogue to their own, then tow him south into the cypress swamp that borders the hourglass marsh.

There are ten of them in the maroon community, seven men and three women. A runaway named Melissa nurses Gustave back to health, wetting his sun-cracked lips with a damp rag, chewing his food even. In a week he is at near-full strength. They ask him his name but he keeps that for himself. Their leader shrugs. Jacques is a veteran of Saint-Domingue. He served under Toussaint. He was captured on the southern slope of Pic la Selle, placed on a slave ship that brought him to New Orleans. His French remains that of the islands. Jacques spits and says, As you wish, young man. We will call you what I have been calling you. We will call you the boy. We will all call you Garçon.

He and Melissa are married. They have a son born dead. Melissa is lost to yellow fever. He has a new name, and this Garçon remains for five years with the maroons. It is a hard life, an Indian life, and he has learned to live wild. There are thirty of them now— men, women and children—but at night he still dreams of Simone and her feathers. In his mind he has killed Trépagnier a hundred different times in a hundred different ways.

The slave revolt of 1811. A mulatto slave named Charles Deslondes lives upriver from Trépagnier, and in the fall of 1810 he is hired out by Madam Deslondes to the plantation of Colonel André for the sugar harvest. Charles is a slave driver—a slave himself, but also an overseer of slaves. The fields have been burned and are ready to strip. Every morning Charles takes his tired slaves to the black and smoking fields.

In December a messenger finds his way to the maroon leader Jacques, and he learns that this Charles Deslondes is planning an insurrection. Many slaves are eager to follow. They will overthrow the masters of the river plantations and then march on New Orleans. They will form a free negro republic at the mouth of the Mississippi River. Follow me. Follow me. Follow me.

Garçon listens as Jacques makes his presentation to the maroons, and then a vote is taken among the men. They will all throw in their lot with Charles Deslondes. New Orleans will be theirs.

January 8, 1811. At first it is raining but then it is clear. The big moon is only a day away from full. The maroons have moved inland and are hiding in a thicket that runs along the river road. They hear scattered gunfire in the direction of the André plantation to the north, and then at midnight the revolutionaries appear on the shell road. Jacques gives a cry popular during the island war. Deslondes is on horseback, and at least fifty men follow him already. They come armed with cane knives and clubs and axes, a few stolen muskets. The bloodied shirt of André's dead son hangs from a pike of red maple, and the maroons fall in behind this banner. Soon others come. Their numbers swell. *Sur la Orleans*, they chant over and again. *Sur la Orleans.*

The slaves loot and burn three abandoned plantations before they at last reach that of Trépagnier. The planter is waiting for them on the veranda, armed with a two-barreled fowling piece. He fires twice and then takes up his sabre. Garçon raises his voice but the others pour forward. Trépagnier is dead before Garçon can kill him. The fieldhands give a cheer. Garçon calls out for his mother but is told by a celebrating uncle that she died that past spring.

A slave stands at the entrance to Simone's bedroom. Garçon pushes him aside and then he sees her. She is crumbled on the hardwood floor, a smoking pistol in her hand, a hole in her head.

Outside they have cut Trépagnier's body into pieces, and Garçon takes the only revenge he can think of on his old master. He collects the planter's arms and legs and head and torso into a cane basket, then carries them down the long road that leads from the house to the river. He throws all of Trépagnier into the muddy water, hoping that with this done the man's scattered soul will never know peace. And then Garçon looks back once at the slave army before he enters the powerful river himself. Even as he swims he thinks that he will drown, but somehow he does not.

Garçon spends two weeks creeping north through the high grass of the riverbank. One night he takes a forgotten newspaper from a plantation dock. When the militiamen came they came hard. In three days the rebellion was put down. Sixty-six slaves were killed in the fighting, another sixteen put on trial. Jacques and Charles were in that second number. They were executed and decapitated, their heads placed on poles along the river road.

The negro fort. Garçon hears a voice that sounds like Simone's telling him to go east. He crosses the river a second time, then journeys for two hundred miles. He becomes an outlier again and is one day taken in by another colony of runaways. They are living atop a shellmound in the delta of the Alabama River when the war with England comes. In 1814 a rumor reaches these maroons. The British have landed in Spanish Florida and are building a fort on the Apalachicola River. They are recruiting negroes to fight the Americans. This is an opportunity for true freedom. This is a chance to be legitimate. The voice comes once more—Simone's sweet voice—and Garçon again pushes east.

The commander of the British fort is a man named Nicholls, and he soon makes Garçon—the genius multilingual, a man with no real name—a sergeant in the Corps of Colonial Marines. Many more runaways arrive. American slaves and Spanish slaves both. Free negroes and Indians, too. Red Stick Creeks. Seminoles. Some Choctaws, even.

The war is over before the fort ever sees battle. Nicholls is ordered back to England, but he hesitates. He seems an honorable man. Again orders are issued, and in the summer of 1815 Nicholls finally relents. There is a speech, a speech about loyalty and duty. Nicholls promises his recruits that he will return for them. Hold this fort for Britain, men.

A mixed-blood trader lives on the river. This man's father was an Englishman. Nicholls commissions him a lieutenant, and the negro soldiers are all placed under his command. Nicholls is gone one week before the soldiers run this lieutenant off. Garçon is chosen as the man they will now follow. He is given the lieutenant's sword, and soon they take to calling him General, their general.

A conversation with Garçon—
A manatí killed

IT WAS THREE days of this parceled hearsay tale before Beah finally
permitted him to speak. She sat on his bedside one morning and
asked him his name. The camp bed bulged under her weight, and
he rolled sideways against her. She put her hand on his chest, then
twisted the front of his nightshirt into her fist. "And don be askin
me to call you Garçon or nothin," she said.

He hesitated. The infirmary was very hot and smelled of sweat.
He tested his plugged voice. "Kau," he whispered. His eyes remained closed as he spoke.

She repeated his name back to him. "So that be African?" she
asked.

He nodded and she laughed.

"I bet you got a wild story too, Kau."

He opened his eyes but said nothing.

"All right. So I see, quiet man. How's that foot doin you?"

"Be doin good now."

"Truly?"

"Truly."

She pulled the thin sheet back and squeezed his sore ankle. He yelped in pain and kicked at her with his good foot—his left foot—but missed. "You lie." She stood and slapped her side as she sang. "You lie, lie, lie."

He tried to turn away from the big dancing nurse. "Lemme alone," he said.

"Look here." She dragged a pair of crutches over from the corner of the infirmary. "Sit up," she told him.

He sighed but swiveled his legs around so that he was perched on the walnut frame of the camp bed. She passed him the wooden crutches, and he saw that both ends had been cut down to fit him.

"Go on," she said. "Test them out."

He gripped a crutch in either hand, then tucked the linen-wrapped rests snug under his arms. She put a hand on his shoulder as he eased clear of the bed. He wobbled across the infirmary and she clapped for him.

"Good," she said. "Now you think you ready to see the General?"

He nodded and she flew forward in a rush. He struggled to escape as she began to wrestle the nightshirt off him, but she kept on until finally he gave up and was naked. She threw the nightshirt aside and laughed.

"What you think? You think I ain't seen all of you yet?" She smiled at him. "You doin good enough down there."

She handed over the clothes that Pelayo's twin daughters had given him. They had been washed and smelled of lye. He put on the osnaburgs and then looked around the infirmary. "Where's the rest of it?" he asked.

"Rest of what?"

"My saddlebags. My knife. My belt."

"And your ugly red club?"

"All of it."

"Questions for the General, I spose."

He looked at her. "Am I his prisoner?"

Beah opened the thick door and its iron hinges squeaked. "Could be, " she said. "But you sure ain't one of mine."

FOR THE FIRST time he ventured outside of the infirmary. It was early morning and except for a sprinkling of negro soldiers in redcoats the fort still seemed empty. He stood with Beah and blinked in the sunlight.

The timber walls of the fort were a doubled layer of pine logs, ten-foot pickets with their ends sharpened into points that were glossy with wept sap. In the eastern corners earthen embankments formed diamond-shaped bastions that rose up fifteen, twenty feet and were crowned with cannons. A hidden sentry whistled down at them from the nearest bastion and Beah giggled.

"Fool," she said.

She began walking west toward the river and he followed after her on his crutches. They passed stables and a stone well—a long cabin she told him served as the barracks for the bachelor soldiers, those men with neither farms nor families. Near the center of the fort an eight-sided earthwork surrounded a low log building. "That be the powder house," said Beah.

They walked on. Closer to the river a large canvas tent abutted the south wall, and a young soldier was guarding its entrance. In the morning sun his dark skin shined the same color as the barrel of the musket he was holding.

Beah approached and the soldier put up a hand. "*Buenos días, Señor Xavier*," said Beah. "Please no shoot us." She laughed. "This here Kau."

The soldier Xavier studied him for a moment and then went into the tent. There came the murmur of conversation, and finally Kau heard the calm, clear voice of Garçon. "Send the man in," he said.

Xavier emerged from the tent and motioned for Kau to enter. "Go on now," said Beah. "And don be tellin him what all we talked about neither." She laughed again when she said this, laughed like she really did not care either way, and then rubbed at the top of his head. He slid out from under her hand and she walked off, still chuckling.

The flap of the tent was tied open and he maneuvered himself inside. Garçon stood behind a wooden table, hatless but in uniform. The tent smelled like dried roses. Garçon took the crutches and then helped him into a shaky chair. There was a pitcher of water on the table, that and the bleached-out skulls of what looked to be a bear and a panther. Garçon sat down across from him and smiled. "You are feeling better, I hope?"

"Yes. Thank you."

Garçon nodded and without the tricorn his pirate braids fell down across his face. He parted them with his hands, then tucked the long strands behind his ears. "Xavier tells me that your name is Kau?"

"Yes."

"Did they give you a slave name?"

"Adam."

Garçon leaned closer. "Adam?"

"Yes."

Garçon touched his own front teeth, then pointed at him. "So you were indeed born in Africa, Kau?"

"I was. Yes."

"And how long since you ran off?"

"The moon be what now?"

"Two nights ago it was new."

"It summer then?"

"Yes."

Kau tapped at his fingers. "Then I left about eleven weeks back." A horsefly was trapped in the tent. He watched it pause then go restless, pause then go restless. "I was a long while with them chickens."

"You know your numbers."

"Some. Enough for countin at leas."

"Where are you coming from?"

"Mississippi."

"And that red bone of yours?"

"Gifted to me."

"By?"

"Indians. Redsticks."

Garçon shook his head. "You must have had a great deal of good fortune on this journey of yours—before you met my farmers, at least."

"I spose."

"Can you shoot a musket?"

"A little, but not really."

"So were you coming to enlist?"

"Enlist?"

"To fight."

"I don understand what you askin me."

Garçon made pistols with his fingers. "This is a fort."

Kau nodded.

"And here you are with us."

"I was jus passin by. Floatin the river."

"To where though?"

"Don know for sure."

"Then it was good you were captured."

"Good?"

"Indians eventually would have killed you or sold you. That or made you one of them." Garçon stood and began to stalk the trapped horsefly around the tent. It flew high into the ceiling and he gave up. "They typically do not abide wanderers," he said.

"I ain't had no real trouble with Indians."

Garçon collected the crutches and handed them to him. "Come along with me," he said. "Please."

Kau followed him outside and they walked past the pine flagstaff to the river. A grassy hillock formed the west wall of the fort, and along its crest a row of cannons sat pointing out over the water. Garçon waited for him and together they climbed to the top. They stood among the big black cannons, and Kau looked down at the brown coil of river.

"Would you ever believe," said Garçon, "that two weeks ago there were three thousand Indians camped across the way?"

The fort was situated on the push side of a slow and easy bend, and the river was about a hundred yards wide from east bank to west bank, maybe more. Kau squinted but saw nothing. He tried to imagine the Indians but could not; all he saw was green forest.

"What kind?"

"Seminoles. Some of what is left of your redsticks."

"They jus gone?"

Garçon spun around and Kau turned with him. The rising sun had cleared the pines behind the fort and now sat throbbing like an egg yolk through a curtain of haze. Garçon pointed toward it. "East and then south," he said. "They are running. Even some of my own men have fled with them."

"From what?"

"The Americans will be coming for us. They all know that."

"And you?"

"Sure. I know it, too."

"When?"

"Soon, I think. Very soon."

Kau was silent as he considered all of this. He had already tried his hand at making war and had failed. He had no desire to fight anymore. As he stared out across that river at the unbroken forest he somehow felt certain that he was close to what he was seeking— too close to risk dying in the defense of another man's fort. He asked if he was free to leave once his ankle had healed and saw Garçon smile. "Yes, of course," said the General. "I do not keep slaves, Kau."

HE WAS GIVEN a small tent of his own in a quiet section of the fort, near the earthwork that protected the powder magazine. Someone had laid his few belongings out on the camp bed for him—his saddlebags and his bone club, his knife and his belt—and he cinched the belt around the waistband of his pants, situating the knife sheath off his right hip. His canteen had been filled for him; he unscrewed the cap and took a long drink.

There was a table and a chair in the tent. He sat down and opened the saddlebags, saw the sling and the tinderbox, an assortment of sling-stones and arrowheads. For the first time in many days he allowed his mind to linger on the dead boy. The canteen had been Benjamin's, a gift from one of the soldiers at the fort near Yellowhammer. Kau took another sip, letting the water fill his mouth before he swallowed. His throat felt much better now, and to be able to speak again took his thoughts to another silence broken.

A bitter winter night, seven moons after he had arrived from the Pensacola slave docks. Benjamin was six years old, and the inn was empty save the father and son. Kau was in the slave cabin eating a scrap-bone stew with Samuel when they heard it—the sound of a table turning over, dishes breaking. Samuel rose from his chair and he followed. They went outside, barefoot in the frost, and pressed their foreheads to the cold glass of the window.

The innkeeper was blind drunk on clear corn whisky, and Benjamin lay collapsed. He was bruised and bleeding. "Oh, my," said Samuel. "Oh, my." The old man moved to the porch, but Kau stayed at the window. A belt was being taken to the cut boy when Samuel knocked at the door. The innkeeper hollered something that Kau could not make out and Samuel entered, his felt hat folded over in his hands. Samuel spoke and the innkeeper came at him, hitting him across the face with the belt. Benjamin yelled but Samuel waved him quiet. The boy went racing out the back door as the slave took his beating for him. The belt rose and fell and rose and fell until at last the innkeeper was exhausted and Samuel allowed to leave. He stumbled past Kau without looking at him; blood was trickling from the corner of his eye.

They found Benjamin in the slave cabin, terror-curled on Samuel's straw pallet. Samuel spread a spare blanket on the dirt floor, but Kau shook his head. He motioned toward his own pallet. "Les share it," he said.

Samuel had only nodded at those first words of English from his silent friend, too beaten to even show surprise. "Thank you now, Adam," he said in a low and tired voice. "Thank you now."

KAU DRAGGED HIS chair to the entrance of the sweltering tent. A soldier—shirtless and pouring sweat—was standing atop the earthwork that surrounded the powder magazine. The young man was holding a cannonball and staring at him, and Kau held his gaze until at last the soldier looked away, leaving with his cannonball in the direction of the river. Kau saw him climb the artillery bank and set the cannonball down, then return to the powder magazine and emerge with another. Finishing with one the soldier would reappear with a next. One after the other until there was a high pyramid of cannonballs piled atop the distant artillery bank.

IN THE EARLY afternoon he heard a sentry blow a trumpet, and then he watched as the dozen bachelor soldiers left the barracks and hurried toward the river. Curious, he hobbled across the fort on his crutches, climbing the artillery bank to where the men had collected. There was something in the river, a big gray beast burrowing like a hippopotamus through far-off lily pads. "*¡Manatí!*" a soldier was shouting over and again.

The soldier Xavier appeared on the riverbank outside the fort, then began launching a canoe into the current. Garçon called out in Spanish, and a man with a longrifle laid himself flat against one of the cast-iron cannons on the artillery bank.

The beast continued with its grazing, and Kau saw Beah come shuffling over. She was breathing heavily from the climb up the steep artillery bank. She jiggled one of his crutches and panted. "How in the world you make it up here so easy?" she asked.

Xavier was halfway across the river when Garçon's sharpshooter shot a hole in the pale head of the manatí. The men cheered but the sharpshooter cursed. He had missed the brain, it seemed. The manatí went to rolling as Xavier dug in with his paddle, closing the distance, and Kau could see blood in the foaming water. Xavier set down the paddle and bent low in the drifting canoe. He was close, an arm's length from the dying manatí. He rose up holding a long wooden spear of some sort, then pumped his arm twice before driving the barbed point deep into the manatí's side. Again the soldiers cheered.

The spear was connected to an empty barrel by a braided length of hemp. The manatí dove for deeper water, and the line disappeared coil by coil from the canoe into the river. Xavier dropped the barrel over the side and it went bobbing along.

Beah chuckled. "Jus like fishin," she said.

It was not long before the manatí bled out and the barrel went still. Garçon sent some men to the riverbank with a brown ox, and a long rope was affixed to the barrel. They dragged the speared and jaw-shot creature up onto the bank like some giant water slug, and then Kau watched as they butchered the carcass, wasting nothing. Farmers' wives and daughters came and went, filling wooden wash-tubs with intestine and bone, flat sheets of skin to be boiled and scraped and fried.

THAT NIGHT BEAH brought him to supper. Garçon had ordered much of the manatí roasted, and the English-speaking soldiers sat to one side of a blazing coal bed and the Spanish to another. Some of the negro soldiers had been slave-marked, and Kau saw shiny cheeks branded with the initials of white men, ears notched in code like those of range stock. Between them all moved Xavier, translating the stories and jokes of one group for the other to enjoy. A soldier tossed the dregs of his rum onto the coals and there came a wet hiss.

Kau searched for Beah but she was gone now. He tried to set himself apart, but Garçon called him over and introduced him to the hungry men. "This is Kau," he said, "and he knows more about where we come from than we ourselves do." Xavier seemed to repeat this in Spanish, and then Garçon asked Kau to please show them all his teeth. When he complied one old soldier touched his forehead then his breast, his left shoulder then his right. The man pressed his thumb against his forefinger and kissed the nail. "*Madre de Dios,*" he said.

The soldiers muttered cautious greetings and though Garçon offered rum he declined, just sat watching as a curled rack of ribs cracked and cooked. After a while he looked down and saw a slight wriggling in the ground between his feet. A small beetle emerged from the hot dirt, then began crawling away from the fire.

Xavier — Pigeons — A Choctaw — A supper with Garçon

THE SKIN UNDER his arms had been rubbed raw by the crutches and so he stayed off his feet and inside his hot tent—though on occasion he would move his chair to the entrance to catch whatever breeze, sit and watch as the same few soldiers came and went, all the while waiting for his ankle to heal.

Often Beah would pull a chair next to his own, and on these visits she would talk and talk and talk until finally one morning he ran her off with his silence. "You always in a spider's mood," she said in leaving.

He realized that part of him was sorry to see the fat nurse go, but he did not try to stop her. He was certain that this strange fort was not where his journey was meant to end, and though his ankle was still hurting him he wondered whether it might be best if he struck out again.

Garçon had left the fort two days earlier. Beah had said he rode north and was headed for the border. Around the fire that night Kau had sat off to the side, listening to the soldiers from Georgia and the Mississippi Territory—Tennessee, even—speculate on Garçon and his purpose. Americans had collected along the upriver headwaters. The General was off to figure their intentions. Them Americans had better stay right where they is, don they come marchin into Florida.

Now, remembering those boastings, Kau thought of Little Horn and his running war, of the lesson that had been taught to the redsticks at Horseshoe Bend. And then he thought further back, to his own ruined life in Africa. He closed his eyes and saw it—this negro fort afire, all of those brave men dead or captured.

HE WAS STILL sitting alone in front of his tent when he saw the soldier Xavier exit the barracks and begin walking toward him. Kau watched as he approached. The young man was barely twenty and had a smooth, rolling walk, a way about him that suggested a thin fish swimming slow, a bass easing along with a current. Xavier squatted down next to him in the dry dirt, then rocked back on his boot heels as he introduced himself.

"I ain't forgot."

"And your name is Kau?"

"Yes."

Xavier began to draw circles in the dust with his long field knife—a small circle swallowed by a larger circle and so on and so forth. Like the other soldiers he wore a British redcoat and pale cotton trousers, a black round-hat fashioned from glossed felt. Sweat dripped from the tip of his nose and landed inside the smallest of the stabbed circles. He looked up. "I think I have heard of you before," he said.

"How you mean?"

"Pensacola. Do you know it?"

"They had me there once."

Xavier nodded. "And I lived in Pensacola. Back before I ran myself."

"So?"

"So I remember some talk. They said a ship once came into the docks carrying a tiny man with teeth like fangs." Xavier slid the blade of his knife between his fingers, cleaning it. "That could have been you, no?"

Kau shrugged but said yes, he supposed that it could have been, more than likely was.

Xavier sheathed his knife and stood. He pointed at the ground with both hands. "Will you be staying?"

Kau looked up and the rising sun forced him to squint. Xavier existed now only as a tall and dark blurring. "No," he said to him. "No."

LATER THAT SAME day Beah came rushing into his tent, her rough dress twirling. She told him he had to get up and stretch his foot. "Scowl all you want," she said. "But you comin."

She stood watching him, her big arms akimbo. He started to argue but then decided she was right. The sooner he got around to walking the sooner he could be on his way. Beah handed him his crutches and led him outside. His ankle felt sore but better. One more day, he figured. Two at most.

He stepped out from the dark and into the light. The heat of the sun seemed almost to push against him as he followed Beah toward the river and the slack British jack. At the base of the flagstaff stood a weather-beaten shack no bigger than the outhouse at Yellowhammer. She pointed at it. "Know what that be?"

"No."

"Come on then."

She took him closer and he saw that narrow windows, barred with thin rods of metal, had been cut into the sides of the shack. Beah opened a leather-hinged door and peered inside. "Lookie," she said. "The British left them behind."

He ducked his head under her outstretched arm and winced at the acid smell of hot birdshit. The shack was full of cooing pigeons. Dozens of the pepper birds sat along a staggered trio of roosts. He looked at Beah. "For what?" he asked. "To eat?"

Beah laughed. "No, no, no. Don you let the General go hearin you say that. Good Lord." She reached inside the open door and grabbed quick hold of the closest resting pigeon. The bird began to flap and struggle, but then she cupped the crying creature in her meaty hands and it calmed. "Close that door," she ordered.

He did as he was told and then turned back to her. The pigeon was enveloped save its delicate neck and tiny head. Beah held it out in front of her like an offering. "Now you watch." She lifted her arms and then spread them wide, releasing the bird high toward the noontime sun. The pigeon rose up nine, ten feet, then started to fall back to earth before it flapped its wings and climbed again. "Keep watchin," said Beah.

The pigeon flew west, crossing the river, and was outlined against a cotton-white cloud forming in the distance. Kau had begun to lose sight of that dark dot on the horizon when it banked left and to the south, then began a slow and lazy arch of a return. The pigeon drifted east over the fields and turned again, flew north and then back west, crossed the river a second time and then commenced another circle in the sky—but closer though this time—on and on, ten times or more, until it was simply skimming along above the pine-wall perimeters of the fort, teasing the soldiers who manned the bastions.

"Here he come," said Beah.

The tiring pigeon dropped lower and then arrived on a bending swoop of a glide. Kau wobbled on his crutches as it shot past. The pigeon slammed down onto a flat ledge that ran beneath one of the windows of the shack, then cocked its head and looked at them. Beah waved her hand, and the shooed bird pushed itself against the metal rods that fell down across the window. The thin bobs swung inward, then fell back into place once the pigeon had disappeared into the shack. Beah slapped her hands together as if she meant to clean them. "You see they can come," she said, "but they can't go. At leas not on they own."

Kau looked at her. "What he got them for?"

Beah laughed. "They is the General's eyes." She pointed to the south. "He keeps them on an island out in the mouth of the river and has a man tie messages to they legs. They come reportin ships and storms and such."

This was too much for him to believe. "And they make they way back here?"

Beah shook her head. "I wonder the same thing you wonderin," she said. "How do they know, right?"

"So?"

"I ain't got the answer to that." She told him all she knew was that once every month or so Garçon would cage all of the birds up and send them with Xavier downriver. And it had to be young Xavier. The General didn't trust too many people to look after his pigeons. She shrugged. "I spose we all got our favorites," she said.

As THEY WALKED back to his tent Kau asked Beah to tell him more about the man downriver, and she explained that the so-called pigeonkeeper was named Israel. A man who, years back as a slave, some rogue Georgia preacher had taught to read and write. Israel now lived alone on a delta island and watched for ships entering the bay. Every day at the initial slight colorings of sunset he would send a message to Garçon, regardless of true news. The pigeon would fly north to its home beneath the flag of the fort, and before Garçon took supper he would check on his birds, untie and read whatever words Israel had committed to him that day. "If they is anythin in this life that truly pleases the General," Beah told him, "you'll be findin it in that pigeonhouse."

WHEN THE DAY finally began to cool he sought out Xavier. The soldier was climbing down from atop one of the bastions when Kau surprised him. "Beah showed me the pigeons," he said.

"*Sí*," said Xavier. "I saw." He slid a finger across his throat. "She needs to learn to leave them alone."

"He back yet?"

"Yes."

Kau laid his crutches down in the dust and rubbed at his armpits. "When you leavin to see this man Israel?" he asked.

Xavier shrugged. "He will need more pigeons soon, I think. The General will tell me when it is time."

"Can I come?"

"For what?"

Kau said nothing. That morning there had been a strong south wind and he had smelled salt air. How to say it? How to say that he somehow needed to see open waters? How to say that after so many failed weeks of searching pine forests and lowlands for someplace like Africa he needed to know that there was some end to this ugly other world, be reminded that this land had shores and boundaries same as all lands? That just as a body could be stolen from one life and dropped into another, so could he one day live free again?

He walked away and left Xavier standing at the base of the bastion. The sun was now setting, and he was limping along on his crutches, headed for his tent, when he saw a played-out pigeon come fluttering down alongside the flagstaff—so marking, he realized, another day for the horizon-watching Israel.

HE LAY ON his camp bed, sweating and still thinking of this man who lived alone on an island, a man sending everyday messages to a fort he could not see—yet all the time trusting that what he did mattered, that his island-dwelling life had real purpose and real meaning. Kau closed his eyes and when he next opened them he found himself staring into the dark face of an Indian.

The Indian spoke to him in clipped English. "Do you remember me?" he asked.

Kau sat up and the Indian moved to the center of the tent. A tallow candle sat flickering on the table and sent bent shadows dancing along the white canvas of the tent. The Indian was not a Creek but a Choctaw, had the long hair and flattened forehead that Kau had come to recognize among the members of that tribe who would sometimes call upon Yellowhammer. Benjamin once told him that Choctaws worshipped the sun.

"No," said Kau finally. "I don remember you at all."

The Choctaw wore a long bright shirt made of striped tradecloth, deerskin moccasins and leg wrappings. "I heard a soldier speaking of you by the fire tonight," he said. "You were in Pensacola once."

"How you know me?"

"I never forgot you."

"You was one of them?"

The Choctaw turned and left the tent.

"Jus wait now." Kau took up his crutches and hurried outside. It was late but between the bright sliver of moon and the dying cook-fires he was able to make his way. He heard movement along the south wall of the fort and went toward it, arriving in time to see the shadowy form of a man slither out through a porthole the soldiers had cut that day, a window through the pine pickets meant to accommodate a cannon. There came the sound of something splashing across the moat and then all was quiet again.

It was only later, after he had returned to his tent, that he realized the Choctaw had stolen his bone club.

THE NEXT MORNING, through Xavier, he would confirm that not all Indians had fled the vicinity of the fort. There were thirty or more Choctaw warriors camped somewhere across the river—men who had broken with their own people when Pushmataha sided with the Americans during the war; men who had pledged their allegiance to Garçon after they had all been abandoned by the British; men who, like the negro farmers, promised to come when called. Kau asked the reason for that loyalty and Xavier shrugged, said only that among Indians a renegade Choctaw was a curious thing. A man who would never again see his home in the Mississippi Territory or Louisiana yet was too proud to throw in with the Redstick or the Seminoles and fall back into the swamplands. "They will fight beside us," said Xavier, "because they feel that they have no other real choice."

"But what would he want with my club?"

"I do not know," said Xavier. "What did you ever want with it?"

HE ALLOWED HIMSELF to believe that his Choctaw visitor truly had been there at the beginning, that he had been one of those faceless and nameless and cruel Indians on that trek from Pensacola to Yellowhammer. He tried to place that man among them but could not. In truth it amazed him to think that any of that party—the smuggler, the Indians, the other slaves—still could be living somewhere.

But of course they were alive, most of them at least.

That smuggler was today living somewhere just as those Indians likely were now living somewhere. And then there were the slaves themselves. By now each had a story like he had a story, and after five years in this second world he had more in common with that miserable collection of stolen Africans that very moment somewhere dragging picking sacks through Georgia cotton fields than he did with whatever Ota cousins of his might still be residing in a faraway forest. It was as if here among the white men a new tribe had been born, a lost tribe, a tribe with nothing more in common than fading memories of Africa and their own tragic pasts.

HE SPENT ALL of the day resting and then Beah came calling again. It was late in the afternoon when she announced herself at the entrance to his tent. "Be very sorry to wake you, Marse," she said. "But the General's requestin the pleasure of dinin with you."

He looked at her. "Now?"

Beah grabbed the sides of her dress and curtsied. "Yessuh."

"Why he wanna see me again?"

"Cause you interestin to him."

"What you mean?"

"Need me to fetch a mirror?"

Though he knew the way to Garçon's tent, Beah insisted on escorting him there. He left his crutches lying on his camp bed and trailed after her. He favored his sore ankle but kept pace all the same. Outside, one of Garçon's brindled hounds was bent double in the shade of a massive oak hogshead, licking itself. They walked on, and suddenly a pebble bounced off Beah's head and then hit Kau in the neck. They both spun around. He thought he heard muffled laughter from atop a near bastion, but could not get a clear look at the face of the man who was taunting them.

GARÇON WAS WAITING for him inside the tent. A stained white cloth had been thrown over his square table, and the yellow-toothed skulls of the bear and the panther were gone now. In the center of the table was a green-glass jug of beer, and beside the jug were a pair of tall glasses, two chipped plates and a large covered platter. Garçon unbuttoned his redcoat and they sat. "Please," he said. "Let us eat."

Kau was hungry. He could smell the tang of cooked meat and his stomach rumbled. Garçon started to pour beer for him, but Kau declined and asked if he could maybe have water instead. A cook entered the tent, a freckled mulatto with the delicate features of a woman. Garçon spoke to the man in French, and he returned with a porcelain pitcher of water that he placed on the table. The cook then lifted the tarnished cover from the silver platter, and Garçon sighed. "*Pintade*," he said. "*Oui, René, oui.*"

Kau saw that it was a bird of some sort. Not chicken or duck but guineahen. A young guineahen braised along with vegetables

171

from the fields—early onions and a few quartered sweet potatoes. The cook produced a large knife and a slotted spoon, then kept glancing over at him as he cut the guineahen in half, dividing the entire dish evenly.

They were served. The tender flesh of the guineahen carried the slight taste of bacon, and Kau began to eat with his hands, slowly at first but then much more quickly. Garçon nodded and seemed pleased. The cook placed a basket of biscuits on the table, and Kau took one of them.

"No crutches, I see." Garçon pointed his fork at him. "Your ankle has healed?"

Kau swallowed a mouthful of warm biscuit. "Almost," he said.

"I sense that I will wake one morning and you will be gone. Maybe tomorrow, maybe the next day, am I right?"

"Could be. But I thank you for bringin me here."

"And of course you are welcome." Garçon brushed crumbs from the tablecloth with the back of his hand. "But perhaps you are wondering whether I did you a favor?"

"Not right now I don."

Garçon chuckled. "Very good," he said. "Very, very good." He lifted his glass, shutting his eyes as he drank the beer down, then licked his lips and poured himself another. "I hear my fat Beah has let you see my pigeons."

"Yes."

"And what else did she tell you about me?"

"She talks morn I listen."

Garçon smiled at him. "I am sure." He folded his arms and leaned back in his chair. "In a few days I will be sending Xavier downriver. He has informed me that you might like to join him."

"I would. Thas true."

"And why is that?"

Kau was quiet. He was imagining the man Israel and his delta island. If there was one such island, then there might be others. A place where he could build a small hut and live alone and unbothered. He would fish and hunt and forage—perhaps even serve as a lookout for his savior Garçon, send word to the pigeonkeeper should there be some sign of danger.

"You are thinking?" asked Garçon.

"Yes."

"Xavier will be leaving in three days. You have my blessing if you would like to go along."

"I think I would."

"You have already decided?"

"I spose."

"Fine. Then it is settled."

Kau twisted a leg bone free from the guineahen and examined it. "Can I ask you somethin?"

"Go ahead."

"I hear them sayin the Americans got soldiers not too far upriver."

"That is correct. At the border."

"You seen them?"

"I did."

"Then was you right?"

"Right?"

"They gonna come down here?"

Garçon tilted his head back and began staring at the ceiling of his tent as if there was a picture painted there. "Oh, I'm sure," he said finally. "And what a fight you will be missing, *mon ami*." He waved his left arm slowly through the air, then lifted his right. His hands collided in the space above him, and he made a sound like the rush of wind. "We will have our revenge." Garçon leaned forward. His hands came to rest on the table, and Kau thought of settling birds. "Understand?"

"I understand."

The heart and liver and gizzard of the guineahen were all that remained on the platter. Garçon speared these one at a time onto the tines of his fork, then offered them to Kau from across the table. "Here," he said. "The best parts are all for you."

XII

The dome swamp — A dead Choctaw —
Parakeets — A bow stave

OVER THE NEXT two days Kau tested his ankle by taking up his saddlebags and walking across the hundred yards of treeless and burnt cutover that lay between the fort and the pine forest to the east. At the far side of the cutover a path began—a trail that pushed through a short stretch of the pinewoods, then turned south to follow the edges of a dome swamp.

The dome swamp was a half dozen acres of flooded cypress and tupelo into which the surrounding uplands drained. Each morning he circled the entirety of the swamp, and then he would repeat this path throughout the day. He noted subtle changes upon each passing: the progress of a dung beetle in rolling a sun-dried deer turd, the soft prints of a gray fox that had left the swamp to hunt rabbits in the wiregrass savanna.

A thick crowning wall of greenbrier separated his walking path from the dome swamp, and beyond the brier thicket he could smell the dank of the standing water but could not see it. Sometimes when he closed his eyes and listened he would hear splashings—a jittery kingfisher diving for minnows perhaps, a moccasin worrying frogs.

On the second afternoon he knelt and peered down a narrow game trail that cut low through the briers. He was curious to see this swamp, and tomorrow he would be departing. Here was his final chance. He stashed his saddlebags in the briers, then dropped to his stomach and crawled forward.

The briers tore at his clothes like cat claws as through the tunnel he went, his knife gripped in his hand. After learning that his bone club had been taken, Garçon had offered him other weapons. Twice the General had presented him with a flintlock, but both times Kau had declined. If all went very well he would one day again inhabit a place where there was no powder and no shot. He had his knife and his sling, and that was enough. It was time to learn how to live quietly again, how not to depend upon the noisy tools of white men.

After ten yards the briers ended and the true swamp began. He gathered his feet under him and rose up. He was standing on a thin lip of black dirt that ran between the brier edge and a flooded stand of wrist-thick tupelos. The water was still and shined like a mirror. He could sense somehow that he was safe here. This was a forest within a forest. He sheathed his knife, then slowly peeled off his clothes.

He stepped into the dark water and let his foot sink. Powdery sediment pushed through his splayed toes until finally the bottom held firm. He eased forward, grabbing hold of saplings to help keep his balance. Rustling one he heard movement in the high branches, then a sunning snake slapped down onto the water and vanished.

He waded ahead, naked and weaponless, and the trees became larger the farther that he penetrated the swamp. Slender tupelos gave way to fire-blackened cypress, and then the trees were all enormous and well spaced and perfect.

The history of the dome swamp was written on these trees. Five or six years ago a lightning bolt had ignited a longleaf somewhere in the summer pinewoods and sent a great fire roaring through the dust-dry savanna. The birds would be the first to raise the alarm. Woodpecker and quail, songbird and turkey, start leaving in waves. The deer and the squirrels and the bobcats mark the exodus of the birds, then smell the smoke themselves. There is a panicked push for the river, and those animals too slow or too confused or too hampered by young to make the crossing are forced into the dome swamp while others burn dead. The briers catch fire in a uniform burst and form one great ring of solid flame around the swamp. When the blaze reaches the water it sizzles and hisses and the animals seeking refuge within crowd closer still—deer and panther, range stock and bear—they all watch together as burning leaves and needles come raining down. The fire kills the outer-edge tupelos but in the end dies out itself. After two days the forest cools and the exhausted and miserable and spared creatures emerge from the ash-crusted water, scattering back out into the smoking gray hellscape of the pine forest to once more hunt and be hunted by the other.

IN THE CENTER of the dome swamp he found a platform of roughly cut saplings, a sturdy square scaffold cinched with vines to a cluster of tall cypress trees. He ventured closer, and when the foul stench of death struck him he realized that this was the work of Indians, that atop that platform they had placed the body of a man to rot.

If what Samuel and the boy had taught him about the strange ways of the various tribes was correct, the dead Indian was a Choctaw—and Kau wondered whether this man's own people would forget him once the fort was attacked, if they would ever remember to return here and collect his bones. A breeze blew across the swamp, and he saw feathers drift down from the platform to then settle without a ripple. He watched them drift toward him and thought not of feathers but of butterflies, a flock of drinking butterflies.

He continued on until he was standing just beneath the platform. The water was at his waist, and he raised his hands high above his head, then curled his fingers around one of the cut saplings. He took a deep breath and lifted himself up out of the water.

Skins and pelts were piled across the platform, protecting the dead Choctaw from the buzzards that would want to pick and scatter him. And then Kau looked closer. His bone club had been placed atop the molting skin of an eagle—a gift, he realized, for this warrior to take with him into the afterlife. Kau thought to steal his club back, but in the end he left it behind. Somehow that seemed the wise and proper thing.

HE DRESSED HIMSELF, and then as he left the dome swamp he saw parakeets and was reminded of Africa. Of sleek green pigeons and noisy gray parrots. Of the beauty of its creatures. He was sliding along the game trail that ran beneath the brier thicket when the flock descended upon him. The adults were green as pickles to the neck, but had bright yellow heads that were browed with a scarlet mask. He rolled onto his back and watched the chattering birds skitter through the thicket, feeding on the cockleburs that grew up into the briers. It was late in the day and darkening quickly. If the parakeets noticed him hidden beneath them, they were fearless and did not show it.

A much larger flock of parakeets had appeared once in a creek bottom near Yellowhammer. He and the boy had spent the afternoon watching the birds, tracking them to where they roosted like bats in the hollow cores of a series of giant sycamores. Benjamin told his father about the flock and that had been a mistake. The next day the innkeeper and twenty soldiers from the fort spread themselves out among the sycamores and waited. At sunset the parakeets came into the grove in an undulating and unbroken swarm. The men began to fire their fowling pieces, and even after losing two or three dozen the veering flock would circle back and then return, the shooters reloading and firing again until finally it was dark and almost all of the parakeets were dead. That night Kau and Samuel lit torches and collected the fallen birds. A wagon was filled and taken to Milledgeville. Samuel told him that the parakeets would be sold to a milliner there—that those feathers were destined to decorate the hats of fancy women in far-off places.

He lay in the game trail, watching the birds move all around him in the briers. A feeding parakeet is constant motion. A spined bur is plucked from its stem by a short beak, then transferred to dusky claws. The pale and naked foot is reversed at the joint, and then beak attacks bur until the husk crackles open to reveal the seeds within. These seeds are removed peck by peck and then the empty shell is forgotten, dropped. The broken husks bounce down through the briers with a sound like falling rain.

Finally the thicket was stripped of its cockleburs, and the flock left him for the branches of a nearby oak. He emerged from the briers and collected his saddlebags. The brilliant heads of the parakeets in the oak shined yellow in the fading light, and he grunted. They looked so very much like candles to him, hundreds of flickering candles.

HE STEPPED OUT of the pine forest and began to pick through the dim cutover to the fort. Teams of oxen were working to wrench burnt stumps from the ground. The smoking bases of the dead pines came twisting from the earth like pulled teeth, their stretched roots so akin to torn nerves that it made him wince. He imagined this land would one day be a tilled field but for now it was just a forest dying. The cooked dirt was hot under his bare feet, and suffering it, he could almost believe in the hell that white men claimed lurked just beneath the crust of the earth, a fire kingdom orange and pulsing. The beating heart of the world.

Farther off the fields and pastures began, and he saw two farmers inspecting a milk cow. One of the men held its tail in his hand while the other pushed at its hindquarters. Kau walked on and soon the farmers and the livestock and the stumps existed only as shadows. He crossed the small bridge over the stinking moat, and as he did the gate opened.

Xavier was waiting for him on the other side of the bridge. "I have been looking for you," he said. "You are still ready to leave tomorrow, no?"

His ankle felt right to him at last. "Be ready now," he said.

"Good. Then I am supposed to tell you that the General wants to see you first."

"When?"

"Soon," said Xavier. "For supper."

"Again?"

"That is what he told me."

Kau nodded. The soldiers had built up their cook-fires, and he made his way through the half-light to his tent. He passed two men tossing dice, and they called out to him with Spanish words that he did not understand. He stopped but the soldiers only grinned and then looked away.

His tent was lit with candles, and Beah was sitting on the camp bed. He placed his saddlebags atop the table and looked at her. She had her wide legs crossed and was rubbing her foot. "Where you been?" she asked.

He motioned back behind him. "Walkin. You needin somethin?"

Beah smiled. "I see you gettin along now, not limpin no more." She patted the bed. "Come here and sit now."

"Garçon waitin."

"So he gonna wait a little more. Come on. I got some questions to ask you."

He sat down next to her.

"What the General see upriver?" she asked. "I believe he told you."

"No."

"You lyin."

"I ain't."

She grabbed either side of his face and then pressed her lips hard against his own.

He pulled away. "What you doin?" He had not known kissing until he became a slave. He had asked Benjamin about it once and the boy had seemed as confused as he was, said only that it was something people did when one loved the other. Samuel had been more helpful. You do it cause it feels good and right, the old man had told him.

"Bed me," said Beah.

He slid away from her and stood. "What now?"

"You gonna need a woman. Every man need a woman."

"Thas what you want? To be my woman?"

She stood as well. She loomed over him. "I ain't aimin to die jus yet," she said. "I ain't like the General."

"Why you think he gonna let you leave with me?"

"He got respect for you."

"And why you thinkin that?"

"Maybe cause you seen things even he ain't never."

He was quiet. Of course he could not take her.

"Well?"

"I'm sorry," he said. "But—"

Beah pushed at him and he stumbled backwards. "Don say nothin else right now," she said. "I want you to think hard on what I'm askin you. We'll talk when you through with the General." And then she turned and laid herself down on the bed to wait, Kau realized, for his return.

THAT NIGHT HE dined with Garçon for a second time. Xavier was summoned to join them at the table, and they were served thin cuts of venison drizzled with sweet muscadine gravy. The pigeons occupied a corner of the tent, secured in a big cage of bent and woven willow, and Kau figured there were close to fifty birds huddled inside.

They began to eat, and then Garçon asked him once more if he might like to take one of the British muskets along when he left the fort. "As a gift," he said.

Kau shook his head. "Thank you," he said. "But no."

Garçon stood in a rush, and the startled pigeons slapped against the ceiling of their cage. A thin white curtain separated the room where the General ate from the room where he slept. He disappeared behind it, and Kau followed the movements of his shadow.

Xavier spoke. "Be more careful," he whispered. "Stop saying no to him."

But when Garçon returned he was smiling. He held a straight length of barked wood in his fist like a staff. "Here," said Garçon. "This is for you."

Garçon walked over and offered Kau the wood. He took it. The heavy pole was almost as long he himself was. Garçon brought his hands together in front of him, then slowly pulled them apart as he spoke: "You once hunted with a bow, correct?" Kau nodded and Garçon continued. "I had my Choctaws bring this from upriver," he said. "Yew. They tell me the finest bows are made from that tree."

Kau turned the wood in his hands. He recognized the pattern of the fissured bark from a species of evergreen he had seen in the slope forests to the north. There had been several such trees in the valley of Elvy Callaway. He wondered if Beah was right—if Garçon really gave him this attention and kindness, offered him these gifts, just because he was interested by him. That seemed impossible to believe. Accepting this gift from the General put him in mind of Chabo and the wife of the Kesa farmer who had once been placed at his feet. From what he knew of gifts they were almost always more than what they seemed.

AFTER SUPPER HE borrowed a whetstone from Xavier and went to his tent. Beah was asleep in the camp bed, but still a candle burned. He removed three biscuits from his shirt and placed them on the table for her. Beah's face was wet with sweat, and he looked away from her.

He contemplated the cut yew. The stave was much too large for an Ota bow and would need to be carved down. He sat in a chair and began to sharpen Benjamin's hunting knife, sliding the blade across the whetstone until he had an edge fine enough to shave the coarse hairs from his arm. Satisfied, he stripped all of the bark from the yew and then closed his eyes. He spoke quietly to his father in Kesa, whispered, Please, Father, guide my head and my hands.

The bruised bark carried a strong odor, though in truth he did not find it to be all that disagreeable. To him the shaved wood smelled of tomato leaves and turpentine—skunk, perhaps—any of which he preferred over the sulfur stink of gunpowder.

He went outside and found a small knob of oak lying loose near a woodpile. He fixed the oak block to the tip of his blade, creating a drawknife of sorts. Returning to the tent, he leaned the skinned yew against the side of the table so that it rose up from the dirt floor at a diagonal. He spread out his horse blanket and straddled the stave—crossing his legs behind him so that the wood was pinned between his thighs—then he took the oak block in one hand and the handle of the knife in the other.

Suddenly Beah began to yelp and buck in her sleep. The damp bed sheet was now twisted around her, and Kau was thinking that he should go to her when she grew silent and settled.

He touched the blade to the top of the yew and then started to plane wood from the belly of his bow. At first he did not trust himself with the sharp knife and so he moved slowly, afraid that he would ruin this rare wood Garçon had favored him with. He tried to remember the dimensions of all the bows he had ever seen in his life: Ota bows but also Kesa bows, Choctaw bows and Creek bows.

In his mind he created a new sort of bow, one that combined the best features of them all. A short bow but a sturdy bow. A bow that was powerful but still not so large that it would slow him when he moved through the forest. With each cut his hands grew more steady and certain. The wood came off in long, yellow curls.

IT WAS VERY late in the night by the time he finished with his initial shapings. The naked stave was heavy with sap and would have to be seasoned before it could launch a fast arrow.

He went outside. It was black dark save a few quivering cook-fires, and he waited for his eyes to adjust. One of the bachelor soldiers living in the fort was also a trapper, and this man had cut himself stretcher boards for mink pelts and fox pelts and coon pelts. Kau filled a wooden bucket with water from a horse trough, then eased his way to the place along the north wall where the trapper kept his supplies. Among the stretcher boards he found a long one that suited his purposes—a five-foot length of pine meant for a bobcat or an otter. The thin board was squared at the bottom and rounded at the top. He lifted it away from the wall and then returned to the tent.

Water sloshed from the bucket when he set it down, but Beah did not stir. He laid the otter board on the ground and placed the yew lengthwise on top of it. The planed side of the stave met flush against the flat otter board, and the snugness of the fit pleased him. He removed the oak block from the end of his knife and stood. The canvas wall of the tent was folded over where it fell down onto the dirt, and he unraveled the fabric, then cut out several long strips of canvas that he placed in the bucket to soak.

Once the stiff strips of canvas had softened in the water he tied them under and over the flat otter board, cinching the bow stave in place. His knots would tighten as the canvas dried, and in three or four weeks the wood might be seasoned well enough for him to be able to finish shaping it. He cut a wider length of canvas away from the tent and then wrapped this around the entire otter board. Beah was awake and watching him now. He pretended not to see her, but then she spoke his name. He set down his bundle and went to her. She forced her hand into his own and then smiled at him. "What you at?" she asked.

"The General gave me some wood for a bow."

She closed her eyes and gripped his hand tighter. "You even ask him?"

He did not answer and she nodded.

"I won't be beggin you no more," she said.

"If I knew for sure I could get us to some safe place I would take you."

"I believe that."

He pointed at the biscuits he had left for her but she shook her head.

"You sleep here tonight," he told her. "I'll go and be by a fire somewhere." He moved away but she would not release his hand.

"I'm scared of what's comin," she said.

"I know."

"Will you stay here?" she asked. "Will you stay here jus till I fall asleep again?"

He sat down beside her and for some reason he thought of Morning Star, of the prophet's death chant. He began to sing this to Beah but in the soft and quiet style of a white man's lullaby. He repeated the Creek verses ten times before her breaths finally became even and her fingers slipped from his hand.

To the mouth of the river—
The pigeonkeeper—St. Vincent Island

HE AWOKE LYING next to a cold cook-fire. It was dark still, but they were to leave at daybreak. He collected his knife and canteen and folded his horse blanket, then walked to his tent. Beah was gone. He stuffed the blanket into one of the saddlebags, then balanced the bundled yew stave on his shoulder and went back outside.

The gate of the fort was open and a sentry was watching him. "*Adiós*," said the sentry. The man seemed exhausted, maybe even drunk.

Kau walked past him and then found the others waiting on the bank of the river. Xavier was in uniform and was holding a long-rifle now instead of a musket. A canvas haversack was resting by his feet. Kau looked at Garçon. He was bareheaded and shirtless, wore only his ivory breeches and black boots. His braids had been tied together with a frayed yellow ribbon, and the matted ropes of twisted hair fell down the center of his muscled back like a cluster of dried tobacco leaves. The General smiled at him. "So you have not changed your mind?" he asked.

"No," said Kau.

"*Très bien.*"

A square raft of milled pine was beached on a slick stretch of hard mud, the same stained spot where the manatí had been dragged ashore and butchered six days before. Garçon kicked at the side of the raft. "You will take this instead of a canoe," he said. "This is good strong wood. I thought perhaps you could use some of it to build a shelter for yourself somewhere."

"Thank you."

Garçon looked at Xavier and laughed. "And then you will walk back to the fort."

"Yes, sir," said Xavier.

Garçon then pointed at the wrapped otter board that Kau was holding. "The yew?" he asked.

"Yes."

"I would like one day to see the bow you make of it."

Kau nodded.

"But probably you will never see me again?"

He thought before speaking. Here it felt right to lie. "No," he said finally. "I think I'll be seein you."

"Wonderful. I will look forward to that then."

"Thank you again for all you done."

"Of course," said Garçon. "It was my pleasure."

Kau helped Xavier load their supplies and possessions onto the raft together with the caged pigeons, and then the both of them stepped aboard. When they were ready Garçon pushed them off, and the raft was swept out into the current.

Xavier poled them toward the center of the river with a long length of wood that had been cut from the trunk of a straight pine. The raft pulled away from the fort, and Xavier corrected their course with punting jabs of the push pole. Kau stood watching Garçon on the bank. A sheet had been thrown over the pigeon cage to calm the birds, and Kau could hear them begin to coo behind him. He wondered whether even penned and in the dark those pigeons could possibly know that they were leaving their home. He kept watching Garçon. They were moving away from him as the sky lightened to show itself cloudless but yet without a sun. In one way the General was becoming clearer to him, in another he was disappearing. They followed the bend of the river, and finally Garçon was eclipsed by the trunk of a big bank cypress. Kau turned and looked to the south. He was facing downriver and the pigeons had quieted. The leaden sky was now blue.

HE SOON SAW that a raft adrift in a deep river is a chore to control. Away from the shallows the push pole was useless, and their awkward vessel was at the mercy of the current. The river would bend and double back and twist like a confused snake, and their raft would stray off course. To their left were negro farms, to their right was all forest. Whenever they neared the shore Xavier would muscle them true—and so they journeyed, bouncing from east-bank farmland to west-bank wilderness as they made their way downstream.

As the hours passed Kau found himself liking Xavier, enjoying the company of the young and cheerful soldier. Kau showed him the leather sling he had carried since Yellowhammer, even sent one of his saddlebag stones sailing from the raft west out over the river. It landed among the top branches of the longleafs growing behind the shoreline cypress, spooking a bronze hawk into flight. Xavier whistled and then asked for a turn.

He passed Xavier the sling, helping him slide the sennit loop onto the middle finger of his right hand. Kau then reached into a saddlebag and produced another round stone. "Here," he said.

Xavier grabbed the knotted end of the second sennit and took the stone, seating it in the sling pouch. "What now?"

"You jus twirl and let go." Kau waved his arm in the air, demonstrating. "Jus twirl and let go."

Xavier whirled the sling twice and on the third revolution the seated stone clipped his ear. He bent over and put his hands on his knees. His round-hat fell into the river and then floated away before Kau could grab it. "*¡Maldita sea!*" said Xavier. A drop of blood splashed down onto the raft and was absorbed by the dry wood. "*Estúpido.*" He was laughing now, and the sling hung limp from his hand. He rose up and a trickle of blood ran from the split in his ear down across his jaw. Xavier wiped it away with the back of his hand. "*Estúpido,*" he repeated.

Kau stared at him. The raft drifted on and Xavier kept laughing. Kau took the sling from him and thought of the Augusta circus as described by the boy. He realized that to someone watching from the bank as they passed—a negro or an Indian, perhaps even some American spy—their crude vessel might have appeared mastered by some manner of lunatic, a cackling lunatic and his silent little freak.

HE SAW THE mouth of a false river entering from the west, a meandering arm of the Apalachicola that had been cut off from the main channel generations before. The old riverbed existed now only as a shallow and silted slough, an expanse of stagnant backwater where heron and egret and ibis gathered for their huntings. He watched them feed and thought once again of Africa. Farther up the false river he could see the monstrous skeletons of water-robbed cypress trees. He heard the booming double-rap of a feeding ivorybill, and then from somewhere distant a beaver alarm-slapped its tail hard against the river.

SOMETIMES ALONG THE east bank the shy children of farmers would emerge from the cornfields and watch them like cattle as they drifted by in the raft. At the scratch farm of a widow Xavier put to shore, and they stood in the shade of a big magnolia that was riddled with brittle cicada husks.

"There is no hurry," said Xavier. "We will go to the island tomorrow instead."

Xavier then knocked on the door of the woman's tiny cabin and a child was sent outside, a blind young girl. She sat with Kau under the tree, sang songs to him in Spanish while they waited. He gave her one of his Mississippi arrowheads, and she smiled at the feel of it.

IT WAS LATE in the afternoon before Xavier finally emerged grinning from the cabin. Kau saw that he had changed from his uniform and was now wearing loose gray osnaburgs much like his own. They led the blind girl back to the cabin, then crossed the river and broke for the day. At sunset they left their raft tied among west-bank tupelos and hiked inland with the heavy pigeon cage into the pine forest, away from the mosquitoes that collected along the riverbank at dark. Kau started a small fire with the tinderbox and they dined on pickled eggs and cured manatí, brown bread and pepper jelly gifted by the widow. After they ate Xavier pulled a stick from the coals. He dropped his pants, then began to burn a tick from the thatch above his privates.

THE FOLLOWING MORNING Xavier said that they needed to release the first of the pigeons. Xavier had been taught to write his numbers, and so to direct him Garçon had penned three notes to himself—thin papers that Xavier said were labeled one, two, and three. Kau listened as Xavier explained their system. How note one was to let the General know they were making progress and doing well; how note two was for when they arrived at the island; how note three was the emergency note, only to be released if they needed saving.

Kau nodded to show that he understood, and then he memorized what the tracks on each note meant—something Benjamin had never got around to schooling him on. Xavier shuffled the rolled bits of paper and quizzed him. "Show me number three," he said. Kau touched the note marked with a balanced pair of half hoops, and Xavier smiled.

THEY STOOD ON the riverbank, and he cupped a pigeon in his hands as Xavier tied the all's well note to its foot with a fine thread of catgut. Once the paper was secured Kau set the frightened bird loose. It flew north and then disappeared into the dim sky.

THEY WERE ONLY a few hours afloat before the river opened into green marsh. He could smell salt in the morning breeze, even taste it in the water.

Xavier put the raft ashore at the very last of the riverbank cypress trees, at the place where the east bank finally yielded to the flooded prairie. Here a small wooden vessel was hidden in the palmettos growing along the bank. Kau helped Xavier right the stashed rowboat, and then they both jumped backwards, wary of moccasins and rattlesnakes and copperheads. Somehow there were none—only a warped pair of oars—and Xavier laughed at their common fear of snakes, serpents.

They dragged the rowboat into the river and waited, checking the hull for leaks. Xavier shared his canteen and then—once he was satisfied that the rowboat was sound—they loaded their belongings and the pigeons on board. When they had finished Xavier fastened a long rope from the raft to the rowboat. "So," he said, "we go now." He removed his shirt and sat down at the oars.

The tide was falling and they went with it. The raft pulled ahead, and the rope connecting it to the rowboat tightened and spun them around. Now and then Xavier dipped an oar to keep centered in the river. Clouds of red-winged blackbirds left the high marsh grass, and on distant mud banks Kau saw sunning alligators—some of them ten, eleven, even twelve feet long and as big around as barrels.

THE PIGEONKEEPER'S SMALL green island sat midway across the mouth of the river, at the spot where the salt marsh ended and the true bay began. Xavier had his back to the south and so Kau sat in the stern and shouted directions for him, a little more east, a little more west.

HE COULD SEE a figure watching them from the island. The man was standing motionless, and it was a while before Kau realized that he had a spyglass trained on them. The pigeonkeeper. Kau told Xavier to keep them straight, that they were on the right course.

THEY BEACHED THE rowboat on the sand shore of the island. The pigeonkeeper Israel was small but wiry, had a bald and shiny head, a full black beard going gray at the temples. Kau guessed him at fifty and was surprised. For some reason he had expected the pigeon-keeper to be much older, and he realized that in his mind he had been picturing a man not so very different from Samuel.

Israel called to them as they approached. "High time you showed," he said. "I ain't got but one bird." He was shirtless and hatless and barefoot, wore only white trousers cut off above the knees.

"You should have five left," said Xavier. "Is our count wrong at the fort?"

"Goddamn mink." Israel spit and then closed his eyes. "Forgive me, Lord. I ain't spoke aloud in over a month."

Xavier went to him and they embraced. Finally Israel turned his attention to Kau. "Well now," he said. "Who are you?"

He stepped forward and Xavier said his name.

Israel studied him. "You a real African?"

"Yes."

"Full grown?"

Xavier spoke: "He might settle somewhere near here."

"That all right with the General?"

Kau nodded. "What he says."

Israel reached for his hand and squeezed it. "Then I say suit yourself, son. I don't own this world, and it sure ain't mine to give."

XAVIER RELEASED THE success pigeon, and they watched it fly toward the tree line and the fort. Once the pigeon was gone from sight Israel took them to his home. He walked with a limp, dragging his left foot almost as if that leg had a weight fixed to it. Kau saw a branch blocking the trail, and so he ran off ahead to clear up their path.

THE ISLAND WAS two or three dry and sand-ringed acres that had been shaped like an egg by the power of the river current. Israel lived in the palmetto-thick core, in a square shack Xavier said had been built from the wood of multiple broken rafts. A cypress cistern stood off to one side, a pigeonhouse off to the other.

Kau listened as Xavier asked after a dog he had brought down with him the month before, a bear-crippled bitch that had belonged to Garçon. Xavier spoke of Caesar and Israel shook his head, told him that the hound had chased a coon into the river and was drowned, that or was taken by an alligator.

IT WAS TRUE what Beah had told him—Israel could read. Could read and write just like Benjamin and the innkeeper, the preachers and the officers who had sometimes passed through Yellowhammer. A desk in his shack held a pendulum clock and a calendar; also quills, ink, paper and a single book—a Bible in English. The calendar, Israel told him, was from London, and the clock he thought was French.

Benjamin and Samuel had explained to him well the meaning of white man's time, but not how to read time. Kau examined the clock. Save the single straight line marking the first hour, the numbers here were different from those Xavier had begun to teach him on the river—but still, by counting the symbols in a circle from one to twelve he was quickly able to place them. Israel then defined each of the metal hands for him and suddenly he had it figured. He could not believe it was so simple.

The pigeons were transferred from their cage into the pigeon-house, and Israel set a small table surrounded by fiddleback chairs. For supper he served a young coon roasted with the peeled tubers of cattails, and later, after they had eaten, he wound the pendulum clock with a key and read to them the parable of a son who comes home to his father. Kau closed his eyes and listened. This story had been Samuel's favorite. "But we had to celebrate and be glad," read Israel, "because this brother of yours was dead and is alive again. He was lost and is found."

THAT EVENING THEY told him that there were barrier islands in the bay to the south. Israel pulled a worn sailing chart from a black sea trunk and spread it out across the table. "Here," he said, "that to the east is Dog Island. There, centered, the biggest one—St. George." Israel then slid a finger farther west, letting it settle onto a triangle of land separated from the mainland by a narrow channel. "St. Vincent," he said. "Follow the coast and in a day you'll be there. On a calm tide even I might could swim to it."

Kau grew excited as Israel described an island close enough to the mainland to have deer, wolves, forest, fresh water, everything. A place where he could maybe make himself a home. "Is it empty?" he asked.

"Empty?"

"Anyone else livin there?"

"Was for sure," said Israel. "But it's been weeks since I've seen sign of an Indian anywhere."

Kau borrowed Israel's spyglass and walked to the thin beach on the south shore of the little delta island. He scanned the salt bay but it was too dark now; he saw nothing that he could say for certain was land. He went back to the shack and Israel laughed at him.

"They is there," he said. "Trust me on that, son."

BEFORE THEY RETIRED for the night Israel asked him if it had been a white man who had cut his teeth like that, and he told him no, that it was the way of his people. Israel laughed, then snarled his upper lip to reveal a single notched canine. "But that," he said, "is the way of some other people, too."

HE LAY ON his horse blanket in Israel's shack and imagined coming home himself. His father is waiting at the place where Kau left him so long ago, still neck-chained to the surviving members of the Ota band. They are all sitting in a silent circle in the forest—hungry and thirsty and tired, but also alive. Kau whistles his whistle, the whistle the elders assigned to him as a boy. His father raises his head and stands, lifting the others with him, and when he sees his son his eyes fill with tears and he goes to him, leading the band in a shuffling approach. They touch hands, and his father asks him where it is that he has been all of this time. Kau has no answer. He finds the scattered remains of the Kesa warriors and then the key. He returns. "Father," he says. "I know now how to release you." And so he does. He applies his new knowledge of chains and keys and locks and sets his remaining people free. That night they carry the molimo down from a high treetop, then make the trumpet speak until they are certain that the forest has indeed been awoken. In three generations there is not one left living who was there that day the Kesa came.

THE NEXT MORNING he went with Israel to the beach and looked due south. It was light now, and even without the spyglass he could see the pine coast of St. George, the closest of the barrier islands. He asked Israel where was St. Vincent and the pigeonkeeper focused the spyglass on a point west-southwest. "Look," he said. "You see?"

Kau lifted the spyglass. It was still hazy and so he saw nothing, just smooth green water under a layer of blue sky.

"Stay on it," said Israel. "It'll show."

St. Vincent came as a shimmering on the horizon, a low smudge line of trees. He looked up from the spyglass and could see the island now with his naked eye. All it took was knowing that it was there. Soon he could not look to the southwest and not see St. Vincent. Again he thought of the man hidden in the moon that Benjamin had taught him to conjure. He had been shown that man just once, but thereafter he could never quite look at the moon the same way again, a moon he had known his entire life.

THEY TOOK THE rowboat out into the bay during the glass of a slack tide, and he sat at the oars while Israel and then Xavier flung a throw net for schooling mullet. It was midday and very hot, but the fishing went quickly. They caught dozens to a cast, and soon the bottom of the rowboat was covered with dying mullet.

AT NIGHTFALL, WHEN the smoke would draw no attention, Israel lit a driftwood fire in the firebox of a tall smokehouse that stood behind the shack, then arranged the gutted mullet on racks of green branches. Thereafter they all went to sleep, but then every hour it was as if some bell in Israel's head would chime and wake him. If it was not his turn he would holler out, and then either Kau or Xavier would rise to rotate the fish in the smokehouse from low racks to high racks, maybe toss another knob of damp driftwood inside the puffing firebox.

KAU WOKE WITH the sunrise and went outside. The fire was dead, and Israel had all of the mullet stacked neatly inside the cold smokehouse. Xavier joined them and that morning they dined on smoked fish and salty oysters that they opened with a chisel, round skillets of ashcake washed down with mug after mug of sweet, sweet storm water.

HE SOON LEARNED that the rhythms of the pigeonkeeper's life were actually quite simple—at dawn, high noon, and dusk the man took the measure of the bay with the spyglass; the between hours Israel would spend reading his Bible. Every day he would write a note to Garçon and send a pigeon. Israel considered himself a Methodist, and so if there was no news of any immediate consequence he shared some scripture in his message to him. In a half hour Garçon would be holding it in his hands. "Only trick," Israel said to them, "is not to stare out at the bay any longer than you have to. That water will ruin your eyes if you let it."

IT BECAME CLEAR to him that Xavier was reluctant to leave, wanted to stay forever it seemed. They passed the days eating mullet and talking, and Israel told them story after story. Old Testament stories. New Testament stories. Georgia slave stories about a trickster rabbit. The story of his learning of the negro fort and deciding to run. "Now ain't it a thing," said Israel, "for a man to read about something in a newspaper one day, then go on and live it the next?"

IT WAS ISRAEL'S idea to smoke the yew stave, as although the pigeonkeeper knew nothing of bows, he understood well the properties of wood. Kau unwrapped the stiff canvas from around the otter board, then showed Israel the yew. It was still damp to the touch and Israel shook his head. "No, sir," he said. "That green stick might never season in this wet air."

There was a scrubbed-out powder cask buried to its rim in the dirt floor of the shack. The inside kept cool and dry, and so here Israel stored cured meats atop corked jars of coon tallow that were intended for candles, soap, cooking. They moved the mullet to the barrel, then Israel nailed the otter board to the inside of the smokehouse. That night they transferred chunks of smoldering wood from their cook-fire to the firebox. They did this every evening and on their fifth day together on the island Israel plucked the yew with his finger and nodded. "Take it down," he told him. "I say it be ready now."

Kau cut through the strips of canvas binding the yew. In his hands the dry wood somehow felt both lighter and stronger. He went to the south shore and sat down alone on the beach. All day he worked. He shaved the belly of the stave flatter still, tapering the limbs evenly from the handle out to either end until finally it was less than the width of three fingers, no taller than he himself in length. He knelt in the sand and bent the stave over his knee. The wood was perfect, limber but not too much so. He nodded and was close to happy.

He was cutting nocks for the bowstring when he looked out in the direction of St. Vincent. Dark shapes had appeared in the bay, and suddenly he flashed to the slave ship that had been waiting off the green coast of Africa. This had become a common moment in the world, he realized—hidden eyes staring out at approaching ships. He saw a dolphin come sliding up out of the water, and then he turned and gave a whistle for Xavier, for Israel.

Ships—An Ota parable— A skirmish—A funeral

H E STOOD WITH the others, watching the bay. The two ships were double-masted schooners, and they were soon joined by a slow-trailing pair of gunboats. Each came from the southwest— through a channel that ran between St. George and St. Vincent— and each flew an American flag.

"A convoy," Israel decided. The four vessels dropped their white sails and lit their lanterns, then sat in anchorage beyond the mouth of the river. Israel assured them that from the bay his island would appear deserted and harmless. He told them not to fret. "We just sit and watch them," he said.

"I should go back," said Xavier.

"No," said Israel. "Maybe nothing will come of it."

Kau saw that the two men were now looking at him. "What are you planning?" asked Xavier.

"I'm stayin here only long as you."

"And when I leave?"

He pointed toward St. Vincent. "Then I'm gone too."

They went to the shack and Israel scratched out a message to Garçon with the flight feather of an eagle. He dipped the quill into a porcelain inkwell and spoke as he wrote, slowly dictating to himself. Kau leaned closer so that he could hear him. "6 p.m. July 10. U.S.A. ships in bay." Then: "Two merchant schooners. Two navy gunboats. So will monitor."

HE HAD INTENDED to borrow the small canoe that Israel kept on the island and paddle to shore. There he would follow the marsh channels to the pinewoods and collect plant fibers for a bowstring, light lengths of softwood for his arrows. But with the arrival of the ships his plans were stalled. He stored the cut yew back in the smokehouse, then set about helping Israel and Xavier in their spyings.

THEY WOULD WORK in eight-hour shifts measured out by Israel and his pendulum clock. Kau had volunteered for the first watch, and so now he sat alone on the beach, staring at the distant ship lanterns glowing in the blackness. When he was lonely he spoke in Kesa to his wife and his children, sometimes to his parents, sometimes to Samuel and Benjamin even. Anything to keep his mind off Beah. The woman who had nursed him back to health, then asked him to help her.

DAWN THE NEXT day. Smoke appeared in the west, at a hidden point where the forest gave way to marsh. He woke the others, and they watched as a smaller vessel—a masted skiff of some sort—was lowered from the davits of one of the gunboats and boarded by four men, one at each oar. The sail was kept furled as the rowers made for the snake of smoke. They disappeared into the marsh and Israel collapsed his spyglass. "I don't know what this means," he admitted, and then the pigeonkeeper limped off to send another pigeon.

THE SKIFF RETURNED to the gunboat with the falling tide, and he saw that a fifth man was with them now. Xavier and then Israel looked through the spyglass. "That is an Indian," said Israel. "A Creek, I think."

Kau took a turn at the spyglass. The Indian in the skiff seemed small compared to the American sailors, and his head was wrapped in cloth the color of cherry. Kau passed the spyglass back to Israel, and they remained on the beach until sunset but saw nothing else to report.

DAYS OF BOREDOM. From sunrise to sunrise they watched the ships, but for an hour each night they would gather together on the beach to share a meal and talk and tell stories. Kau kept mostly quiet until supper on the third evening when Israel insisted that he offer up some tale of Africa. He begged off but Israel would not take no. "I know your people had stories," he said. "All people got stories."

Kau thought a moment, then swallowed the last of his ashcake and told them an Ota parable. A story that had been one of his father's, a story Kau would sometime tell to his own children:

There is a Kesa farmer. He has grown tired of farming and wants to be a hunter like the Ota. The farmer goes to the Ota and they take him in. He is eager and the band begins to teach him, then finally the time comes for the farmer to go off hunting alone. The elders tell him that he has learned much but there is really only one big, important lesson. You must give yourself over to the forest, they tell him. Submit yourself fully and completely and you will be protected. The farmer is told then of the molimo—how in times of trouble the Ota need only to call upon that wooden trumpet to remind the forest to care for them. When we wake the forest we dance, say the elders. We dance because we know the forest will now remember us, we know we will now be saved.

And so the farmer goes, and he is not away very long before he sees a honeybee. He follows the bee deep into the forest but then night comes and he realizes that he is lost. A dog wanders upon him, one of the small hunting hounds from the Ota camp. The dog tries to lead him to safety but the farmer frightens it off. He spends a long night hungry and terrified, chanting aloud to the forest. He screams and screams as he tries to wake it.

The next day a foraging Ota woman happens upon him. She invites the farmer to go with her back to the camp, but even though he is still miserable and afraid he refuses. "No," he says to her. "I will trust in the forest."

The Ota woman returns to the camp and tells of the lost farmer. The elders agree that maybe it is because a woman found him that he will not return. He is proud, they decide. In the morning two of the young hunters are chosen. The woman describes to them the place where they will find the farmer and they know it very well. They leave the camp and reach his bed of leaves. The farmer is missing and so the hunters begin to track him. He takes them on a long journey through the forest, and when they finally overtake him he is crying. They sit with the farmer, say, Come with us now and we will help you. Again he refuses. "This is a test," he says. "The forest will provide."

The hunters leave the farmer and share this with the others. The elders shake their heads in confusion. The following morning they depart together—a group of old men led by the two young hunters. They find the farmer and he is dying. He roamed in the night and was bitten by a forest viper. He will not live long. The elders do what they can to make him comfortable. His leg swells until it blackens and splits, and as the venom takes root in his head the farmer sees the forest for the web of connections that it is. He speaks to it, says, I had to send away a dog and a woman and two hunters—why did you do nothing to save me? The elders hear the question hidden between his moans and are angered by it. The forest sent one dog, a woman, and two young hunters, what more did this man need from it?

THE SHIPS HAD been four days in the bay when Garçon came. It was late in the afternoon and Kau was on watch. He turned and the General was there, on the river in a long canoe. Two of the Choctaws were with him, a pair of longhaired and bare-chested warriors. The canoe kissed sand and Garçon regarded him. His hand rested on the hilt of his sword. "Please," he said. "Go and wake the others."

NIGHT FELL. THE waning moon was almost at last quarter, and he saw its twin reflected onto the water. Israel had put on a fraying redcoat in addition to his cut trousers, and was now speaking alone with Garçon on the beach. Kau sat on a length of driftwood and slapped mosquitoes. Xavier was beside him, wearing his own crimson jacket over his gray osnaburgs. Both were staring at the silent Choctaws. The two Indians had dragged the canoe into the palmettos and were crouched beside it, smoking a long pipe. Xavier spoke. "Are either of those the one who came into your tent?" he asked.

Kau studied the Choctaws' faces. "I don believe."

"Are you certain?"

"I'd know him."

Xavier threw a forked stick into the river and it was carried off by the current. "Maybe you should have left, no?"

"Yes. Maybe."

Garçon called them over. He had received Israel's pigeons announcing the arrival of the ships, the rendezvous with the lone Indian. Now he had a report for them from upriver. "The American soldiers are preparing to march south soon," he said. "In three or four days they will be coming for us at last."

Xavier spoke: "And then how long, sir?"

"Once they break camp? Another three days, I would say."

Kau stared at him. He was thinking of Beah. He felt like he had murdered her. "Till they make the fort?"

"Yes," said Garçon.

"You gonna fight them?"

"Of course."

"What about them boats? What they doin out there?"

Garçon shrugged. "We will know soon enough." He pointed to the black south. "In the morning we will ask those sailors just what their intentions are."

AT DAWN CAME the doldrums of the slack tide that Israel had promised them. The rowboat had been hidden on the north end of the island, and they all went to it now. Kau stood watching with the Choctaws as Xavier and then Israel stepped on board with their longrifles. Several big muskets were already lying in the hull. He spoke to the Indians in English, and when they did not respond he tried addressing them in their own language. They ignored him, then one Choctaw whispered something to the other and they both laughed.

Garçon had prepared himself in the shack. His sword and boots were now polished and he was wearing a clean uniform—a white waistcoat and breeches, a long-tailed redcoat. His tricorn held his long braids in place, and a longrifle was cradled in his arms. He walked over to Kau and smiled at him. "Will you join us?" he asked. "We have room for a small one like you."

"I'm thinkin I'll jus leave off."

"Or you could fight."

"I don think."

"You do not understand me."

"How you mean?"

"St. Vincent—Israel tells me that you intend to live there."

"Yes."

"But, you see, that is my island you think so freely of having."

"Your island?"

"Correct."

"You sayin I can't?"

"I am only saying that you have to earn such favors." Garçon touched him on the shoulder. "Please come," he said. "We will need you there with us."

BOTH XAVIER AND Israel frowned but said nothing when they saw him coming to join them. He settled in the bow with Garçon, and they pulled away from the island. Garçon asked if it really was true that he could shoot, and when he nodded the General handed him one of the heavy muskets lying at their feet. Kau brought the flintlock to his shoulder but could not reach the trigger. Garçon told him that it was a Brown Bess, smoothbored and inaccurate—but also much more powerful and quicker to reload than their longrifles. A soldier's weapon. Garçon patted him on the ribs. "Shoot it from your hip if the time comes. Then start reloading for the rest of us." The General then gave him a leather-bound box. Inside, wooden dividers held rows of paper tubes. "Have you ever used these before?" he asked.

Kau shook his head. "What they?"

Garçon lifted the nearest Bess and explained that each paper cartridge contained powder and a single lead ball. "Now watch." He bit the end from a cartridge, then primed the musket's flashpan with a quick splash of powder and closed the frizzen. "You try," he said.

Kau took up a musket and a cartridge and did the same. The rowboat rocked and he spilled some powder but not too much.

"Perfect," said Garçon. "Now for the rest of it." Garçon removed the ramrod from the underside of the Bess, then forced the torn cartridge down the length of the barrel. Kau copied him and Garçon smiled. "Perfect," he said again. A gull flew past them and screamed.

HE LOADED THE final Bess, then rubbed a wet hand on his neck to cool himself. He had moved to the stern with Israel, and the three muskets and the three longrifles were all arranged at their feet. Xavier faced them as he rowed, and Garçon remained in the bow, watching the Americans.

Mullet were feeding in great dimpled schools where the brown water of the river melded with the green water of the slack-tide bay, and when the crowded rowboat pushed in among them they scattered in eruptions of white froth. Israel pointed and told him he had just missed seeing a far-off tarpon dance on its tail. "It was something," he said. "Believe you me."

KAU SAT WITH his elbows on his knees. They were well into the bay—maybe two hundred yards from the American ships—when a skiff was lowered from one of the gunboats. Garçon ordered Xavier to stop with his rowing, then called to Israel. "How long?" he asked.

Israel gathered a handful of dead cypress needles from the floor of the rowboat and sprinkled them overboard, testing the tide. There was a slight chop to the water now, and the needles began a slow inch back toward the river. Israel squinted, watching them, then looked up at Garçon and spoke. "It's begun," he said.

Garçon told Xavier and Israel to take up their longrifles, and then he trained Israel's spyglass on the approaching skiff. He laughed and said that an ugly man was staring right back at him with a spyglass of his own. "Listen very close for my orders," he told them.

Kau shielded his eyes with both hands and the sailors in the skiff began to come into better focus. All five wore blue and white uniforms and varnished black hats. A man stood at the bow, his arms folded, mirroring the posture of Garçon. On his side was a sword, and he had the cragged features of a carved statue. Garçon spoke. "That man would be the one to kill first," he said.

THE AMERICANS PULLED to within seventy-five, then fifty yards. A beige pelican fell from the sky, slamming into the water between them. Two of the Americans were now kneeling with their muskets, and Kau saw the officer say something to his men. The officer spoke again and this time his words carried. "Steady," he said. He then raised his voice and called out to Garçon: "Announce yourself."

Garçon did not respond and so the American brought his hands to his mouth and called out again. "I am an officer of the United States Navy," he said. "Announce yourself."

The skiff sat facing them, its oars splayed out high like the wings of a colossal courting bird. The sky had settled into a deep blue, the morning haze gone, burned off by the big yellow sun. Kau let his hand come to rest on a musket, and there was a metallic click, the sound of either Xavier or Israel full-cocking his longrifle.

At last Garçon answered the officer. "I take no orders from Americans," he said, "as this is not America."

The officer nodded to a pair of big-backed sailors who had remained at the oars. The sailors leaned forward and two of the oars came down quickly. They began to spin the skiff clockwise, turning it broadside to the rowboat. Sailors lined the rails of the distant ships, and there came a low noise like the music that lives in a seashell. The sailors had begun to cheer. Garçon crouched down at the bow. "Fire," he ordered.

Kau was first. He threw up the Bess and pulled the trigger. A yellow blaze appeared on the side of the turning skiff, then Xavier and Israel lifted their longrifles and fired as well. Both men missed. Kau passed Garçon's longrifle forward to him and then handed loaded muskets to Xavier and Israel. A dull cloud of powder smoke hung over the rocking rowboat. Garçon shot and another chip appeared in the wood of the skiff. The Americans had come around complete, and they responded with their own volley. Kau heard the musket balls crack past, and then the smoke from the skiff lifted to mingle with the smoke from the rowboat. Israel pointed at a streak of red on his black and wrinkled neck. "That one there tasted me," he said.

Xavier fired his own musket and then began heaving on the oars. Their rowboat sat low in the water, but the tide had made its switch and was slowly drawing them back to the river and the island. The sailors looking on from the closest of the gunboats had quit cheering, and Kau saw them running to man their cannons. The skiff was retreating to the fleet, and Israel and a stern-riding sailor traded parting shots but without effect.

Kau passed Israel one of the spare muskets, exchanging it for his spent one, and then he bit the end off a cartridge and set about reloading. Xavier was watching them as he rowed. He was openmouthed and breathing in gasps. Kau saw a flame lick and then white smoke puffed from the nearest gunboat. A cannonball passed high over the Americans in the skiff, but then it splashed down far behind the rowboat. The skiff was a hundred yards off now. Israel fired again and Garçon shouted that maybe this time he saw a sailor slump.

And then Xavier screamed out in Spanish. Kau looked up from the Bess he was loading and saw that Israel lay dead, his forehead smashed by a musket ball. The back of his skull was missing, and his blood was spreading across the bottom of the rowboat. Kau turned away and saw Garçon sitting at the bow, quiet.

Xavier continued rowing them back toward the island, until finally they were well beyond the range of the both the skiff and the gunboats—but even as they fled the firing from the near gunboat persisted, only now Kau realized that its cannons had been aimed away from the retreating rowboat. For reasons known only to the Americans they were instead shelling the empty coast, firing incomprehensibly into the continent. He watched cannonball

216

after cannonball punish the green coastline as the tide carried the rowboat north.

THEY CIRCLED BEHIND the island before they beached—a ruse meant to fool the Americans into thinking that they had fled even farther up the river—and later, after the rowboat had been washed clean and emptied, Kau helped Xavier dig a grave behind Israel's shack while Garçon and the two Choctaws watched. They did not dig very long before they hit water, and so it was decided that the grave would have to be shallow.

Xavier fashioned a cross cut from raft wood, and after the hole was dug Garçon placed the pigeonkeeper's Bible in his stiff hands and a blanket was wrapped around him. The body was maneuvered into the grave, and then they covered Israel with dirt, more scraps of raftwood to discourage scavengers. When they were finished Xavier hammered his cross down into the ground.

They both stepped back so that Garçon could say words. With the Bible buried Garçon could only preach from memory. The General began to speak of a man walking alone through the valley of the shadow of death, and Kau let his mind drift. He remembered another story—Samuel's favorite story—the story of a bad man who returned to his home and became good. Kau realized then that he was living the opposite sort of life. Here he was, a good man stolen from his home and turned bad. A tiny cursed child-killer fated to traipse alone witnessing evil after evil after evil until at last his own time came to suffer, like Israel, some remote and terrible death. This was not a life worth living.

As he watched Israel be put to rest he recognized the mistake he had made in refusing Beah. She had offered him a way to save not just her life, but his own life as well. Garçon finished with his preaching and Kau went to him. "I believe I gotta go back," he said. "I believe I gotta go back and fetch Beah."

PART THREE

A RED FLAG

A watering party—Up the river—
An ambush

A T FIRST GARÇON hesitated, but in the end he agreed to let him take Beah away from the fort before the battle came. Kau nodded and then went off with Xavier to spend the day watching the American ships. He washed Israel's blood from his osnaburgs and then sat naked in the sun while they dried.

Xavier had listened to the conversation with Garçon and seemed troubled. Several times he asked about Beah, but Kau would not discuss her. In truth he was afraid that if he did speak of her some spell would be broken—that not Garçon but he himself would change his mind, that he would make for St. Vincent without her, abandoning her to die in the fort with the others.

That evening they all met together in the shack. At dawn Garçon would leave with the Choctaws in their canoe; Kau and

Xavier were to remain behind for now. Garçon pointed in the direction of the ships. "When they come," he ordered, "then you come." Kau frowned at this, but Garçon only handed him Israel's longrifle and powder kit. "Do this for me," he said. "Do this for me and I will keep her safe for you."

THE ISLAND WAS theirs alone now, and one would sleep while the other sat on the beach and stared at the ships. Every six hours they would switch out with the tide change. One man waking the other and passing him the spyglass.

IT WAS THE morning following the departure of Garçon. The warm night peeled back like some dark hide, and the land and sea were revealed. He trained the spyglass on the fleet and saw activity aboard one of the gunboats. The sailors were preparing a skiff. He hurried down the dirt path to the shack. The pendulum clock showed five o'clock, and he woke Xavier. "They comin," he said.

Xavier went with him to the beach, then took a turn at the spyglass and described what he saw. The skiff held a number of wooden barrels. Xavier lowered the spyglass and spoke. "*Sí*," he said. "They need water, I think."

THE ROWBOAT WAS still beached at the north end of the island, and it had been loaded with their effects since the day of Garçon's departure. Kau stood by the water and waited for Xavier to release the pigeons. Finally Xavier came running through the green palmettos, and Kau looked up at the sky, watching as the entire flock left the island for the fort.

He had thought of bringing along the bow stave, but there was no real point in that. He had his knife and a longrifle. What purpose would an unstrung and arrowless bow stave serve in the world of war and metal to which he was returning? No, he decided, let it wait for me here in the smokehouse.

He sat in the bow as Xavier worked to keep the island between them and the American skiff, blocking the rowboat from the view of the approaching sailors. The tide was coming in, and so the current pushed them north. Kau had the spyglass, and he leveled it on the upriver spot where the marsh surrendered to trees. Cardinals were flitting back and forth through the cypress and the long moss, a bright red male chasing after a bright red male while a fawn female watched.

Xavier pulled them into the shelter of the flooded cypress just as the skiff appeared around the side of Israel's island. The skiff's sail was raised, the Americans taking advantage of the steady breeze blowing in from the bay. He helped Xavier conceal the rowboat far back onto the shore, and then they unloaded their things.

They were watching the Americans glide slowly closer when Kau looked up and saw an Indian—a dark Choctaw, shiny with sweat—sitting astride the high branch of a cypress. The warrior was staring down at them. He pointed north. "Go," he said in English. "The General waits."

THEY TOOK THE horse path that ran along the river. He was thinking of the Choctaw. That had been him—the one who had visited Kau in the night, the one who stole his bone club and then left it as a gift for a dead man. After a while Kau spoke. "That Indian in the tree," he said. "It was him."

Xavier stopped and looked at him. "Him?"

"The Choctaw."

"From your tent, you mean?"

"Yes."

Just then Kau heard a slapping sound from back down the muddy trail. He turned with Xavier, and they saw the Choctaw approaching at a run. The Indian had a tomahawk in his hand and was almost upon them. Xavier leapt to one side of the trail and Kau to the other, but the Choctaw raced past them and kept on.

SOON THE HORSE path bent with the river, and they arrived at the first of the negro farms. Kau saw Garçon standing by the edge of a lush cornfield, surrounded by forty or fifty men. There were six Choctaws mixed in with the soldiers, and though the sentinel Choctaw was nowhere in sight, he must have reported that Kau and Xavier were coming. No one seemed surprised to see them, and when Xavier waved to Garçon from the horse path the General only smiled and said, Join us.

KAU WAITED WITH the others in the rows of corn that ran alongside the riverbank, and it was at least an hour before the skiff appeared. Garçon ordered everyone to keep hidden. The current was beating back the tide and the Americans had lowered their sail. Four men struggled at the oars; a fifth sat at the bow. On the west bank—directly across from the cornfield—a creek spilled into the brown river. The skiff turned and then made for it.

The river was wide here, and Kau sat beside Xavier in the hot cornfield, watching as the Americans unloaded their water barrels onto the shore. A tiny beetle was climbing one of the sleek cornstalks, and Kau flicked at it with his thumb. The beetle went careening through the rows, then landed near the edge of the river.

Soon the Americans would sail back out to the bay and be gone, and one of Garçon's soldiers seemed to be begging the General for something. Xavier translated the man's Spanish for Kau. The soldier wanted for them to try an across-the-river volley; he said they all felt lucky this morning.

Kau was far down the line of men but now saw Garçon creeping toward him. The General knelt with him in the dirt and then whispered in his ear. "So," he said, "the time has come for you to prove to me just how much my Beah means to you."

THE AMERICANS WERE sealing the last of their barrels when Kau hollered at them from across the sliding water. He was standing alone and unarmed on the strip of beach that ran between the river and the cornfield, Garçon and the others concealed behind him. He yelled and then waved. The Americans were watching him now, and he began to dance from side to side. "Hey," he shouted, "hey, hey."

He was thinking of the bright yellow tip of a young copperhead's tail, the way the snake could make it wiggle and writhe like a caterpillar, a lure to catch lizards and frogs. He was that tail tip, behind him was the snake.

The Americans seemed to be arguing among themselves. He danced faster, throwing his hands from the south to the north, slapping his knees to his chest as he jumped. This had become a dance not for the Americans, but for the forest. He screamed, Please, in Kesa. Please, he called out, please wake and remember me. He danced until he was exhausted and then, when he could dance no more, he sat down on the brown sand and waited. The Americans had left their water barrels by the creek and were at the oars. They were at the oars and they were coming.

He sat and watched. The bow of the skiff had been fitted with a small, wooden-handled cannon that moved on an iron swivel, and at about fifty yards one of the Americans stood and came forward to aim it at him. The man grabbed hold of the firing lanyard while four sailors kept the skiff stable in the current.

Kau raised his hands above his head. The sailors at the oars were very young—boys, really—and seemed afraid. The American at the swivel gun was older but only slightly, and this man had cupped a hand to his mouth to speak when there came a whistle from the cornfield. Kau dropped flat onto his stomach, then gunfire erupted behind him and the skiff was raked. The sailor collapsed at the swivel gun, and the firing lanyard slipped from his fingers.

Garçon and his men came pouring out of the cornfield, and the sailors took up their muskets but fired in a rush. The six Choctaws splashed into the river waving tomahawks and knives. Xavier knelt beside him in the sand. "How are you not shot?" he asked.

The sailors had thrown down their empty muskets and started rowing. The skiff was pulling away. Xavier helped him to his feet, and they watched as the swimming Choctaws overtook the skiff and began trying to slither over the sides and board. The four sailors quit their rowing and beat at the glistening warriors with the butts of their spent muskets. The skiff rocked hard and a sailor fell overboard. A Choctaw reached out but the boy dove and then resurfaced downriver.

Garçon drew his sword and gave orders to his soldiers on the bank. They reloaded and began firing at the sailor in the river. The boy was a strong swimmer and so they seemed to find sport in it. He would rise up for air, then dive back merganser-quick so that the soldiers never quite knew when or where he would reappear. Finally he made it safely to the far side of the river. Garçon laughed as he clapped for the boy. "It is impossible not to be glad for him," he said.

Kau looked to the drifting skiff. All six Choctaws had boarded. Three sailors were now huddled in the bow with the dead man, and the smallest of them was dragged by his ankles into the mass of Indians. The warriors went at him with their glinting knives, and soon they were all glossy with his blood.

The last two sailors watched the killing from the bow, and one of them seemed to be crying. Kau realized that they could not swim.

The weeping sailor pulled a pistol from his belt, aiming the black barrel at one of the Choctaws and then at himself. The boy stood up, shot a ball into his own chest and fell overboard. He disappeared into the river, and the final sailor lifted an empty musket. He grabbed the barrel and swung it at the Choctaws like a club. From the bank Kau could hear the warriors laughing, and they sounded almost like feeding gulls.

The musket-swinging sailor was soon exhausted and sat slumped at the bow. The Choctaws started to move forward, but Garçon yelled out and they stopped. Four of them crouched down at the oars and began rowing the skiff back upriver. Kau watched as the General slowly turned to him. "And you," he said. "My, my."

When the skiff reached the shore the sailor tried to run but was quickly caught. Kau saw that the boy was indeed young, but he was also big and angry. He had long, powerful arms and a thick neck, a block of a shaved head that bristled with tiny black hairs. The Choctaws threatened him, and he spit in their faces but did not speak. Garçon ordered the sailor's hands tied, then pinched his red cheeks when he struggled.

The skiff was dragged ashore, and Kau looked on as the two dead sailors inside were scalped by the Choctaws and then stripped of their uniforms. The sailor was watching from across the river. He alternated between cursing them and shouting to his caught friend. "We'll be coming for you, Edward," he yelled. "Don't you worry none."

Garçon ordered a volley to quiet him, but when the hollering sailor saw the men level their muskets he retreated into the forest before they could take aim and fire. "Fly away," said Garçon, and then as an amusement the soldiers aimed the swivel gun out over the river. Garçon tugged at the firing lanyard, and the little cannon boomed. Kau flinched as grapeshot sprayed out across the water like some great handful of cast gravel.

He kept quiet as the soldiers hauled the skiff up into the corn-field to hide it. The six Choctaws were left to watch the river, and the bloody Indians sat themselves in the cool water. Garçon began walking to the north, and Kau followed with the others. They soon reached the cabin of the soldier who worked that stretch of the land, and they emptied his smokehouse, feasting on ham hocks and oxtail that had been cured to the color of cinnamon.

Kau was the dancing hero of the fight. Garçon presented him with one of the American scalps, and he saw that it had already been scraped and salted for him. Later, he threw the scalp behind a woodpile but Xavier retrieved it. "Now listen to me again," said Xavier. "You need to learn to stop refusing his gifts."

"I don want it."

Xavier shook his head, then tucked the sailor's scalp into his own haversack as they prepared to set off. The captured American was glaring at them both from atop a braying mule. Kau looked away and saw Garçon mount his copper gelding. The General raised his sword three times, then began marching his men to their fort.

North — The torture of Edward Daniels — Juaneta — Samuel

THEY MARCHED NORTH along the dry road that connected the negro farms. The sun had long ago cleared the tree line and the soldiers were sweating like horses. The bayonets of their muskets shimmered and flashed.

Kau sipped warm water from the canteen that hung from his neck. The countryside was empty, and the farms lining the bank of the river had been deserted. He heard Garçon consider aloud whether he should raze the crops before the siege came, then decide against it.

"No," said Garçon. "We will not cut ourselves to injure them." The General said this in English and then again in Spanish. The men broke into halloos and hurrahs. These were their farms, their crops.

Kau held Israel's longrifle propped against his shoulder, same as the marching soldiers with their muskets. Xavier walked beside him. They passed abandoned farm cabin after abandoned farm cabin. He turned to Xavier and asked where all of the women and children had gone. "The fort," Xavier told him. "Everyone waits for us there."

IT WAS EARLY in the afternoon when they at last reached the fort. The gate was opened and the prisoner Edward pulled from the tired mule, his nose bloodied before Garçon could protect him. The soldiers were greeted by their comrades from the northern farms, and then the men with families went off to find their wives.

Kau surveyed the dusty fort. In his absence it had become crowded with the camp tents of Garçon's farmers. A blinding sea of white. And he saw that the renegade Choctaws had finally been forced from the forest. Thirty or so warriors had laid claim to a grassy area along the south wall. Four of them sat hunched on their heels nearby, gambling with musket balls on some Indian game of chance.

In a river corner of the fort stood the barked-pine slats of new livestock pens that had been filled with hogs and horses and cattle. Two tall girls moved among the nervous animals, steadily shoveling shit into a crooked wooden cart. Marcela and Ramona. The twin girls caught him watching and disappeared among steaming cattle.

A treble blast from a trumpet announced Garçon's review of his troops, and all gathered on the last square piece of open space in the fort. The soldiers were divided into four lines of twenty to twenty-five men, and Kau sat down against a tent and looked on from the shade. A crowd formed, some two hundred negro women and children. Their men had put on their uniforms—apple-red jackets, polished black boots and crisp white breeches. "My Lord," said a woman with green eyes. "Now ain't that the handsomest bunch."

Garçon walked back and forth in front of the soldiers, and in two languages he spoke of the ships in the bay, the death of Israel, the skirmish in the river. "Make no mistake," he told them. "There will be a reckoning." He ended his speech by invoking God. He told them that for every giant there was a David awaiting, that victory always went to the righteous. Kau shook his head. He was thinking that no one could possibly believe that.

The soldiers were dismissed and the crowd dispersed save one—Beah, watching him. Her coarse hair was brushed back in a stiff wave, and her osnaburg dress was a riot of wrinkles and folds. He went to her and she pushed at the longrifle in his hands. "You think you a soldier now?" she asked.

He looked around and felt his knees give a quick buckle of exhaustion. Most of the men had retired to their tents, others to the barracks, and soon they would be sleeping through the worst heat of the day. But not Garçon. The General was kneeling in the shadow of a wagon with Xavier, interrogating the sailor. The American sat with his head bowed, and Garçon slapped gently at the underside of the boy's chin as he spoke to him.

Beah snapped her fingers in front of Kau's face. He flinched and then answered her. "No," he said. "I'm no soldier."

She shook her head. "That general has him a silver tongue."

"It weren't him."

"Thas a trick of his, makin you believe that. Thas a famous trick of his."

"No," he said again. "It jus seemed to be right. Comin back."

"Why? You was gone."

"I know."

"So then what you gonna do?" she asked. "Fore you die here with me."

"I need to go and rest a bit."

"That why you come here? To rest?"

"I'm here cause I need to talk to you about somethin."

She folded her big arms. "So talk."

"Later," he said. "Please. We'll talk jus a little later."

HIS FORMER TENT was now occupied by a farmer and his family, and so Beah had insisted that he follow her through the maze of bright canvas to her own. Once inside, he stashed his saddlebags and Israel's longrifle in a corner, then spread his horse blanket out on the swept dirt.

That same morning a man had been kicked in the head by a mule, and Beah went to tend to him in the infirmary. She was still gone when he awoke to the sunset squeals of a dying hog and the lowing of frightened cattle. He stepped outside and began walking toward the river and the livestock pens. In places the tents were spaced so close that he had to turn sideways to pass between them. He dragged the corner of his foot in the dirt, leaving a scuff trail that would lead him back to Beah.

At the edge of a freshly dug sewage ditch he stopped and covered his mouth and nose with his hand. Black flies swarmed around him but then settled back into the sludge. Across the way were the livestock pens, and he saw that Pelayo's daughters had taken knives to a big chocolate barrow. They had the fat hog hanging from an iron gambrel with its throat slit. Blood was collecting in a washtub, and the twins were smiling.

HE SAT ALONE by the cook-fire in front of Beah's tent, roasting a ration of the butchered hog on a forked green stick. He had just pulled the meat from the flame when Xavier came and joined him.

Xavier had spent all day with Garçon and the caught sailor. He explained that at first the young American had told them nothing, but then had told them everything. The General knew well that every man has that which he fears above all—snakes or knives or God, for example—and for the boy prisoner apparently it was fire that came in his nightmares.

His name was Edward Daniels and he was sixteen years old, an ordinary seaman from some small place in Louisiana called Madisonville. According to the terrified boy, one month ago a pair of merchant schooners had set sail from New Orleans. The two ships were accompanied by a naval gunboat and were soon joined by another in Pass Christian.

Daniels served on this second gunboat under a man named Loomis, commander of the entire expedition. It took the convoy over two weeks to reach the mouth of the Apalachicola, and from there they were to transport supplies to the American soldiers garrisoned upriver. "Do you see now," asked Xavier, "how all of this is a trap?"

"How you mean?"

"They are only waiting for the soldiers to get into position across from our fort before they sail up." Xavier was slurring his words slightly, and Kau realized that he had been drinking. His eyes were glassy and red. "They are expecting to provoke us. And when they do—"

"I understand." Kau bit a clear corner of fat from his pork-steak. He swallowed and then spoke again. "Makes sense."

"*Sí.*"

"They gonna win."

Xavier looked at him. "We have a strong fort."

"It won't matter none."

"Why do you say this?"

Kau ducked into the tent and began to search through his saddlebags. Only one of Benjamin's sling-stones remained. He went back outside and tossed the smooth stone over the fire. Xavier caught it with both hands.

"What?" said Xavier.

Kau moved the flat of his hand through the air. "Study on that," he said. "See what a river do to a rock over time?"

THAT NIGHT HE saw one of the Choctaws come galloping through the open gate on a lathered horse. Again Garçon gathered his men. Activity upriver. The American soldiers were finally on the move, and from the northeast came a mixed-blood chief named

McIntosh and a hundred and fifty Lower Creeks. Soon this would be a siege. The last wagonloads of firewood were collected and the gate secured. No one was to leave without the permission of the General.

Kau watched as they prepared to more properly torture Daniels. Xavier told him that the soldiers were demanding it—as they had convinced themselves that this boy had fired the shot that killed the pigeonkeeper, a man most of them had never even seen. And that none of the other soldiers had been there with Israel on the water that day was not important. They wanted revenge and Garçon promised them that they would have it. He ordered the execution of the prisoner that same night and there was ceremony to it. The boy feared fire and so fire was chosen.

A bonfire was built and a vat of black tar set to bubbling. The soldiers cheered as Daniels was taken in chains from the small stockade attached to the barracks. The boy saw the fire and began to sob. Because most of the soldiers had been slaves, Daniels was treated as a slave. His hands were tied to the pine flagstaff, and Garçon whipped him bloody. Shifting to protect his shredded back, Daniels would be beaten across the side and sometimes the face. Twenty lashes from the whip and the boy fainted. The Choctaws were waiting nearby, and at last Garçon called for them.

Kau had heard that they were experts in torture, these renegade Choctaws. The boy was given over to them, and the warriors sat with him for a while, treated his wounds even. Once Daniels was strong enough to stand they brought him closer to the fire. He was stripped naked and his penis cut off, thrown into the coals to blacken, shrivel, and burn. They were painting the blistering sailor with tar when Kau finally walked away.

BEAH HAD REFUSED to watch the slow killing of Daniels and he found her in her tent, staring at a flickering candle. He sat beside her on the camp bed and told her that soon he would be leaving again. "But I'm wantin you to come with me," he said. "I think I've found a place for us. An island."

She leaned toward him and her loose dress rode low across her chest. He looked down into the black space between her large breasts as she kissed the side of his face. He waited for her to speak but she said nothing.

"I believe we could be safe there," he said.

"No," she told him. "I don't wanna go with you no more."

"Why not?"

She pulled away from him. "What all you know about me? I mean you know anythin about where I come from? How I done got here?"

"How would I know any of that?"

"People talk."

"You talk."

"Not jus me."

He shrugged. "You speakin English, I always figured you come from Georgia."

"Well, you right." She picked a ball of brown lint from the flat of her dress. "But you ain't never heard nothin more, that so?"

"I ain't heard nothin at all about you."

And so she told him, told him how she had been working in the house of a plantation near Augusta, how she had a husband and five children living there, a mother and a father. There was a trader she came to know and trust, a freed slave who sold venison in the market. He was the one who had told her about the British and their negro fort, and this had been a curse. The fort had haunted her, dominated her dreams and distracted her days—until finally one morning she filled a basket with all the house silver and went running to the market.

Beah placed her hand on his knee. "What I'm tellin you is this—no, I can't leave after all. But it be real good you turnin back to ask me."

"I don see it," he said.

"I left them all behind, understand? Wagoned out that same night hid under a pile of deer hides." She tapped at his leg. "But you see you askin means at leas maybe you still got a soul worth savin." She smiled at him. "You was a selfish one."

He made to stand but she grabbed hold of his hand and pulled at him.

"Don pout," she said.

"You was wantin me to take you and now you sayin no." The tent had cooled with the night and felt something like a cave. "What gone changin?" he asked. "What of your own soul?"

"Thas the thing of it." She lifted his hand to her mouth and kissed it. "I get now that I need to die here jus like you needed to risk comin back for me."

He looked at her. "You sayin you ain't scared?"

She stood and blew out the candle. It went dark and he heard her dress drop to the dirt. A moment later and she was in the bed and on him. She whispered in his ear and he felt smothered by her, buried. "You know I'm scared," she said. "But I got my penance to suffer now."

IN THE MORNING he found Garçon at the pigeonhouse, doting on his birds. Kau walked over to him, and from somewhere distant came the sharp crack of a man splitting wood. Garçon opened his hands and a pigeon went fluttering off.

Kau spoke: "I might be goin fore long. Is that all right?"

"What of Beah?"

"She stayin."

Garçon shut the door of the pigeonhouse. "That does not surprise me," he said.

Kau looked up and realized that the entire flock had been set free; a black ball of birds was circling the fort. "It does me."

"But that changes nothing for you?"

"I spose it don."

Garçon nodded and began walking back to his tent. Already the first of the released pigeons had dropped down exhausted onto the perch that marked the trap-entrance of its home. At twenty paces the General turned and spoke. "Then join me this evening for a meal," he said. "Join me just one last time."

HE SAT IN front of Beah's tent and let his thoughts extend beyond the nurse. He felt that Garçon was probably in some part insane, but still the man had taught him things. From studying on this general he had learned what it meant to look forward with one's life and not back. He experimented with a vision of his own future. Beah had refused to go with him, but he began to ponder whether it might not be so impossible to leave with another sort of person. And in fact Beah had suggested that very same thing. When he pressed himself against her she had said, Go on and find youself someone greener than me. Someone without no real sin. Over and over she had said that, moaned that. Go on and find youself someone greener than me. Someone without no real sin.

There seemed to be women everywhere in the fort now. A pregnant pair hurried past to fill buckets from the well, and he watched them come and he watched them go. They were married no doubt, the wives of soldiers. That those two women—that all of them—would be widows or dead soon enough was meaningless now. The wives would remain with their doomed men and so instead he considered the younger ones, the girls too old to be children but not yet married, those still living in their fathers' cabins. If he could have one of that class, just one, he could maybe start another family. Yes, they were horrified by him—he knew that well enough. They quivered when he looked at them, changed their course when they saw him coming. And then there was the fact that he was small, that he was a tiny man. Still, he decided that if the opportunity arose he would try to take one of those handsome daughters with him to that St. Vincent Island. Perhaps in time she would come to see that he had saved her, that he was not the dangerous little man she had thought him to be.

At midday Xavier sought him out in Beah's tent. Kau was lying in her bed with a mug of water resting on his bare chest. Beah was gone, off to care for the kicked man in the infirmary. Xavier dragged a chair closer and sat. "I hear that she will not leave?"

"No."

"We have no chance here."

"Thas true."

Kau drank his water down, and Xavier lifted a pitcher from the table and refilled the empty mug for him. It was very hot. "He would never allow me to go," said Xavier.

"You gonna ask him?"

"No."

"Then don. Jus run." Kau set the mug on the table and then propped himself up on his elbows. "In a minute he'll be dead and ain't none of it will matter."

"Do not talk like that."

"Don wish it. It jus be."

Xavier lifted his hand to quiet him. "Stop," he said. Then, in a low voice: "I have already decided to join you."

"Yes?"

"Yes."

Kau spun sideways in the bed so that he was now sitting up and facing him. "I'm leavin tomorrow," he said. "Come and meet me here after dark, after evbody done gone off to sleep."

That afternoon he saw a girl in a long green dress. She was standing in one of the alleyways that ran between the tents, talking with the twins Marcela and Ramona. She teased them and they teased her right back. He realized then that this was their kin, a pretty older sister he had somehow never seen. The twins spotted him, and when they warned their sister of his presence he heard them say a name—Juaneta. She was fine-featured and dark, saw him staring but did not look away. Of all the young women in the fort this Juaneta alone seemed not to fear him. He watched her finally slip into a tent with her sisters and remembered what Beah had said about finding himself a green girl. He wondered what should amaze him more—the green dress, or that he would happen upon someone with a name so similar to that of Janeti. Someone prettier than any woman he had seen since Africa.

THE FINAL MEAL he shared with the General was extravagant—a courtboullion, Garçon told him—thick steaks of bass poached in a red gravy of crushed tomatoes. The mulatto cook began to prepare their plates, but Garçon dismissed the man and called for Xavier.

Xavier was posted outside, and when he looked into the tent his head seemed to be cut off and floating against the white canvas. "Sir?" he asked.

"Help us with all of this," said Garçon. "I think that maybe I am safe from rebellion for at least through supper."

Xavier leaned his longrifle against the wall of the tent, then removed the round-hat he had found to replace the one that had been lost in the river. He sat with them at the table, and Kau saw that his hands were shaking slightly. "*Gracias*," he said. "Thank you, sir."

"As you likely know," said Garçon, "our friend here will be leaving us soon."

"Yes, sir. He has told me that."

"Right." Garçon filled a second glass with beer and passed it to Xavier. "And that is a shame, is it not?"

"It is. Yes, sir."

Garçon lifted his glass and Xavier did the same. Kau realized that they were both looking at him, waiting for him to follow. He raised his glass of water and Garçon continued. "But he is with us now," he said. "And so we drink to him while we still can."

The three glasses clicked together. Another toast. "And to Israel," said Garçon. "A man who laid down his life for us." The glasses collided once again, and now the General was staring at Xavier. "There is simply no greater love," he said.

He sat waiting, and at some lost hour after sunset Juaneta finally emerged from her tent. She wore only a thin nightgown, and her feet were bare same as his. She walked across the fort, and he followed by the light of the high moon. She went behind the artillery bank, and he crept up to the top. The girl was crouched down below, urinating near a ditch that drained into the river. She finished and he approached, shuffling his feet so that she would hear him coming. She looked up and saw him. "*¡Quieto!*" she said.

He stopped halfway down the back of the artillery bank, then patted at his chest and spoke slowly. "My name is Kau," he told her.

"What do you want?"

"You know English?"

"Go away."

"Don be afraid of me." She threw a clod of dried dirt at him as he said this. It hit his chest and exploded into dust. He wiped his shirt clean with the flat of his hand. "You that man Pelayo's daughter?" he asked.

"I am."

He pointed upriver toward the farm, the chickenhouse. "How come I never seen you?"

She did a quick twirl on her toe tip and her loose nightgown billowed high around her waist. "I was gone."

"Gone where?"

"I live here."

"At the fort?"

"At the fort," she said.

"What you do here?"

She smiled. "*El General*," she said, "he teaches me." She climbed up the artillery bank until she stood in front of him. She was his height but she was also only thirteen, maybe twelve even. In another summer she would pass him and in three she would tower. Already she seemed to understand this. "I asked you what you want."

"I—"

She laughed and then spoke before he could answer. "Oh, I know what you want." She sat down in the wet grass. "I see how you are looking at me right now, *hombrito*."

He glanced around. A sentry was watching them from farther down the bank. "Easy," he said.

She poked him in his leg. "Maybe *you* do not be afraid of *me.*"

"What you mean he teachin you?"

Again that laugh. "What I mean, *hombrito,* is that he runs a schoolhouse for us in that tent of his."

"You tellin a riddle?"

"No riddle."

He knelt down next to her. The grass was slick as pond lilies. "Tomorrow night I'm leavin," he said. "You want you can come."

She pulled slowly at her hair, letting it slide between her fingers. "Why would I do that?" she asked.

"If you don you gonna die. At best you gonna die."

"No." She shook her head. "I would never leave him." She rolled over onto her knees and then lifted her nightgown. She was staring over her shoulder at him now. "*Esta noche, sí*" she said, "*pero mañana no.*"

He stood and walked away, leaving her half naked on the slope of the artillery bank saying, Last chance, last chance, last chance. She belonged to her general, he realized.

HE SPENT A second night in bed beside Beah. In the morning she was gone and when she returned it was to tell him that the mule-kicked soldier had passed. She waited for him to dress and then asked if he would help her attend to the body.

Together they filled a bucket at the well and went to the infirmary. The soldier was an older man he had not seen before. His face was swollen and his eyes were black. They pulled off his clothes and

Beah washed his skin. When she was finished they wrapped the body in a clean white sheet. Word had spread. Garçon appeared in the tent and said something in Spanish to the dead man. His name had been Roberto.

With Lower Creeks about, Garçon feared that any fresh grave dug beyond the walls of the fort would be desecrated, and so instead he ordered that Roberto and two cannonballs be sewn into a length of canvas and then sunk into the river.

Shooters took positions on the artillery bank as Xavier and three other soldiers carried the bundled corpse outside of the fort to the riverbank; two more soldiers trailed after them, dragging a canoe. Kau searched the gathered crowd and saw Juaneta. She was wearing that same green dress and watching him. He nodded to her, and she put her hands on her hips and rubbed them.

The corpse was placed inside the canoe, and then Xavier paddled the dead soldier Roberto out to the middle of the channel. As the current pulled the canoe south Kau saw a single arrow launch from high atop an upriver pine. It sailed well past Xavier and then entered the water without a splash. He turned to Beah but realized she had not seen it, that no one else had seen it. Xavier muscled the body out of the canoe, and when the river finally took Roberto the soldiers lining the artillery bank let fly with a salute volley.

And then Garçon came up beside him; he was holding Juaneta's hand. The General asked Beah to leave them and once she was gone he pointed to Juaneta and spoke. "Listen very closely to me," he said. "No."

AT THE FIRST shadings of night he went to collect logs for his cook-fire so that he could eat and then begin preparing to leave. He was sorting through the woodpile when the gate of the fort opened and two Choctaws led a stooped negro inside. The man was bare-foot and unarmed, his osnaburgs tattered and filthy. White hair. A cotton beard. Kau stood amid the scattered wood and stared, unbelieving.

Samuel.

He rushed over and saw that his old friend was wearing a pearl-gray top hat of dyed beaver felt. A white man's hat. Samuel lifted his hands and pointed with two fingers. His eyes were red-rimmed and watery. "You," he said.

They embraced and Kau held Samuel long enough to smell Yellowhammer on his skin and be reminded of Benjamin. He pulled away. The gate had been closed and Garçon was now standing with the two Choctaws and watching. "You know this man?" he asked.

"Samuel his name."

"Who is he to you?"

"He's my friend. My friend from back in Mississippi."

"Amazing," said Garçon.

Samuel spoke. "Adam," he said. "So you do live."

Garçon waved the Choctaws away, and as they slunk off Samuel turned to the General as if seeing him for the first time. He tugged at the sleeve of the British redcoat. "My," he said. "And what you meant to be, son?"

Samuel tells his story — Garçon at play — Beah is swayed

H E WATCHED AS Samuel yawned and then scratched at his head with both hands. They were in the tent with Beah, and the old man was sitting on her camp bed while she doctored the cuts and sores and blisters on his feet. Several times Kau tried to ask Samuel questions but Beah always hushed him, telling him to leave her patient be. As she worked Samuel's breaths became longer and then the sweat-stained top hat fell from his head.

Kau ate another square of the ashcake that Beah had found for them, but finally he could no longer stand the waiting. Beah left them to tend to a sick child, and once she was gone he shook Samuel awake but in a gentle way. "How is it you here?" he asked.

"What is this place, Adam?"

"Kau."

"What?"

"Kau. Call me that now."

"Thas your true name, ain't it?"

"Yes."

Samuel shrugged. "All right," he said. "What is this place, Kau? Tell me."

He explained to him about Garçon and the fort, about the Americans who would soon be coming. There was a tin mug of cold coffee on the small table beside the bed. Samuel asked him if he could have it, and Kau nodded. He drained the mug in a single swallow, then wiped his thick beard with his sleeve. "So listen," he said.

IT HAD BEEN a Friday night when Kau left Yellowhammer with the boy, and since the innkeeper knew it was in the habit of the pair to spend long days together—catfishing and exploring and what all—it was not until Saturday supper came and went that he became concerned over the whereabouts of his son and the little slave. Samuel was on his knees and praying when the innkeeper at last called for him.

Samuel readied a pair of horses and the two men rode off together. At dusk they found Benjamin's mare idling riderless beside the river, and even before they came upon the puddle of stinking blood, Samuel had begun to sense just what Kau had done.

After Samuel was whipped and Lawson's body found—the trail of Kau lost—the soldiers returned to this place on the river. A grapple hook was dragged twenty times across a deep blackwater hole, and on a last fortunate cast it hooked into a leg. The sunken corpse of Benjamin—a fraction eaten by mud turtles, the chest infested with minnows—was pulled dripping onto the bank. The innkeeper collapsed onto his dead son, and Samuel cried for them both.

The innkeeper was a Jew. This was something he had never even told Benjamin—yet in his grief the man quit his drinking and became devout, found the god he had abandoned after his wife died in childbirth. Benjamin was laid carefully across a table inside the inn, and from notes that had been handwritten inside a beaten copy of some holy book the innkeeper tried to teach himself how to prepare the body in accordance with the laws of his people. There were faltering prayers in a language Samuel did not recognize, and the corpse was washed and dried as best they could manage. Samuel helped dress Benjamin in fresh white linen, and then a blue sash was tied around the boy's waist. The innkeeper fastened and unfastened the strip of silk as he struggled to arrange the knot into some specific and special shape. When he was satisfied he pointed to the knot and looked up at Samuel. "This is the name of God," he said.

It was here Samuel realized that his master had become crazed, and he wondered what would become of him—the slave of a madman.

The innkeeper went into his bedroom and began to search the same cedar chest that had held the ancient book. When he returned he was carrying a corked vial of khaki dirt that he said came from some sacred land. He sprinkled the dirt onto his son, and the body was at last buried at the base of a gentle green hill. Afterward the innkeeper told Samuel that he would grieve as a Jew should. For a week he received the sympathies of visitors—the soldiers and Indians and traders who had known the boy—and then at midnight on the seventh day he went into his bedroom with the book.

At dawn and at dusk Samuel would bring the innkeeper a meal and empty his chamber pot. Travelers seeking lodging were turned away, and from time to time Samuel pressed his ear to the closed door and could hear his master chanting aloud. The innkeeper's short hair went uncut; he grew a shabby beard. A month of this and then he emerged from his room. That same day a wagon merchant appeared with a top hat the innkeeper had requested many weeks before. "Vanity," said the innkeeper. He paid the merchant, then gave the hat over to Samuel.

And next the innkeeper freed him, apologizing to the man he had owned for all of the sins that he had committed against him. Then he left. One morning Samuel awoke and the innkeeper was gone. The rumor along the federal road was that he had fallen in with a small band of Coushattas relocating west to Louisiana. It was said that in his month of solitude and grief the innkeeper had come to a conclusion about the Indians still living wild in the Americas, that he had decided they were the last descendants of some greater, lost tribe of the Old World—that therefore those migrating Coushattas were somehow related to his own ancestors. His mind was addled.

Samuel spent only a few days living alone at Yellowhammer. Pioneers bound for Texas presented. He apologized and told them that the inn was now closed. An hour later the failing farmers kicked in the door and told him that the inn was now theirs. He was left with nothing, nothing save his freedom papers and the clothes on his back, the hat on his head.

So as an old man Samuel started his life anew. He was a third-generation slave with no understanding of how to exist free and independent. He walked the federal road east, sought charity but received none. Twice he offered himself as property, but both times he was judged useless and denied. He was a man without any value—and as if to prove this point his freedom papers were finally taken from him by a soldier near Fort Mitchell and burned. A near four-score years as an owned man, and now at long last he had his liberty not as a reward or a gift but only because there were no white men left who wanted him as their own.

At the border to Georgia Samuel sat on the bank of the Chattahoochee, the top hat in his hands as he watched the ferry take livestock and horses and men back and forth across the river. He himself had no money to pay for the crossing, and so he prayed and he waited. After several hours of this a long black racer slithered out of the forest to then lie motionless in the sun. Samuel bashed the basking snake's head with the edge of a flat rock, and later he saw two Indians dressed as white men paddle a canoe to the downstream shore. They made camp on the riverbank, and because he was very hungry and had no tinderbox, Samuel was fearless and went to them. He made gestures meant to ask if he might share their fire so as to cook his snake. The Indians were happy with drink, and though on most other nights they no doubt would have ignored him, on this night they were kind and made room.

Samuel soon recognized that these two Indians were Creeks, and though he knew their language well he did not let on—even as one of them spoke to the other of a strange thing he had seen on one of his furtive excursions downriver into Florida: a tiny sharp-toothed negro caught and kept chained in a chickenhouse. "They thought he was one of their angels," said the Indian. "I have bought three runaways from that farmer, but this small one he would not sell."

That night Samuel gnawed snake and watched from the forest as the Indians laughed and continued on with their drinking. Once they were asleep he returned, stole their canoe and began drifting south, following the river, searching for his friend.

Samuel went quiet, and Kau looked up from his chair by the table. "I'd done more to stop you if I'd known," said Samuel.

"Known what?"

"That he be leavin with you. Why do that? Why take him jus to kill him?"

"That ain't it."

"What ain't?"

"I mean I ain't sure I ever meant to cut him."

Samuel shook his head. "At first I was only wantin to find you so I could ask you that. Maybe make some sense of what you done."

"And now?"

"Now I think it don really matter." Samuel pointed at the ceiling of the tent. "I believe now that all this was meant to happen, that this be God's plan for you and me both."

SAMUEL KEPT PUSHING south in the stolen canoe because with the boy dead and the innkeeper gone Kau was all he had for family left in the world. His friend had killed a child and for that he was damned, but still Samuel was determined to find him, help him, as in truth over time he had come to see a sort of blessing in the murder. Though he had loved Benjamin, he knew that the boy would one day be a man molded by his father—that most all that had been pure and perfect about him soon would fall away like velvet rubbed from buckhorn in the late summer woods. So yes, damned, for certain Kau was damned. But in killing the boy Kau had also saved the boy, kept him from becoming another evil man. Though Benjamin was the son of a Jew, Samuel was certain the boy would see heaven. He refused to believe that a Christian God would punish a child of any sort, and so in that Samuel rejoiced and was glad.

But with Kau it was different. Time and again Samuel had tried to school him on the Lord Jesus, but he could never reach him. Kau had rejected God at every advance, and so, for Samuel, that his friend was fated to forever burn in hell made his earthbound years that much more precious. If Kau was really being kept chained in a chickenhouse that could not be allowed to stand. He should have some comfort in this life, as later he would only know even worse suffering.

The canoe sank a few miles past the headwaters of the Apalachicola, its hull busted by a collision with a log. Samuel dragged himself onto the east bank and then began walking south atop high bluffs that looked down onto the big river. Three days later the land flattened into pinewoods, and upon reaching the first of the negro farms he was captured by Garçon's Choctaws. That he had made it so far was one miracle, yet another was that he should arrive the very same day that Kau would be planning to leave. He offered these up to his friend as proof of God's mercy, explaining that perhaps it was not too late for him to be saved. To be saved all one must do is believe. Such was the appeal of Christianity to a man born a slave.

SAMUEL WAVED HIS finger at him. "I think thas what's off about you," he said. "That you weren't born no slave. That ain't all you ever knew."

Kau only nodded. Though he remained doubtful of a heaven in the sky, he had amended his own opinion on the subject of hell in the three months since leaving Yellowhammer. He had seen enough now to believe that, yes, there was a hell. But not an unknown hell, not a thereafter hell. A hell right here in the pinewoods. He had come to believe that in this hell-life he was paying for sins perpetrated in some better life before, things he had no memory of doing but that must have been evil indeed.

Still, he could guess Samuel's reply to that. "Thas all jus fine," Samuel would say. "But what about all the evil you doin here?"

IT GREW LATE. Beah had returned to the tent, and Samuel had given her the bed. Now she was asleep and snoring.

Kau sat with Samuel at the table. A candle burned between them, but because it was hot and still in the tent the flame did not flicker or even waver. He put a choice to the old man—Samuel could leave with him or he could stay. "But I'm hopin you gonna come," he said. "I really am."

Samuel coughed into a yellowed handkerchief. He spit again and wiped his chin. "You told me I was a coward. You recall that?"

"It was wrong sayin that."

"No, no. You was right in a way. I spent too much of my life thinkin on things. Not doin nothin." Samuel laughed. "But all I know of dreams is that things never come about the way you see them in your head."

"I spose."

"So then a dream ain't nothin but a chance erased. You wanna stave somethin off then go on and picture it." Samuel rubbed his hands together quickly and then slapped them. "It won't happen. At leas not the way you seen it happen."

Just then Xavier came into the tent. He stared at Samuel, and Kau stood to introduce them. "Xavier, this here Samuel."

Xavier was wearing osnaburgs and black boots. He had his canvas haversack slung across his shoulder, that and his longrifle. "*Sí,*" he said. "I have heard already."

"Hey there, boy," said Samuel.

Kau spoke: "I think he comin with us. Yes?"

"Yes," said Samuel. "Yes."

Now he sat with Xavier at the table, and they let Samuel rest on a blanket spread across the dirt floor. They would leave just before dawn, and so to stay awake they spoke in whispers. Samuel had

begun to snore in rhythm with Beah, and finally Kau came around
to asking about the girl Juaneta.

"You know her?" asked Xavier.

"Only some. We met up once."

"I could probably show you all about her if you truly want to
know."

"I do."

Xavier blew out the candle. "Then follow me," he said.

THE FORT WAS asleep save the on-duty sentries, and a man was
guarding the entrance to Garçon's tent. The sentry grinned at
Xavier. "They in there," he said. "But be careful now."

Xavier nodded and gave the sentry some tobacco, then they
were allowed to venture around to the narrow gap of space between the wall of the fort and the backside of the tent. From within
the tent Kau heard the murmur of a man speaking. Xavier pointed
to a walnut-sized hole in the canvas and mouthed a single word:
"Look."

Kau pressed his face against the canvas, centering his eye on
the peephole so that he was looking into Garçon's private quarters.
He saw a camp bed lit by a collection of oil lamps. Garçon was in
uniform and pacing. Three naked girls sat on the bed—Juaneta and
her twin sisters—and they were close enough for him to see beads
of clear sweat on their smooth brown skin. Ramona held Juaneta's
right hand, Marcela her left. Garçon was lecturing Pelayo's daughters in Spanish and they were listening. He finished his speech, then

slipped behind the curtain that kept his quarters shielded from the rest of the tent. When he came back he was carrying a chair and several strips of bright cloth. Garçon sat down in front of the three girls, and they went to him without a word. Juaneta removed the tricorn from his head and Ramona sat in his lap, straddling him in the chair as Marcela stood beside them and watched. The girls set about unraveling his braids, brushing them out one at a time before retying them oiled, exact, and perfect. Garçon spoke to them as they worked, saying more Spanish things. Juaneta's small breast passed close to his face and he lashed out snake-like with his tongue, sliding it across her dark nipple so suddenly that she gasped and then giggled. Garçon rotated the girls, and Juaneta climbed onto his lap as they all traded places. She now had the stunned eyes of a doll, all three of them did. They moved as if in some trance.

The girls had taken up the strips of thin cloth, and they were tying Garçon's ankles and wrists to the chair when Kau turned away from the peephole. He looked around for Xavier and saw him farther down the wall, staring through a peephole of his own and rubbing his crotch. Kau crept over and when Xavier heard him coming he rocked back, embarrassed.

Kau spoke into his ear. "I'm goin," he said softly.

Xavier nodded but stayed where he was.

"Don be long." Kau turned, but then he stopped and went back. "What all he tellin them?"

"*Dios mío.*" Xavier made a big circle with his hands. "Everything," he whispered.

HE OPENED THE flap to the tent and saw that the candle had been relit. Beah was awake and talking to Samuel at the table. Her face was wet with tears, and Samuel was holding her hands in his own.

Kau stepped into the dim space and the two of them went quiet. Finally Beah stood and went to him; he saw that some of her effects were laid out across her bed.

"You really got a place we can go to?" she asked.

He nodded. "You comin now?"

"Yes," said Samuel. "She comin."

"That right?"

Beah took him by his chin and forced him to look up at her. "Why you didn't tell me all you done? You done some bad things, too."

"Hell things, you mean."

"Yes, hell things. Jus like me." She kissed him hard on his lips until Samuel said, Oh my, and she pulled away. "Come and help me pack up," she said. "We need to be leavin."

A desertion — In the American encampment

H E WIPED ISRAEL'S longrifle down with an oiled rag while Beah collected her few possessions, and when she was finished she came and sat with him and Samuel at the table. Together they all waited, and in the last dark hour before false dawn Xavier finally returned to the tent. Kau told him that now Beah would also be joining them, and Xavier shook his head but was quiet.

They made their way to a porthole cut into the north wall, and Xavier was the first to slip outside the fort. Kau passed him their belongings, and then Beah struggled her big body through the porthole as well. For a moment he thought that maybe she would not fit but somehow she did.

Samuel was next. He passed Xavier his top hat and then leaned forward. Xavier dragged him outside, and Samuel began to mumble and pray. Kau could hear Beah trying to calm the old man. "Please keep quiet now," she told him. "Don fuss."

After Samuel was through Kau turned and saw that a soldier had crept close and was watching him. The man raised his musket to his shoulder, and they stood staring at each other. He had splotches of white on his face and his neck. The sentry looked twice behind him, then jerked the barrel of his musket toward the porthole. "*Vayate*," he said. "*Ahora*."

HE WADED ACROSS the moat and joined the others. The sturdy funeral canoe still sat beached on the shore, and they loaded their things and pushed off. Kau heard a whistle as they pulled away. He looked and saw the faceless figure of the sentry standing alone atop the artillery bank, his thin arm held high and waving. Kau answered back with the warble of a redbird, then gave a farewell wave of his own and looked away, focusing on the wide and shining river that lay spread out before him.

THE CURRENT CARRIED the canoe south, and he sat in the bow, watching in the dark for logs as Xavier steered from the stern. Samuel and Beah slept hunched over between them. Earlier they had all agreed that it would be wise to quit the river before full sunrise, and so when the sky began to bleed red Xavier put to the western shore—the wilderness shore—and Kau woke the others.

THEY DECIDED THAT he would venture inland to scout for danger while the others waited by the river. He began loading the longrifle while Xavier concealed the canoe with armfuls of cut palmetto and long moss. Beah had taken up a push pole and was using it to fish moss from the cypress trees. He watched as she pulled at one big tangle and a large bat came tearing out from within it. Beah screamed into her fist as the disturbed bat dropped low, almost to the ground, then went flapping off into the daylight to search for some new roost.

FOR THE FIRST time since his day in the dome swamp he found himself walking alone in the forest. A horse path ran north-south through the pines, following the river from a distance. He checked the trail for sign and saw that it was riddled with the fresh tracks of both shod and unshod horses. He considered the tracks and decided that they should make camp farther to the west—staying well clear of the daytime comings and goings that seemed to be required of men preparing for battle. He leapt across the path, careful to leave no prints of his own in the dry dirt.

He heard the horse before he saw it, a drumbeat rolling down on him from the north. He lay flat in a palmetto grove with the longrifle, watching as an Indian in a black turban blew past, bareback on a brown and white pony. The rider had the reins clinched in his teeth, and a loose end of his turban streamed behind him like a banner, mingling with horsetail. The pony continued on but in its wake a cloud of dust had lifted, refracting the light that came glinting through the high green pines. Kau rose up and again jumped the path. The forest quieted and he turned for the river, off to gather Samuel and Xavier and Beah.

THE INDIAN HE had seen was a Lower Creek, Xavier figured. Hurrying to bring some news to the American ships.

THEY HIKED INLAND for at least a half mile. Xavier led and then came Samuel and Beah. Kau followed with a bough of cut pine, sweeping away what tracks the others had left. The sun was well up when they finally stopped and he caught up with them. They were standing in pure pine forest, a flat savanna of wiregrass and longleafs.

A warm wind blew and the trees sang their whispery song. It was very hot now. Xavier had stolen bread from the fort, that and some salty strips of dried meat. Kau passed his canteen, and they ate clustered beneath the shade of a stunted pine. Eventually Xavier and Samuel left to find shade of their own, and Kau laid himself down beside Beah, listening as the two men arranged their bodies under whatever particular shadow that they themselves were chasing.

MIDDAY. HE AWOKE to a feeling that something was out of balance. He left Beah sleeping and went to check on the others. A short ways off through the wiregrass he found Samuel on his back beneath the trunk of a fallen longleaf, the top hat perched over his eyes, a blanket from Beah spread out beneath him. The old pine was held up by only a few rotting branches, and Kau wondered how Samuel could ever have fallen asleep there—knowing that at any moment those branches might break and the tree would collapse like a deadfall, crushing any deer or bear or freed slave foolish enough to seek shelter underneath.

Nearby, hidden among palmettos, he found the flat nest of pine needles where Xavier had bedded down through the morning. But Xavier was gone. No Xavier, no haversack, no longrifle. No blanket, even. Kau cut for sign and found tracks leading east toward the river. He bent two thin saplings to mark this spot, then went back to wake Samuel and Beah.

BEAH WAS PACING around the stunted pine when he returned. She saw him and threw up her arms. "You off and left me," she said.

"Xavier gone."

A ray of sunlight split through the pine branches and settled on Beah's round face. She shielded her eyes with the flat of her hand. "Gone?"

Kau pointed toward the river. "He done snuck away."

"How come?"

"He say somethin to you?"

Beah shook her head. "Nothin. He took the canoe?"

He knelt to collect his saddlebags and the longrifle. "Don know," he said. "Come on."

SAMUEL WAS STILL asleep in his suicide shelter beneath the dead pine. Kau asked Beah to ease him out from under there, then he set off through the wiregrass alone. In soft and sandy places Xavier's boots left clear tracks that had just begun to crumble at their edges. Kau compared the progress of their deterioration against one of his own small footprints, and decided that Xavier had only been gone a few hours at most. He checked the prime on the longrifle. Xavier was a free man free to leave and go wherever—but to take the canoe from them would be something altogether different.

At the horse path he saw that Xavier had turned to the north, back in the direction of the fort. Kau quit the trail and went to the river. He found the canoe as they had left it and looked up at the sky. The sun had just begun its slow fall west. Kau closed his eyes but still saw orange and red and yellow.

He told Beah and Samuel what Xavier had done. Samuel said that he would pray for the boy, and then they all walked back to the river and sat down together on the bank. Beah was washing Samuel's feet in the shallows when they heard the faint boom of a flintlock echo down to them from the north.

They remained on the riverbank, listening. Samuel spoke first. "That has somethin to do with him," he said. "You know it do."

"Yes," said Beah. "We know it."

The day was still very bright and without clouds. Kau told himself that they should stay put until dark, push off at sunset and never look back at this place. But no. He stood up and Samuel nodded. "You'd be doin right."

Kau looked at Beah. "What you think?"

She sighed. "Xavier a good enough boy. Go on."

"You sure of that?"

"Yes."

He tried to give Samuel the longrifle but the old man refused. "No," he said. "That'd be useless to me."

"You jus keep safe," said Beah.

He took her hand. "I'm not back here fore dark, you two gotta go and leave on without me."

"Quit with that."

"Promise."

Beah turned away from him but gave a slight nod. "All right," she whispered. "All right, all right."

He walked over to Samuel. The old man squeezed his shoulder, and they both looked out from the bank at the river flowing past them. Kau told him how to find Israel's island, then explained that there was a shack there with a dry bed and a cistern filled high with rainwater, a buried cask of food. "Stay to the inside of that island till them ships are gone," he said. "Ain't nobody cept me ever gonna even know you there."

Samuel touched the brim of his gray hat. "I'm obliged," he said.

Kau forced his canteen into Samuel's hands, then took one long last look at Beah before he turned and went running into the forest.

He studied a short length of cut rope left lying in the thicket, then saw where a stray shot had slapped off the side of a pine.

Tracks and these scattered bits of sign told him much of the story:

Xavier walks the horse path for a long while before he is surprised by a rider on an unshod horse—the same black-turbaned man from early that morning, perhaps—coming hard from the south. Xavier hides himself in the sharp heart of a blackberry thicket, but then the rider at last spots the bootprints and dismounts in a rush. He is wearing moccasins, the rider, and has the pigeon-toed gait common among Indians. The rider hitches his horse beside the trail, then creeps forward carefully on foot. The path crosses through the blackberry thicket, but Xavier misses his ambush shot and is captured. His hands are tied and he is marched to the horse, made to mount first so that the rider can straddle him and then carry his prisoner north.

Kau began to jog the path, masking his own footprints within the tracks of the horse. Even under the weight of the saddlebags and the longrifle his breaths came easily. He felt the strength in his legs as he ran. He was an Ota again. An Ota, hunting.

Though slowed by his prisoner the rider kept a quick pace. The horse waded warm black creeks that drained into the river, and at those crossings not spanned by fallen-pine bridges Kau would shed his osnaburgs, then move forward with all of his belongings held high above his head.

After several miles he looked to the east and saw smoke collecting in the blue sky. He untangled Benjamin's sling and looped it around the wide trunk of a tall pine. The leather was at first stiff in his hands but soon it began to loosen slightly. He tied both ends behind him and leaned back, walking up the trunk in the manner of the Ota. Every few steps he would straighten his legs against the tree and jerk himself forward, releasing the tension on the sling so in that weightless instant he could throw his arms up and slap the sling higher still, gain purchase and ascend.

Soon he was in the canopy sitting astride a sturdy branch. The tree swayed in the breeze and something clicked *kuk kuk kuk*. Above, a gray squirrel—its shoulders bumpy with the larvae of botflies—was perched on the rim of a dead-twig nest and watching him. Kau shifted and the startled squirrel bolted off along the branch. It leapt for the next closest tree and went falling before its claws hit bark, scratched and then stuck. Kau moved again and the squirrel scrambled away, terrified.

In the treetop he was a surveying eagle. He looked to the south as if searching for Samuel and Beah, and he believed that he could see the curvature of the world. Portions of the federal road were sometimes hard and smooth, and one day Benjamin had taken a stick and drawn a big circle in the dust. Inside this circle the boy marked Yellowhammer and the Americas and Africa, the ocean Kau had sailed across. The boy then drew the sun and the planets and convinced him that the earth was round. And indeed—gazing upon the moon and the sun thereafter—it had seemed ridiculous ever to have thought differently.

Though of course by then he had also learned of the vastness of the world.

The forest thinned a short distance to the east. In a space between trees he saw the rising thread of wood smoke that was coloring the sky. He moved to another branch and spotted the British jack that flew over Garçon's fort. He shook his head. He was back. Twice now he had left the fort and twice now he had returned. He walked himself down the rough trunk of the pine, and then again took up the trail that would take him to Xavier.

ABOUT A MILE north of the fort, the sounds and smells of many men and many horses gathered made him realize that he had come upon the American soldiers, camped along the river. He figured that there would be sentries posted, and so when he glimpsed the first of these white men he quit the trail and climbed another tree—though a shorter one this time, a scrub oak growing alone in a thicket that separated the pines from the river.

He hid himself in the dense foliage of the oak, lying limb-draped as he watched the American encampment from a safe remove. At least a hundred soldiers were standing in a cluster, and a collection of Indians moved among them. He saw Xavier as well as the rider from that morning. The Indian in the black turban had cinched a belt around Xavier's neck and was now leading him about like a dog, a bell cow. The soldiers pushed at Xavier until he swung at them with tied hands and was tripped. He sat down hard in the dirt.

The American soldiers wore dark blue coats and high leather hats adorned with a single egret plume. Most of them seemed very young, younger even than Xavier. The Indian in the black turban waved them away, then he squatted down beside his prisoner. He was inspecting Xavier's longrifle when another soldier appeared. This man wore white trousers and a navy shortcoat, had a red sash tied around his wide waist. Thick brown sideburns ran down from under his black bicorn, framing his pink and glistening face. He was not very old himself, but from his dress Kau figured him for an officer.

The officer spoke to the Indian and then to Xavier, and when Xavier did not respond the Indian kicked at him until he screamed out in Spanish. The officer turned to the gathered soldiers, but they all shrugged in confusion. The officer spoke again, and soon a soldier presented with a shackle and a length of chain.

Xavier was secured by his ankle to the wheel of a nearby fieldpiece, and thereafter the soldiers seemed to lose interest in him. Kau watched as they began to peel away in groups of three and four and five, ambling over to their cook-fires to fix their separate suppers.

THE SUN WAS setting when the scalp of the sailor was found. The Indian in the black turban pulled it from Xavier's haversack and let out a whoop. Some soldiers hurried over and then the fat officer stepped out from his tent. The Indian tossed him the salted scalp, but the officer let it drop. He knelt in the dirt to examine the scalp, and when he finally rose up he seemed very angry. Again Xavier was interrogated, but again he would answer only in Spanish. Orders and five of the Indians left south in a long canoe. One of them was carrying the scalp. Kau watched the Indians paddle away and was reminded of Garçon's pigeons. Back and forth, back and forth.

HE HID THE longrifle and his saddlebags near the base of the oak. It was a dark night; clouds covered the moon. The sentries were spaced too far apart at their posts and—moving slowly with the breeze, pausing during the lulls—he was able to creep past them in time.

The soldiers were asleep in their tents. He went to the center of the camp and knelt down among the cannons. Xavier opened his eyes but kept silent. Kau tugged at the shackle and chain, then looked up. "This a fix," he said quietly.

"Leave me," whispered Xavier. "Please."

There came a noise from one of the tents—a soldier moaning in his sleep. Kau waited for the man's nightmare to play itself out and then spoke: "Why you done this?"

"You will think I am crazy."

"No. Go on."

"I heard him in a dream. The General."

"So? Evbody dream."

"He was calling for me." Xavier waved his hand in front of his own face. "Everything was black but I could hear his voice."

Kau grunted.

"You do not believe me," said Xavier.

"I believe you fine." Again Kau looked at the shackle. "We gonna figure this."

A breeze blew in from across the water, carrying a rank scent that teased his memory. Bear grease. He turned and saw two Indians coming over the top of the cannon. Kau put his hand to his knife as they leapt for him. The Indians were big men and soon he was dragged far away from Xavier and pinned. They began to mock him in Creek. So these were indeed Creeks, he realized. Lower Creeks. There came the shouts and curses of soldiers as the camp stirred, and he was thinking of the redsticks he had known—how remarkable it was that, in the end, they should come to share the exact same enemies.

HE SAT WITH an Indian on either side of him, his arms locked in their own. Torches had been lit, and a soldier was studying him.

The American had a scar that ran from high on his neck to the corner of his eye. He asked question after question but Kau would not to speak.

They were ringed by tired soldiers, and soon the officer came pushing through. He seemed upset. "You wake me to see a child?" he asked.

One of the Lower Creeks hooked a finger in Kau's mouth and pulled. His cut teeth were revealed and the soldiers began to murmur among themselves.

"Jesus," said the officer.

A tall soldier interrupted: "We caught him sniffing at the prisoner, sir."

The officer demanded his name, but Kau still would not answer. Finally the officer sighed and began walking back to his tent. "Then put him alongside the other one," he ordered. "We will see to him tomorrow."

THE SHACKLE WAS meant for a full-sized man, and placed around his ankle it slipped off his foot. After arguing on the matter the soldiers found that the iron coupling fit perfectly around his neck. He was chained beside Xavier to the wheel of the fieldpiece, and then the few remaining soldiers extinguished their torches and returned to their tents as well.

The sentries stationed around the perimeter of the camp were beyond earshot, and so once they were alone Xavier spoke out in the darkness. He asked after the others, and Kau told him that he hoped they were already on their way to Israel's island. For a moment Xavier was quiet and then he spoke again. "I am sorry for this," he said. "You should have left me to die."

OF COURSE TO be chained by his neck as a prisoner brought the killed Ota to his mind. He remembered his people lying in that dead tangle, connected by a necklace made of necklaces, and all he could think was broken necklace, broken necklace, broken necklace. A broken necklace he had buried with them, but that two days later scavengers had no doubt unearthed. Now nothing would remain but the chain itself, and he imagined that in some distant year it would be found by another make of people moving through his lost land. These trespassers would examine those rusted loops of iron and see no evidence that they had ever held lives at all.

William McIntosh and the Lower
Creeks — A failed negotiation —
A gift from Garçon

THE SUN ROSE hot over the trees and the brown river shined. He sat huddled beside Xavier in the tight shade of the fieldpiece, watching as the Americans emerged from their tents. For breakfast a cook had set water to boil in an enormous pair of footed kettles—one for coffee and another for a thin gruel of cornmeal. A soldier brought two bowls over to Kau and Xavier, then spit into each before setting them down.

Earlier this same soldier had traded with one of the Lower Creeks for Benjamin's hunting knife. He had long black hair, four dead teeth that sat like gray pills in his mouth. He dragged the point of the knife against Xavier's chest, then flicked the blade toward Kau. "Compared to you, he's lucky," he said.

"*¿Qué?*" said Xavier.

"He might get to be a slave again, *amigo*." The soldier laughed. "You just a dead man."

Kau lifted his bowl and began to eat. Others came to sit atop the cannons and watch them. There were here and there questions that went unanswered and soon the talk turned to other matters and curiosities. Kau kept his head bowed but was listening.

A soldier claimed to have seen Dolley Madison up close once. She brushed against him on a muddy street in Washington. Her dugs were as big as wineskins. . . . The fat officer's name was Clinch. A born leader, him. . . . Chinamen saw 1816 as the year of the fire rat. They did that, named their years for animals and elements. . . . Chief McIntosh and his Lower Creeks were camped across the river. Clinch had met with him and two lesser chiefs just that morning. . . . Up north the weather had turned backward, and some were already calling this the year without a summer.

The sunburnt soldiers laughed as one of them began to joke about frozen fire rats.

NIGHT CAME, LEFT, and then came again. At times he would fall asleep with his arm pinned beneath him so that when he woke it would feel numb and useless—like now his arm belonged to some other man—and so he would rise and wait for the blood to flow back down to the tips of his tingling fingers.

XAVIER HAD USED the scuffed heel of his boot to scratch a hole in the soft dirt, and into this shallow pit the two of them would aim their piss so that to the blind creatures of the world below their hot urine must have seemed like summer rain. Kau watched as duped earthworms wriggled to the surface to writhe and struggle. At times he and Xavier would speak in whispers, but for the most part they were silent.

AT DAYBREAK HE heard the roar of cannons to the southeast, and later a soldier rode into camp and was met by the officer Clinch. From the piecemeal of the man's drawling report Kau learned that McIntosh and the Lower Creeks had surrounded the fort after sunset—and then at dawn the Indians had moved through the wiregrass and palmetto and pine in a false charge, whooping as they crossed the burnt cutover separating the forest from the fort. The American soldier had watched this from across the river. He told Clinch that the fort's cannons fired and the bluffing Indians had been pushed back. The negro soldiers cheered their retreat, and soon the world was again quiet other than the callings of scattered Indians meant to mimic nature. The soldier laughed at that. "Hell, Lieutenant," he said. "Even I know turkeys are done gobbling come July."

THE NEXT MORNING he looked on as the five Lower Creeks returned from the south in the canoe. Clinch invited them into his tent, and Kau imagined the news they would be bringing him from that man Loomis, the commander of the American convoy. That there had been a massacre of a watering party; that an American had been taken prisoner; that it had been a tiny dancing negro who had lured them into the ambush.

AFTER A SHORT while the five Indians emerged from the tent and then Clinch appeared. The officer stood a long time alone at its entrance, and Kau saw that the man was watching him and Xavier. Finally orders were issued, and a soldier brought a brass bugle to his lips, blowing seven short notes that were quickly answered by the pounding of drums to the east. The separate instruments of the separate armies spoke back and forth to one another in a confusion of codes, until at last three figures appeared on the emerald bank of the opposite shore. An eye-patched soldier pointed. "There they is again," he said. "The chiefs."

The Indians swam the wide river, and Clinch greeted them on the bank. They had stripped down to their breechcloths, and though two of the chiefs were shaven-headed like most of the Lower Creeks in the camp, the third man had thick, reddish hair and was lighter in color than his companions.

Kau soon realized that the large mixed-blood was McIntosh himself. He was at least ten years older than Clinch, tall and muscled with the sharp features of a hawk. McIntosh nodded to Clinch, then requested blankets with which they could dry themselves. He spoke English and sounded just like what the whites would call a gentleman.

THE CHIEFS REMAINED in Clinch's tent through the morning, and Kau listened as two nearby soldiers whittled pine knots and talked. After a while they began to speak of Chief McIntosh. His mother had been a Lower Creek, his father a Tory from Savannah. He had led the Indian troops under Jackson during the Creek War, was commissioned a goddamn American general after Horseshoe Bend. Among the redskins he was not William McIntosh but White Warrior. The soldiers laughed. "General White Warrior," one said, his head shaking. "You believe that?"

But this made great sense to Kau—that a man moving between worlds would require a name for each. The two soldiers left and he leaned back against the hard fieldpiece. He began to imagine Samuel and Beah together on Israel's island, watching the ships. A tired old man and a frightened woman. Xavier asked him what he was thinking and he told him.

Xavier shaded his eyes from the sun. "You really think they could have made it?"

Kau shrugged and the shackle pinched at his neck. "I don't know."

"That would be a miracle."

"Yes."

Xavier went quiet and Kau looked up. Clinch and the three Lower Creek chiefs had come out from the tent. The four men were staring at them, and it was clear that some course of action had been decided. They stepped closer, and Clinch spoke to McIntosh. "Perhaps take the small one," he said. "He should be easier for you to control."

Xavier covered his mouth with his hand and began to whisper. "I heard of you years ago," he said quickly. "Do you remember me telling you that?"

Kau nodded.

"I do not think that was an accident."

Two soldiers approached and Kau covered his own mouth. "No," he replied. He started to say more but there was no time. He touched Xavier's hand as the soldiers removed the shackle from around his neck, and then he was pulled away.

HE WAS GIVEN over to McIntosh and the two lesser chiefs. They bound his wrists with twisted lengths of leather and then placed him in a canoe borrowed from Clinch. As they pushed free from the beach he looked back and saw Xavier slumped against the field-piece. His head was between his knees; his shoulders were rocking. The canoe drifted farther and farther away. There was a small comfort in this, he thought—that after all those angry years as a slave perhaps he had found his way into Xavier's heart, made a man he hardly knew sorry to see him carried off to die.

THEY CROSSED THE river and he was tethered to a tupelo as the chiefs collected their hidden weapons and adornments. It was a very hot day, but still they changed into buckskin leggings dyed scarlet and beaded moccasins. Over their breechcloths they pulled long hunting shirts striped white, yellow and red, cinching them at the waist with wide leather belts.

Three blue scarves were draped over a snarl of muscadine that stretched between twin pines. McIntosh took one of the long scarves into his hands and then wound the silk tightly around his head. The other chiefs did the same, and as Kau watched them tie their shiny turbans he was reminded of a white-robed man he had seen executed by the Spanish at the African barracoons. The more he saw of the world the more he was staggered by its congruities.

THEY WENT EAST in a single-file line. McIntosh led them through the abandoned farms and fields and pastures of Garçon's soldiers, then they entered the shade of the pine forest and turned south. Each of the chiefs held a longrifle in one hand and a turkey-feather fan in the other. They worked these fans steadily as they walked, so that among their bright colors and preening ways Kau came to feel as if he were being guarded over by some strange race of fluttering birdmen.

LOWER CREEKS WERE sprinkled through the flatlands in small clusters. Hobbled horses pawed at the lime wiregrass, while others scratched their ribs against flinty pines. Braves stood among the trees, staring—then ten rushed forward with their wooden war-clubs raised. The chiefs calmed them, and then the braves fell in behind.

They moved on, continuing south. Soon they entered into a part of the forest he recognized from his wanderings. The fort was near. At a creek crossing someone fired a flintlock at them. Smoke lingered within the branches of a distant oak like a fallen cloud, and as it slowly cleared he saw a negro dangle one-handed from a limb and then drop. Four braves splashed through the creek to pursue the sniper, but McIntosh called them back. One of the braves was wearing a loose white shirt and McIntosh asked him for it. The brave gave the shirt over to him, and then McIntosh wrapped it around the end of a broken branch. A dog barked to the west as McIntosh forced the branch into Kau's tied hands. The dog barked again and they angled toward it, Kau leading.

They skirted the thicket of greenbrier that ringed the dome swamp. Kau thought of the Choctaw on the platform, dead and rotting, and at times he could even smell him. He held the branch high above his head and waved the white shirt. Twice more snipers dropped from trees and ran, but no other shots were fired.

Finally he saw it—the fort. The gate was shut, and soldiers were watching from the bastions. The Indians halted at the tree line, then pushed him forward out into the burnt cutover. He was alone and in the open, holding his flag. He spotted Garçon a hundred yards off, standing atop one of the bastions with a spyglass trained on him. Kau stared back and saw Garçon turn and shout down orders. The British jack was lowered to half-mast on the distant flagstaff and then raised again. Their signal, he realized, to approach.

McIntosh and the two lesser chiefs left their longrifles with the ten braves and stepped out into the cutover as well. Unarmed, they followed Kau across the black and broken ground. He looked back and saw the braves watching them from the pinewoods. The Ota had not been real fighters in comparison and so this amazed him— that men who lived to kill other men could also have it in them to trust the other, to live under some code of temporary peace. A peace they would refuse to break—not only for their own benefit, but also for the benefit of those killers who would come after them. He once again found himself thinking of a chain.

He could see Garçon more clearly now. The General was in full uniform and had his sword strapped to his side. His oiled hair fell down from under his tricorn in a loose and untied river. They stopped at the edge of the moat, and Garçon called down to him from the bastion, ignoring McIntosh and the other two chiefs. "Caught again?" he asked.

Kau quit his silence. "Yes," he said. "Me and Xavier both."

"So you do speak," said McIntosh.

They went to the bridge and the gate opened. Kau saw a negro crowd gathered in the sun. He blinked and then coughed as the stench of livestock and sewage washed over him. Three frightened soldiers were sent walking across the cutover—toward the waiting braves—before the chiefs would agree to enter the fort. McIntosh made to include Kau with these collateral prisoners, but Garçon spoke out. "No," he said. "He comes along."

GARÇON LED THEM inside his tent and Kau stood by the table, his hands still bound in front of him. Garçon went to him. "Are you hurt?" he asked.

Kau shook his head. "No."

"But of course you are not well either."

"No."

Garçon walked behind the table and faced the three chiefs. In their striped shirts and blue turbans and scarlet leggings they looked like magicians from one of Benjamin's fairytales, the wise men described in Samuel's Bible stories, those three kings from the East.

"I know Creek," said Garçon.

McIntosh spoke: "English will do."

"Wonderful." Garçon sat and then began to drum his fingers on the tabletop one two three four, one two three four. "You have come here to surrender?"

"The reverse."

Kau saw Garçon's eyes narrow. "I have heard of you," he said. "White Warrior, is it?"

"If you prefer."

"I believe I do."

McIntosh lowered himself into a chair as well, but the two lesser chiefs remained standing behind him. He said something to them in Creek and they left the tent. There was a silver knife on the table, and Kau watched as Garçon plucked at the handle with his fingernail. The knife spun like a blurring chance wheel, and no one spoke until it finally slowed and then settled. The blade was pointing at Garçon and he shuddered. "Well then," he said. "Your terms?"

McIntosh talked of Clinch and his soldiers across the river, Loomis and his sailors in the bay. He brushed dust from his leggings. "Surrender and I promise you will be treated fairly."

"Just me?"

"I do not know really."

"So an offer of nothing." Garçon sipped water from a glass, then twisted a finger in his long hair. "Let us begin again," he said. "Under whose authority do you come here to negotiate with me?"

McIntosh sighed. "The United States and its army."

"But you are not in America."

"And you are not in England."

Garçon looked over at Kau. "What do you think?"

He could hear a quiet sound coming from behind the white curtain that hid Garçon's quarters—a girl, whimpering—but if McIntosh could hear her he did not show it. Both men were watching him. The crying stopped and Kau spoke: "I think you gonna die if you fight them."

"Quite correct," said McIntosh. "Very good, you."

"And that is why you left us?" asked Garçon.

"In part."

"Yet now you are in a worse situation than me, true?"

"No better."

"And what of Beah and that Samuel?"

"Gone. Dead."

Garçon nodded. "And my Xavier? You took him from me, remember?"

"He made his own mind."

"And then changed it perhaps?"

"He did."

"And where has that led him?"

"Caught like me."

"I see."

McIntosh interrupted: "There is another matter for us to discuss."

"Then speak of it," said Garçon.

"I have been told that your men attacked a party of American sailors."

"Attacked, you say?"

"A prisoner was taken, an Edward Daniels."

"Oh, my. Poor boy."

"Indeed," said McIntosh.

"Quite amazing."

"In what way?"

"That your armies would know to be waiting here in the wilderness. That they would anticipate the disappearance of this sailor. Amazing."

Kau saw McIntosh wipe at his eyes. The man looked tired. "Just say what you mean," said McIntosh. "There is no point to these games you are playing."

"Fine." Garçon walked his fingers along the length of his sleeve. "I am saying that your Daniels was bait on a hook. I am saying that this is not my game but yours."

"What do you know of him?" McIntosh leaned forward. "Men will live or die based upon what you say to me today."

"I would agree," said Garçon.

There was a pause and again Kau could hear quiet crying from behind the curtain.

McIntosh stood. "What is your decision?"

Garçon rose up himself. He walked behind Kau and let his hands rest down on his shoulders. "Tell your American masters this, White Warrior."

"Yes?"

"Tell them that this is a British fort occupied by British subjects. Tell them that our presence here on Spanish soil is of no concern to anyone but King George and King Ferdinand. Tell them that they have allowed for the invasion of a sovereign nation."

McIntosh laughed. "And yet you are no more a Spaniard than you are a British general."

"You call yourself an American general, do you not?"

"I do indeed."

"And yet your mother was an Indian whore."

McIntosh's face pinkened. He took a step toward Garçon but then turned to leave. "I will see you again very soon," he said.

"Wait," said Garçon. "You have already forgotten what you came for." He spoke quickly in Spanish, and Kau watched as the curtain rippled and then parted. A child in a white dress moved forward, a dark young girl with red and swollen eyes. She was balancing a human skull on a flat velvet pillow, and she placed the pillow on the table and then left as she came. The skull had been boiled clean and bleached, and Garçon tapped at the scraped bone and smiled. "So," he said to McIntosh, "do you think that maybe this might be your Edward?"

The parley ended with the appearance of the skull, and Kau thought that McIntosh seemed more saddened than angered. McIntosh told Garçon that the Americans' prisoners would receive no better, but Garçon only nodded and said, "I should hope not, White Warrior."

Garçon then went to Kau and took his hands into his own. "I am very sorry for you," he said, and Kau felt a piece of cool metal press against his palm as Garçon spoke to him. "But I could not keep on saving you forever, my strange, strange friend."

THE CROWD OUTSIDE was still gathered, and the cranberry coats of the men made their wives and sons and daughters look faded in contrast. An illusion: uniformed soldiers moving among phantoms draped in spent fabrics, apparitions shrouded in shabby gray clothes like he himself wore.

The witnesses split into silent halves as the three chiefs led him toward the gate. He saw a dozen of the renegade Choctaws. Pelayo and Elisenda. Marcela and Ramona. The twins watched him move past, and they seemed unsure of whether he was still favored by Garçon. One girl sneered at him as the other girl cowered.

Juaneta. He saw her last. She stood closest to the gate and was again wearing her green dress. She bit her lower lip as he went by, and in that moment she was his dead wife Janeti. This did something to him, and inside he felt a tearing, a breaking. At their last supper together Garçon had spoken to him and Xavier on the subject of love, claiming that he had studied on it. "You see," he had lectured, "there is really no such thing. A white man lusted after someone and invented the idea of love. It helped to justify the fool he had become."

But it was from Samuel that Kau had heard the word first—the old man explaining his feelings for his own Lord Jesus. Later, Benjamin would say he loved his dead mother without ever having met her. Of all Kau had learned in this second world that word was one of the few things that made sense to him. A word that tried to explain how a man could look at a girl and see a grown woman—Janeti—the wife taken from him so long ago. And perhaps it also helped explain why he knew he would never forget his last glimpse of Xavier or Samuel or Beah. The face of the dying boy. His daughter Tufu begging him to dance for her. His infant son Abeki smiling up at him. Love. What other unnamed forces might exist? Forces that once defined by words would wrap themselves around his mind and change the way he saw all else thereafter?

THE CHIEFS CROSSED over the bridge of the fort and then signaled to the braves hidden in the pinewoods. The three soldiers they had been guarding appeared, and the released men raced over the cutover—running, running, running—swinging wide around the chiefs as they passed, their eyes big and white, the dry ash erupting beneath their boots.

The broken tip of a knife blade, no bigger than a small coin. As the soldiers went by Kau lifted his tied hands to his face and slipped it into his mouth. The cold metal warmed on his tongue as he followed McIntosh forward. They were halfway across the cutover when the braves began whooping from the pines. McIntosh stopped, and Kau turned with him. The British jack was being lowered inside the fort, and one of the lesser chiefs spoke to the others in Creek. "Look," he said. "That man is a coward after all."

But then the jack was raised for the third time that day, and fastened above it now was a new flag, a red flag more crimson than the coats of the soldiers even. The pigeons were released to circle—by Garçon himself, Kau knew—and then the soldiers watching from the bastions began to cheer and shake their flintlocks. On the high flagstaff behind them the flag of no surrender hung limp in the dead summer sky, smothering the nation banner that was suspended beneath it.

Cranes—An escape—
The future glimpsed—An obliteration

McIntosh and the ten braves led Kau back toward the section of pinewoods where the Lower Creeks were camped. The two lesser chiefs had already left to tell Clinch what had happened at the fort, and Kau now pictured the deadly news moving like a stone skipped down the river—a rock traveling from Garçon to McIntosh to Clinch to Loomis.

It was dark when the lesser chiefs finally returned from across the river, but from the stump where he was made to sit Kau could not hear the substance of their report. Regardless, he knew there was a fair chance that he would be ordered tortured or even executed. He sucked on the blade hidden in his mouth and watched.

HE WAS WRONG. Although some of the young braves taunted him, his captors did not appear eager to abuse him, and—for the moment, at least—any orders to that effect were ignored. The fate of the watering party seemed to mean very little to these Lower Creeks, and so for a prisoner they treated him well enough—better, he was certain, than the Americans were now treating Xavier.

McIntosh retired to his bedroll hidden somewhere in the wiregrass, and Kau saw one of the lesser chiefs select three young braves to serve as his guards. They initiated a rotation—two sleeping while the third kept watch, a single fierce and serious boy who would occasionally strike at the air with his war-club as if challenging him to run. Kau closed his eyes and hoped that somehow while he slept he would know not to swallow Garçon's blade, cut the inside of his throat, choke on his own blood.

AT DAWN HE was brought only a tin mug of water for his breakfast. He spit the blade into his palm and found that it fit perfectly there, that even with his hand open flat the sharp bit of metal remained in place. He drank the warm water down, and soon McIntosh moved them all to within sight of the fort.

A LONG TETHER connected his tied hands to the trunk of a young pine growing near the edge of the cutover. The waiting Indians stretched out along the tree line, and he juggled the blade throughout the morning—from his palm to his mouth and then back again, from his left hand to his right. A magician in his movements as he watched the dark fort.

AT SOLAR NOON a pair of gray cranes landed in the blackened cut-over between the forest and the fort. The birds began to scratch for field mice, and Kau saw that McIntosh was looking at them as well. A pair of braves spoke to the chief and he nodded.

The two braves crept from the pines to the field edge and took aim with longrifles. On some whispered count between them they fired and the cranes toppled. The shot birds began flapping and clouds of ash were sent rising into the hot air. From the bastions of the fort came the sound of soldiers laughing, and then one fired at a crippled crane but missed. McIntosh cut Kau loose from the pine and told him to stand. "Get them," he said.

At first Kau gave no response, but then he decided there was no longer any advantage to silence. Because of Garçon they now knew that he could speak, that he could understand. "For what?" he asked.

McIntosh pointed toward the cranes. "Go," he said. "Now."

Kau stepped out into the field, his tied hands clasped in front of him. He saw the soldiers in the bastions level their muskets, but they did not fire. He moved forward and McIntosh called out to him. "Run," he said, "and you will be shot down as well."

And so he walked slowly across the cutover until he had reached the fallen birds. The cranes seemed almost as long as he was. He slipped Garçon's blade into his mouth and stood over them. Their sleek heads were white at the cheeks and crowned rust red at the forehead. One was alive and the other was dead.

The wounded crane lay still in the ash and the dirt, watching him with a wet and yellow eye. He kicked at the bird with his bare foot, and suddenly it rose up on stilt legs like a crumpled puppet lifted and began to lope away, a broken wing dragging. The soldiers were laughing again; he could hear them as he gave chase. The panicked crane ran until it had reached the moat of the fort and then, trapped, it turned and waited for him.

Even more laughter from above. He came at the crane and it leapt high into the air and then fell. A toe raked down his chest, tearing his shirt and his skin. He staggered backwards and the crane advanced hissing, its long neck weaving as it pecked at him. The bird's dark beak looked as sharp as a snapped buck tine.

And then there was a burst of feathers and the crane lay dead; a single shot had been fired. Kau looked across the moat and saw Garçon standing with the soldiers atop the near bastion, a smoking longrifle in his hands. McIntosh's hundred and fifty Indians had stepped from the pines with their own flintlocks trained on the fort, but in the end they did not engage. Kau collected the dead cranes and walked back toward the tree line. Both birds seemed to be mature adults, but one was well larger than the other. A mating pair, he figured. Sweat had seeped into the cut on his chest, and he winced at the salt sting of it.

HE HAD BEEN tethered again to the same young pine and now sat watching as McIntosh and the two lesser chiefs decorated their turbans with the longest and most perfect plumes from the cranes. The braves took what remained, then set sections of the skinned breasts to roast over a bed of glowing embers. At the insistence of McIntosh he was given a portion of the crane for his supper.

He tore at the meat with his teeth, and it came off in shreds in his mouth. The taste was close to liver and he wondered if this, here, would be the last meal of his life.

IT WAS NEARLY dark when he finished eating, and he could hear the negro soldiers singing over the crickets and the cicadas, the trillings of toads. Above him he saw a large spider—speckled in oranges, browns and yellows like Indian corn—suspended between the low branches of the pine. Kau slapped the spider to the ground, then gathered up its web and spread his torn shirt open.

He sat with the balled web in his lap, picking it free of mosquitoes and gnats and moths. Once the web was mostly clean he pressed it carefully against his bleeding chest, arranging the spider-silk across the crane-cut to help clot the wound. A new collection of braves had come to guard him through the night. They built a watch-fire and were just as vigilant as the three who had served before them.

AT SOME LATE hour McIntosh appeared. The fort had gone quiet, but the forest was even louder now. Kau was slumped against the small pine, and when he pushed at the tree it would flex and then push back against him. McIntosh motioned to one of the braves, and the guard stirred his sleeping companions.

After the three braves were gone McIntosh knelt down before him. "What do you know of the fort?" he asked.

Kau saw the evicted spider emerge from the shadows beyond the light of the watch-fire, then creep carefully across the forest floor, searching for another tree that it might claim for itself. "What you mean?" he asked.

"How many soldiers are there?"

"You saw."

"A hundred?"

"Maybe."

"And some Indians?"

"About thirty Choctaws."

"No Seminoles? No Red Stick Creeks?"

"They all done left off already."

"So then no more than a hundred negroes and those thirty Choctaws?"

Kau nodded. "For fighters. But they is women there, too. Children."

"And what about cannon? Powder?"

"Looked to be plenty of both."

"You deserted?"

"Deserted?"

"Left without asking."

"I never joined up with them."

"Hardly, dancer."

McIntosh stood and placed a green log on the fire that sent sparks chasing sparks up through the trees to then die among the planets and stars. The wet wood hissed and Kau was reminded of the angry crane. McIntosh knelt back down but said nothing. After a while Kau wondered whether the chief had somehow fallen asleep in a crouch. The blade was hidden between the fingers of his right hand, and Kau considered it. Suppose he cut himself loose and attacked this big kneeling man, could he kill him?

He glanced down at his tied hands and then up again. McIntosh was watching him now. The chief removed his blue turban, and without it he looked more like a white man than an Indian. McIntosh ran a finger across his teeth and then pointed at him. "Tell me something about where you are from," he said. "Tell me about Africa."

"What of it?"

"How long has it been since you were taken from there?"

"Five years. At leas five years."

"So you know your years as well?"

"Do now."

McIntosh unraveled the turban in his hands until it was just a long blue scarf again. "Were you a warrior in Africa?" he asked.

"A hunter."

"And your people—all of them were small, small like you?"

"Yes, they was all jus like me."

For a second time McIntosh lowered his head and was quiet.

Kau watched him for a moment and then spoke. "Was you at Horseshoe Bend?" he asked.

McIntosh looked up at him. "I was."

"Across the river? Blockin the retreat for that Jackson?"

"How do you know this?"

"I was caught by redsticks once. I heard them tell of it."

"Well, then I hope they also told you that we killed them like dogs."

Kau nodded. "Morning Star. You knew him?"

"One of their supposed prophets." McIntosh pointed toward the fort. "A fraud just like your British general." He stood. "Do you have anything else to ask me?"

Kau shook his head and McIntosh walked away. Once he was gone the three braves moved back in from the shadows with their war-clubs and longrifles, appearing so quickly that Kau thought that perhaps they had been listening the entire time. The braves checked his restraints, then two went off to sleep while the other sat and watched him.

IN THE MORNING came reports that the gunboats had sailed upriver with the bay winds. He overheard the braves talking. Clinch had marched his men south to meet with Loomis. The American sailors and soldiers were together now, camped just a few river bends below the fort. Soon.

THOUGH THEY FOUGHT on the side of the white men, like with most Indians there were ways in which these Lower Creeks reminded him of the Ota. What a white man might persecute an Indian might celebrate, and so as these braves waited for the assault to come they examined him the same as McIntosh had. They were fascinated by his size, his cut teeth. He heard them say that there was good sense in it—his smallness. A young brave shared a story from his grandfather, a story about how at one time their own people had not been much larger, that it was only when the white men came that the ancestors had begun to grow.

Kau considered this and thought on the surviving bands of Ota that might still roam the forest. He wondered whether the very same thing could be happening right then in Africa—an entire tribe of people, growing.

THE SUN BORE down on the pinewoods as they waited. He stared out across cutover at the fort. On occasion careless soldiers would appear atop the bastions, and the braves who believed themselves marksmen would ask McIntosh for a chance at them. The chief refused, and it became clear to Kau that the role McIntosh was to play in this battle was not altogether different than the function he had served at Horseshoe Bend—stay close but let the American soldiers lead the fight.

THAT NIGHT THERE was hardly a moon. The eyes of Benjamin's laughing man were hidden, and Kau wondered what they now watched from the shadows. He pulled his ripped and bloodied shirt up over his nose to protect his face and neck from the mosquitoes that swarmed around him. His hands were tucked into the waistband of his pants, his feet buried in a mound of pine needles. He heard some of the braves begin to play a courage game, taking turns rushing forward to splash their hands in the water of the moat. He listened as they went off in a hollering relay—a man leaving, a man returning, a man leaving, a man returning—daring the soldiers to fire upon them.

The three guards collected around the watch-fire, and Kau feigned sleep as they began to argue. Finally two of them ran off yelping to join in the game, and the remaining brave sat with his back to him and sulked. Before long the fire began to die down, and Kau decided at last that he would run as well. He had a black night and a failing fire, a distracted guard and a means to cut himself free. To linger any longer would be foolish. He thought of the Ota parable. The story of the Kesa farmer who died demanding that the forest provide him with more than he ever truly needed.

He spit the blade into his tied hands. When forced, the thin metal could be made to fit between his filed front teeth. He wedged the blade into place, then tasted blood from torn gums as he lowered his head and began to chip quietly at the leather binding his wrists.

HIS GUARD WAS still focused on the gaming Indians, and so Kau kept on with the blade until the leather had been sawed down to a single stretched thread. He pulled the blade from his teeth just as one of the negro soldiers finally fired a frustrated shot into the darkness. Kau spotted the muzzle-flash in the bastion before he heard the powder blast. His guard charged a short ways out into the cutover and began to shake his war-club at the fort. For a moment Kau was alone. He jerked his wrists apart, and the bindings broke and then unraveled, releasing him from the tree.

The dome swamp, he decided. He would make for the shelter of the dome swamp. He dropped Garçon's blade and stood, hurrying away from the fire and into the forest. The wiregrass was damp with dew and occasional palmettos stabbed at him. In a small clearing he stepped over a sleeping Indian. The man grunted but did not wake, and then from the field edge came frantic screaming—the guard announcing his escape. The forest erupted and soon Indians were moving all about. Kau began to run, and twice he brushed against braves rushing past him in the night.

From the fort came the shoutings of the negro soldiers, and Kau realized that the clamoring of the Indians had Garçon's men preparing for an attack. A volley of their musket balls slammed into the trees, but over all of this he could hear McIntosh, calling out the names of the braves who would go and hunt him. Kau stopped and saw pitch torches being lit. He turned and continued running but then collided with a pine and stumbled. He sniffed the air as he limped on, following the faint scent of decay that would lead him to the dome swamp.

FOUR LIT TORCHES came floating through the pines, and he stood against the high wall of greenbrier that separated him from the dome swamp, watching them approach. The braves were hunched over and cutting for sign. One called out, and at the sound the others collapsed in closer so that, pressed together, their torches seemed to form one giant ball of fire in the night. The braves looked up, faces aglow as all four stared in his direction. When they moved toward him they moved in synch, low and with their footfalls in rhythm—longrifles in their right hands, torches in their left.

The braves advanced and he dropped down to his knees. A rabbit trail led into the dome swamp. He wormed his way through the briers and then went crawling onto the mud. The black water was reflecting starlight and he lay back in it, filling his lungs with air. He came to a float. He was suspended. The water seemed warmer than the air even. He stretched out his arms, and with slow steady strokes he began to ease himself deeper into the dome swamp.

The water flowed past his ears and he could hear nothing. His soaked osnaburgs pulled at him and so he slid his shirt over his head, then unbuckled Benjamin's belt and struggled free from his pants. With the belt abandoned and sunk everything he had taken from the boy was gone now. He closed his eyes and let his hands guide his naked body through the maze of cypress and tupelo, careful not to leave any sign that the braves might spot with their torches—no bloomings of disturbed silt, no bent saplings or dampened trunks.

As he drifted he wished that he could stay like this for all time, a fetus in a womb, and he could feel the water washing him. A mosquito landed on his cheek and his eyes flickered open. A meteor streaked across the sky, and he tracked it through the hovering tangle of branches. He drifted on a little farther, then stood up slowly in the shallow water and listened to the loud collapse of briers. The four braves, coming for him. He hid within a cluster of young tupelos as they went sloshing past, their torches held high. They were chanting, and he tried to make out the words they were singing but could not.

Suddenly the chanting ceased. There was silence and then from the heart of the dome swamp came the sound of something heavy splashing down into the water. The sound, he realized, of the dead Choctaw's enemies pushing him free from his platform forever.

HE STAYED HIDDEN within the tight circle of tupelos. For a long time he watched the torches of the braves travel back and forth until finally they burned to nothing and all was blackness. Crouched low in the water, his head plastered with lilies, he had the sensation not of being caged by the tupelos but of being housed, protected. He slid his tongue past his lips and tasted the water, slow-drinking the sour swamp like a lizard, like a snake. It was quiet and dark, but still he could sense the four braves nearby and listening, waiting for him to make some mistake of sound.

AT SUNRISE THE motionless braves were revealed, and with the light they separated and again began moving through the swamp, flipping dead logs and staring up into trees. Fatigue and frustration had made them hurried and careless, and several times they peered in among his tupelos but did not see him.

HOURS PASSED, THEN late in the morning the braves met as if to discuss the status of their hunt. The shortest of the four was punching at the water when the roll of drums sounded from somewhere in the pinewoods. The braves all went still, their heads cocked and listening—and then the drums grew louder and he watched as they turned toward them, filing off in a line like the called hogs of a farmer.

ONCE HE WAS certain that the braves had left him he emerged from the tupelos. The drums had quit and he felt himself calming. The dense saplings dwindled as he neared the center of the dome swamp, and he waded in among the mature trees until at last he arrived at the Choctaw platform. The dead man was gone, but the air still stank of him and his crude scaffold remained. Kau circled beneath the platform three separate times before his foot collided with the tight cocoon of blanket and hide that held the warrior's corpse.

And then his foot settled upon something smooth and solid. He ducked below the surface of the water and came up holding the bone club. It had found its way back to him, or he to it, and felt almost hot in his hands. He heard the whispered voice of the redstick prophet, then closed his eyes as the first vision came:

He sees an endless cotton field. Slaves move through the rows and the last of them is Pelayo. An overseer slaps at him with a whip and says, Hurry up now, nigger. Hurry up now.

He sees the American encampment. The soldiers are gone. Xavier's body hangs from an oak branch, and the salted scalp of the sailor has been pushed deep into his mouth.

He sees Garçon made to stand before a line of American soldiers. They are holding muskets, and Clinch is pacing behind them. The General is blindfolded and his hands are tied. Clinch says, Fire, and Garçon's chest is blown apart.

He sees a very old man on a beach. His father, alive many years beyond his African death. White men in dull gray uniforms are approaching him. His father is holding a bow, but when he makes to draw it the soldiers laugh and shoot him down.

HIS SKIN HAD cooled slightly and so he opened his eyes. The shadow of the platform now covered him, and he pinned the bone club against his neck and climbed up onto it. He looked around. There was a gap in the canopy above and the sun bore down on him. All around him the swamp was glistening.

He set down the bone club and sprawled out naked in the sun, drying in the heat as he thought on his situation. If the braves came for him again he would hear them in the water and have time to hide himself. They had lost whatever advantage they had held over him. The dome swamp was his alone.

He began to ponder the visions that Morning Star had decided to share with him from the other side. So Xavier and Garçon would die badly, and Pelayo would be a slave again. But what to make of that glimpse of his father? A man he had already seen die once before? The strange bow his father had been holding fixed in his mind. The yew stave, he realized. He had not seen his father but he himself as an old man. He had seen his own death, and though it frightened him he now wanted to see more. So maybe he would survive this day and this dome swamp. But what of Beah? Samuel? What else might the prophet have to tell him? He touched the bone club to his cut chest and again closed his eyes:

It is a crisp autumn day. The sky is blue. A forest, aflame with color, stretches from horizon to horizon. In the center of all of this an enormous granite mountain, treeless and smooth, sits like a tooth. Thousands of Indians stand upon it. They are cheering a game between boys. Young braves not so much older than Benjamin scramble by the dozen over and across the surface of the mountain. They charge over fields of bare rock, splash through clear pools of rainwater. On either end of the mountain stands a high wooden pole pinned between boulders. Atop each pole is mounted the skull of a buffalo. The boys all carry a pair of stout sticks affixed with webbed baskets. They are chasing a small deerskin ball. One of the boys towers over the others. That is me, says the voice. Morning Star. The young prophet is from a western village; his team represents the setting sun. Along a wide crack in the stone, yellow daisies are blooming. Morning Star bursts through the flowers and the air fills with pollen. He has the ball cradled in one of his sticks; he is being chased by the Rising Sun. They are almost upon him when he spins and flings the ball. It goes streaking across the sky. For a moment both the crowd and the players are silent, all of them watching the tiny ball make for the horned skull staring back down at them from atop the distant pole.

BUT HE LEARNED nothing of the fate of Samuel and Beah. After that final vision—one of the past, not of the future—his mind went dark, and so he set the bone club down. He was very tired, and he slept until late in the day. When he awoke he shimmied to the top of one of the tall cypress trees that supported the platform, and then he sat in the crook of a branch. The crane-cut had opened and blood ran down his chest. He could see the fort. Negro soldiers had congregated on the artillery bank, and they seemed to be looking out across the river. He followed their gaze. There were flashes of movement along the opposite bank—American soldiers taking positions behind trees and stumps and logs—and he remained in the cypress, watching soldiers watch soldiers until night fell and the world went dark.

THE LOWER CREEKS seemed through with hunting him, and so he considered slipping away in the night, leaving the dome swamp to head south yet again. He doubted that they would ever resume their search for him. With all the prisoners they and the Americans would soon have in shackles what could one tiny man be to them? Twice he waded to the brier edge of the dome swamp, but each time he turned back. The truth was that he needed to see the battle, had to know for certain how this would finally end. He climbed up onto the platform once more.

Awaiting the assault on this fort reminded him of another sort of fort—one he had helped Benjamin build atop a ridge that ran behind Yellowhammer. Their fort had stacked-stone walls and a swept-dirt floor, a sod roof that sprouted sticky green weeds. When the innkeeper's drinking made him violent Benjamin would sometimes run there, and if the boy ever went missing Kau knew that this was the place where he could find him.

Though he had never seen a ghost he now thought it doubtless that they existed in some form or another. The best sense he could make of it was that when a man died his soul flew back to that place where he had come to feel the most safety or comfort or bliss in life. If he went now to that child's fort he was certain some piece of Benjamin would be waiting there for him, even if it was just as a chill wind on the back of his neck. And maybe Morning Star's past was also his future. The prophet would spend eternity as a boy playing stickball on his stone mountain, and for the next thousand years Garçon might be haunting the high ground beside this river. Kau looked up at the stars. So when he died where would

he go? Africa, he figured. But perhaps not. Perhaps instead it would
be to that island—St. Vincent—a place he had never even been yet.
Perhaps somehow, after so many years of horror, the site where his
own soul would choose to rest itself was somehow still to come.

No, he decided. Of course it would be Africa, to some clearing
in the forest where his wife and his children were waiting for him
to finally come and join them. But maybe St. Vincent was a place
where he might find some kind of near peace until at last the forest awoke to end his suffering and the day arrived for him—just as
Morning Star had once sung and then done—to return to some far
corner of the world.

THE FIRST CANNONS fired in the brightening twilight before true
dawn, and he climbed to the top of the cypress. The two American
gunboats were now anchored across the river from the fort, and
Garçon was firing upon them. White smoke belched from the artillery bank and again the fort's cannons boomed.

But the negro soldiers were poor gunners apparently. They
overshot the ships and instead pounded the trees growing on the
far bank, showering broken branches down onto the American
soldiers collected along the riverbank. Kau searched for Xavier
somewhere among those Americans but could not find him. From
inside the fort a Choctaw was launching arrows wrapped with
flaming long moss at the Americans. In places the forest was already burning.

He saw Garçon moving among the cannons with his sword
drawn, and the negro soldiers were reloading when the nearest

gunboat fired its first shot. A cannonball flew low over the river and smashed into the artillery bank. A dropped flintlock went spinning through the air, then bayoneted the throat of a roan steer. Garçon rose up. He slashed out with his sword and his cannons fired a third time. His men seemed shaken. Their shots again felled trees and splashed water but none found the gunboats.

The Americans' next shot was angled higher. This cannonball lobbed into the fort and then bounced once before crashing down onto the roof of Garçon's pigeonhouse. The shack caved in on itself, and a single surviving bird came fluttering out, dazed but alive, a dancing black speck that flew toward the rising sun, then turned and began to circle.

The American cannons fired twice more, and each shot struck a few lengths farther into the fort, closer to the mass of women and children huddled against the east wall.

As the pale smoke lifted from the near gunboat Kau saw leather-gloved sailors loading a red-hot cannonball. They hurried off with their hands covering their ears, and the cannon snapped back on its tracks, puffed smoke and then roared.

The hot shot cut a hellish cherry tracer across the sky, and the negro soldiers watched as it sailed over them. The cannonball hit the ground and then leapt, killing two men and a horse as it careened and slowed but kept on, traveling to the top of the earthwork that surrounded the powder magazine. And there it appeared to pause almost. A young woman—Juaneta, Kau realized, Juaneta in her long green dress—made for the glowing hot shot, and she had nearly reached it when the cannonball went rolling down the opposite slope of the earthwork, through the open door of the powder magazine.

There was a clock tick of nothing—no shots, no yellings of men, no callings of birds—before the explosion. The air seemed to suck out from the dome swamp, but then a hot wind rolled back over him and there came a blast like a direct strike of lightning that sent his cypress rocking. He stared down through a rain of green needles and saw the bone club go tumbling off the platform to then sink back down into the water.

He gripped the cypress tighter, and there was a steady ringing in his head as he waited for the forest to recover. He looked up and thought of the molimo, of a sleeping guardian awoken. The smoke had begun to clear. It was a landscape changed. One moment a fort was there, in the next it was not. Men floated in the river, their skinned backs shining red in the morning sun, and he could see a woman's bare torso dangling from the branch of a blast-slanted tree.

And then he saw one of the twins—either Marcela or Ramona—wandering alone and stunned as McIntosh and the Lower Creeks flowed out of the pinewoods. The girl spotted them coming and gathered herself. She ran south into the forest but was not followed. Kau watched as the Indians picked their way through the remains of the fort. The American sailors were ferrying men across the river in skiffs. If what Morning Star had shown him was correct, Garçon would soon be captured and executed. More of the forest was burning now, and Kau saw the lone last pigeon finally quit circling its ruined home and break for the horizon. It was time for them both to leave.

On their solitary way

THE GIRL WALKED the road that followed the river, and he tracked her bare footprints. He suspected that eventually she would come upon an American or perhaps some Indian, and so he kept to the far left side of the road, ready to bolt naked into the forest should danger present.

It was growing into another hot day. Smoke from the destroyed fort had softened the sunlight, and he watched as bits of charred log and wood floated past him on the river. He thought of Samuel and Beah. If they were alive and on Israel's island then they would have heard the explosion. They would understand that the fort was no more, that the battle with the Americans had ended. Though likely they had already suspected him and Xavier to be dead, now they would be certain. He would take the hidden rowboat to the island, find them mourning him when he came slipping through the palmettos.

Soon the land seemed to fall slightly. The river bled over the bank, and the road curved around a flooded pocket of cypress. He pushed on. Water frogs were croaking—fooled, he realized, by the smoke-dimmed sun. He figured that they would keep at this for hours, waiting for the strange and sudden dusk to finally darken and end.

And then the land rose again. The swamp ended and the road joined back with the river. He reached the first of the southern cornfields and found the girl standing alone on the bank. He crouched in the road and watched her enter the muddy water. Her thin cotton dress was stained nearly black with ash, and for a long time she stood in the shallows, scrubbing at the fabric with handfuls of wet sand. He whistled but she kept on with her cleaning. He whistled again but louder, yet still she ignored him.

He left the road and went down to the bank of the river. The girl had her back to him, and as he came closer he saw that she was bleeding from both of her ears. He clapped his hands together, but she did not turn. He feared that if she saw him now, this close and unannounced, that she would panic, and so he returned to the road to sit and wait for her to notice him.

The girl waded deeper into the river. Her dress was off, and now she was naked same as him. She soaked and then wrung the dress over and again. Each time she twisted the osnaburg in her small hands the expelled water would run a little clearer, until at last she raised the gray dress up to the sun and was done. She walked back onto the bank and he stood up in the road. She saw him and he motioned for her to come closer. He thought that probably now she would run or swim from him but she did not. Instead, she dropped the dress in the dirt and began to cry.

He left the road and went down to her for a second time. Though he was certain that she could not hear him he spoke anyway. "Marcela?" he asked. "Ramona?"

She did not reply and so he picked up her dress for her. It was heavy with dirt, but he found a clean corner and pressed the damp fabric gently against her face. He washed the dust and tears from her cheeks before erasing the streams of dried blood that had painted forked deltas along the length of her neck. When he was finished he held the dress out to her, but she would not take it from him.

Again he asked the girl her name, as if with the blood gone her hearing might somehow have returned. She saw him addressing her, but when she tried to speak herself there came only a loud braying of Spanish words.

He put his finger to her mouth and hushed her. She shivered when he touched her lips, and just then a wind blew in from the north and rippled the river. There came the faint and far-off slappings of several flintlocks firing almost at once, and though the girl could not have heard either the shots or him, he told her that the fort was now really finished, over.

"General Garçon," he said. "He dead now."

She blinked but did not speak again. He held out his hand but she stepped away from him, and so he walked alone to the road. Before continuing south he turned and looked back at her. She was still by the river but she was watching him. He walked on a few steps and suddenly she came running. She flew past him, then stopped on the road to wait. He pulled alongside her and felt a hand curl itself into his own. She fell into step with him and he saw her staring at the river as they walked, either at the river or at their twin shadows, the linked silhouettes of a small man and an orphaned girl, sliding together naked across the flat, dry land.

EPILOGUE

St. George Island. 1833. The lighthouse keeper watches the workmen sail themselves back to the mainland. For the first time he is alone on the island. The keeper spends his days sleeping and then at night he tends to the new lighthouse—trimming wicks and cleaning lenses, hauling the wooden buckets of whale oil that feed the thirteen lamps.

To the northeast he can see the snaking smoke of steamships working the river. Their cotton cargoes are loaded onto schooners, and some days a dozen of these bale-laden vessels shuttle through the narrow pass separating his own island from the smaller one named St. Vincent. The captains doff their hats for him as they make for the enormous three-masted ships that sit anchored in the deeper waters offshore. In thunderstorms the blue lights of the corposants sometimes dance along their riggings.

He is two months alone before the figure appears to him. Sunrise. The keeper is extinguishing the lanterns when he perceives a faraway noise and looks west across the half-mile pass to St. Vincent.

In the gray twilight he sees something moving along the beach. He searches with his spyglass but the dark form is gone.

This happens again on the cusp of the next morning, so that on the third dawn the keeper is waiting, has his spyglass trained on the white beach when the sun first cracks in the east. He sees him clearly now—an impossibly small negro in a ragged top hat, naked save a swathe of some fabric or hide. The man is dragging a long length of wood. He brings the end of this log to his mouth and his shoulders seem to heave. The keeper swears then that he hears music. He cups his hands to his ears, and when the man lurches again he is certain—a deep sound carried by the wind across the water. This is not so much a song as a prayer. Somehow the keeper knows that.

The tiny man lets his crude trumpet fall to the sand and moves closer to the water. He is facing the rising sun. Waves wash over his ankles. He stands motionless and then seems to convulse, his entire body quivering. Seawater splashes beneath his stomping feet. The dancer's head lolls back and he stretches his arms. He begins to swoop and spin like a circling eagle, and as the sun clears the horizon he soars out of the water. He pauses on the beach for his trumpet, then vanishes back into the green interior.

Sometimes the man comes at dusk and is with others: a large woman and a thin woman, two boys who are almost men themselves. They collect flotsam along the shoreline, hunt gulls with an Indian bow. Though they are no doubt runaways who might bring some reward, the keeper lets them be, never mentioning them to the merchant who comes every month with the supply boat. He clings to this secret because it always moves him, cuts at his own loneliness and desperation, to spy that bantam man each morning, blowing his trumpet and then dancing, dancing for the attention of some heathen god.

ACKNOWLEDGMENTS

I WOULD LIKE to thank Jack Shoemaker, Charlie Winton, Trish Hoard and the excellent and hardworking people at Counterpoint and Publishers Group West. My appreciation also to Nat Sobel and the team at Sobel Weber, as well as the Stanford Creative Writing Program and the Martha Heasley Cox Center for Steinbeck Studies at San José State University for their remarkable generosity and support.

Thank you as well to Eavan Boland, John L'Heureux, Elizabeth Tallent, Tobias Wolff, Adam Johnson, Tom Kealey, Scott Hutchins, Josh Tyree, Molly Antopol, Stacy Swann, Abby Ulman, Mike McGriff, Sarah Frisch, Jim Gavin, Vanessa Hutchinson, Stephanie Soileau, Justin St. Germain, Mary Popek, Christina Ablaza, Phil Knight, Paul Douglass, Tim Cahill, Laura Mazer, Mikayla Butchart, Roxanna Aliaga, Julie Pinkerton, Tiffany Lee, April Wolfe, Sam Douglas, Judith Weber, Adia Wright and Julie Stevenson.

Also, for their hospitality, patience and guidance during my time in Africa, I owe a huge debt of gratitude to Rosmarie Ruf, Marc Kupper, Jon and Cher Cadd, Lary Strietzel and Okapi

Wildlife Reserve rangers Michel Moyakeso and Ungoboma—as well as to my wonderful Mbuti hosts in the Ituri Forest, for being kind enough to share a small part of their amazing lives with me.

Finally, as always, my deepest thanks to my family and friends for their unwavering encouragement, and to my wife, Sylvia, for continuing to be the best thing that has ever happened to me.

ABOUT THE AUTHOR

SKIP HORACK IS the author of the story collection *The Southern Cross*. He is currently a Jones Lecturer at Stanford, where he was also a Wallace Stegner Fellow. A native of Louisiana, and a graduate of Florida State University, he now lives in the Bay Area.